*Pointe*

# Pointe

BRANDY COLBERT

G. P. Putnam's Sons
An Imprint of Penguin Group (USA)

G. P. PUTNAM'S SONS
Published by the Penguin Group
Penguin Group (USA) LLC
375 Hudson Street, New York, NY 10014

USA | Canada | UK | Ireland | Australia
New Zealand | India | South Africa | China
penguin.com
A Penguin Random House Company

Library of Congress Cataloging-in-Publication Data
Colbert, Brandy.
Pointe / Brandy Colbert.
pages cm
Summary: Four years after Theo's best friend, Donovan, disappeared at age thirteen,
he is found and brought home and Theo puts her health at risk as she decides whether
to tell the truth about the abductor, knowing her revelation could end her lifelong dream
of becoming a professional ballet dancer.
[1. Kidnapping—Fiction. 2. High schools—Fiction. 3. Schools—Fiction. 4. Emotional
problems—Fiction. 5. Anorexia nervosa—Fiction. 6. Ballet dancing—Fiction. 7. African
Americans—Fiction. 8. Family life—Illinois—Fiction. 9. Illinois—Fiction.] I. Title.
PZ7.C66998Poi 2014
[Fic]—dc23
2013020689
Printed in the United States of America.
ISBN 978-0-399-16034-9
1 3 5 7 9 10 8 6 4 2

Design by Marikka Tamura.
Text set in Simoncini Garamond Std.

*For Emily B.,*
*my good friend and fellow book addict*

# Part One

# CHAPTER ONE

I WISH I COULD SAY THE DAY DONOVAN CAME HOME was extraordinary from the start, that I woke up knowing something special would happen that Thursday evening in October.

But the truth is, it's like any other day of the week.

I go to school, then I get on the train and go to ballet.

People fawn over the beauty of dance. The long legs and elegant shoes and expertly twisted buns. And it's not that they're wrong. Those are all part of the reason I was drawn to ballet at the age of three. But I'd be willing to bet those same people have never set foot in the dressing room of a dance studio. Because you can't quite look at it the same once you've been to the other side.

Straight chaos.

And I'm late, because the Metra never wants to run on schedule when I actually have to be somewhere that matters. I squeeze into an empty corner by the lockers and toss my coat to the floor as I step out of my flats. Everyone is chattering away in various stages of undress, but I'm the only one still wearing all my street clothes. Phil once mentioned he'd like to be a fly on the dressing room wall, and I laughed in his face when I realized he was serious. It's all A-cups and square hips in here and he said it didn't matter, that boobs are boobs, but I think he'd be underwhelmed. Also, it reeks of body odor and feet.

I glance to my right, where Ruthie Pathman perches on the edge of the bench, already slipping on her toe shoes. Her back is set in a perfectly straight line and there's not a curl out of place in her tight, tight bun.

"Staring at me won't help you get dressed any faster, Cartwright." She says this without looking in my direction.

"Not all of us have the luxury of driving ourselves into the city," I say as I tug on my tights. "The train was late."

But I pull them up too fast, and a run appears mid-thigh, fast and final. I probably have a new pair somewhere in my dance bag, but I don't have time to deal with that right now. The other girls are already beginning to file out of the room and I'm not even in my leotard.

Ruthie shoves her bag into her locker. "You'll have to think of a better excuse than that. Nobody likes the blame game."

She winks at me after reciting one of our ballet instructor's favorite lines, then snaps her combination lock shut. In a certain light, Ruthie looks like one of those angels pictured in the Bible—pale skin and wheat-colored curls and big, soulful blue eyes. But the only angelic thing about her is her dancing. She's tiny but she's been in more physical fights than anyone I know, guys included. And that's saying a lot—I go to school with a disproportionate number of assholes.

She walks through the doorway, then pokes her head back into the dressing room. "Three minutes." Her lips curve into a canary-eating smile before she closes the door firmly behind her.

I can get away with lacing my shoes in the studio, but I still have to put up my hair, and Marisa flips when she sees so much as a stray hairpin. It's all regimented: solid black leotard, blush-pink tights, no loose hair. I am so screwed. I gather up the pile of clothing pooled around my feet and throw it all in my locker. And I'm just going to have to chance being screamed at about my hair, because I'll be locked out if I don't run.

The ribbons on my pointe shoes tangle around my ankles and heels with every step, conspiring to trip me as I dash down the corridor. Thanks to the snug elastic against my ankles, I manage to stay upright and fly into the studio only seconds after the official start of class, before Marisa will lock the door for the next hour and a half. She never lets anyone watch the senior company practice.

Marisa is also very serious about punctuality, so much that if you are even two minutes late, she will open the door only to stare you down and ask you to leave. We all learned long ago to set our watches to the studio's clocks. I'm never late and I am her favorite, so I expect a warning at the most. But she's not standing near the door at all. Instead, she's in the far front corner of the room, going over sheet music with an accompanist I've never seen before. She's so preoccupied that my lateness doesn't even register. I smirk at Ruthie as I use the extra time to tie up the ribbons on my shoes and fashion the thick black hair that crests my shoulder blades into an acceptable bun.

This place feels more like home than home sometimes. There are three studios in the building and they all look the same: sprung floors to absorb shock and protect our feet and joints; long wooden barres running along two sides of the room, their surfaces worn from the grip of so many hands; one whole wall made of mirrored panels that can make you feel like the Swan Queen on your best day and a bloated, dizzy mess on your worst. This is the only studio without windows and it's my favorite because it means there are no outside distractions.

There are twelve people in the senior company, and most of us have danced together since we were kids. Nine girls, three boys; attitude and ego for days. Caryn has amazing turnout, and some days I'd kill for Elissa's arms and the height of Toby's leaps as he propels himself into the air. But I have good feet— these arches were *made* for pointe shoes—and good musicality, and it may sound conceited, but I know I'm one of the best dancers in this class.

Ruthie stands at the barre, stretching her hamstrings. "Saved by the substitute accompanist. Impressive."

"Where's Betty?" I ask as I take my spot next to her. Kaitlin is on the other side of me, sitting a few feet away from the barre

4

in her right split. I can see the muscles in her legs tense under her tights as she stretches to the tips of her toes.

Ruthie shrugs. "No idea, but where'd they find this guy? He looks kind of . . . grungy."

"You're a snob."

But then I turn my head to get a better look at him and—oh.

Ruthie looks at me curiously. "You know him or something?"

I do. He goes to school with me in Ashland Hills, our little suburb outside of Chicago. He's a year older. A senior. And he is Phil's dealer.

"I think he goes to my school," I say, and face the barre so I don't have to wonder what he's doing in my ballet class.

Marisa finally crosses the room to close the door, then stands in front, waiting for our attention. She doesn't have to wait long; she's the kind of person who commands attention, whether she's trying to or not. We're all intimidated, but not because she's scary, not like the tales of evil ballet mistresses patrolling the room to poke us when we mess up. More because she's a former professional dancer and this is her studio and we've all seen what she can do on a stage. I found her old bio once, and according to my math she's in her mid-forties now. She doesn't look much older than her twenty-year-old head shot, though.

"Before we start today, I'd like to introduce you to our new accompanist," she says.

New? Marisa is careful with her words. She would never

introduce a substitute as someone "new." When I glance at him, his eyes are already on me. I turn back to Marisa. She tells us Betty's husband is sick. Alzheimer's. Everyone is quiet because we know Betty has been with her husband since high school. They never had children and she always said the only two things that mattered in life were her husband and the piano, in that order. It's not fair that she won't always have both.

Josh Barley's shoulders slump with the news. Betty loves him most of all and he knows it. He's kind of hard to resist with his red hair and freckles. There's something wholesome about him, like he should always be eating apple pie or hanging out at a church picnic.

"In the meantime, everyone please welcome Hosea Roth, the newest addition to our studio family," Marisa says with a smile. "Hosea comes with a strong musical background and we're lucky to have him."

A strong musical background? Either this is the best-kept secret in all of Ashland Hills High or Marisa is totally fucking with us, because I wasn't aware he could play any instruments. Hosea gives us a nod followed by a smile you would miss if you looked away for even a second. His dark hair is long and pulled back from his face. He wears the same clothes I've seen him in for as long as I can remember: faded jeans, a black T-shirt, and black boots with a heavy sole.

Our eyes meet again. He knows me. Not very well, but I see him at school sometimes and at most of the parties. And once, I went with Phil to pick up an eighth at his house, and

Hosea looked out at the street from beneath the hood of his sweatshirt and saw me sitting in the passenger seat of Phil's car. Hosea is pretty much focused on pills and Phil usually sticks to pot, but they're friends, so he makes an exception for Phil.

Until now, my school and ballet worlds have been segregated, except for a handful of recitals Sara-Kate has talked her way into attending. But now Hosea is here and I don't know how I feel about it and he just keeps staring at me, until I give in first and look away. Ruthie catches all this and flicks her eyes to the ceiling as we line up at the barre in first position for plié.

I've been dancing so long that ballet has become an extension of me. I can no longer stretch my legs without pointing my toes, and I'm always aware of my arms, my back, the roll of my shoulders. As I walk between classrooms, while I'm rinsing dishes, even when I'm picking out apples with Mom at the market.

Some people associate memories with music, but I can align most of mine with dancing. The mere mention of chicken pox sends gold-sequined swatches through my mind as I remember secretly suffering during my fourth-grade recital, how I dug my fingers into the stretchy fabric of my costume again and again when no one was looking, because if they knew, they wouldn't let me dance. The slightest whiff of menthol reminds me of two years ago, when I developed tendinitis and kept slathering my ankle in smelly ointment to numb the pain.

Dancing on pointe reminds me of Trent. I got my first pair

of toe shoes when I was twelve and he became my first boy-friend a year later. It's not just the timing, though. I fell for him nearly as fast as I grew to love pointe work, so for me, the two are forever linked. He asked to see my pointe shoes a couple of weeks after we'd been together. I slowly pulled them out of my dance bag in the front seat of his car and slipped one onto his lap, the ribbons swimming between us in silky waves. I'd just gotten a new pair, so they were still unmarred; a soft, sweet pink against the dark blue of his jeans. He slid his hands around the satin almost wonderingly, then looked over and said they were pretty, like me. Sometimes I'd complain about the pain in my feet and he'd say I should quit if it hurt so much. I don't think he understood that it was all worth it, sore feet and ankles included. The only thing *he* seemed at all passionate about was *me*.

Some days, in the beginning, I was so tired from dancing on pointe that I didn't feel like going to class. And some days, I didn't feel like doing what I did with Trent. Lots of times, he was exactly what I wanted, and I felt sexy when he pinned me to the backseat of his car with just his torso as he whispered in my ear that I was special. But sometimes I wished we could go back to the kissing and slow touching with all our clothes on. On those days, I couldn't understand why sex with him made me feel a little dirty. After all, we'd been doing it for months.

We stretch and strengthen our ankles and feet as we work through tendu and dégagé, rotate our hips through the arc of rond de jambe. My favorite barre exercise is grand battement.

It's so powerful, thrusting one leg as high in the air as you can and returning it to the supporting leg quickly, but with total control. To really pull it off, both legs have to stay perfectly straight as we execute grand battement devant, à la seconde, and derriére—to the front, side, and back—on both sides.

Once we're finished at the barre, we move from our place along the wall to start center work. The center exercises are similar to what we just finished, but we're warmed up now, so we can perform them without the additional support of the barre.

By the time we get to allégro, my muscles are limber and my legs lengthen straight and assured. I hold myself up with the invisible string Marisa always talks about, the one that makes my leaps sky-high, my neck long and elegant. Even now, even with his music serving as my soundtrack, I am able to put Hosea out of my mind and dance like no one else is in the room. I feel Marisa's eyes on me. I'm worried she thinks I look tired, so I make my next jeté count even more than the others.

I allow myself to sneak another look at Hosea. He's good. Very good, like he's been playing piano as long as I've been dancing. It's the same classical music we've danced to for years, yet there's also a personal connection that makes each note seem fuller, more meaningful, as if the piece was crafted specifically for our ballet class. I couldn't be more surprised, and I wonder if there are rules about revealing that kind of thing in his world. Like piano is for pussies and you'd damn well better hide it if you don't want to be labeled as such.

I'm exhausted when Marisa dismisses class. I dance three nights a week and every Saturday. Each time, I leave dripping with sweat, my chest heaving and my legs burning. Today, I wonder just how bad I look and avoid glancing at the piano before I leave the room.

I have a standing dinner date with Sara-Kate and Phil after ballet on Thursdays. It sounds fancy, but it's not like we're sitting in a dimly lit restaurant with tablecloths and heavy flatware. It's always Casablanca's and always the back booth with the cracked vinyl seats and a dirty sugar dispenser in place of sweetener packets.

Sometimes we drive around and smoke a bowl before we go into the diner. Today would've been a good day for that. The winters are shitty, but nothing beats October in Chicago. I know it means everything is dying, but I could stare at the leaves for days—the burnt gold and burgundy and flaming orange hues bursting from tree branches. I like the fat pumpkins perched on front porches and how the air is perfect—cool but not freezing, warm enough under the sun but not stifling.

But we can't drive around today because Phil has a trigonometry test tomorrow and wants to study. His boxy sedan and Sara-Kate Worthington's powder-blue Bug already sit in the lot when I arrive from the train station. I slide into the booth just in time to hear Phil extolling the virtues of Goodwill over independent thrift stores. Phil Muñoz has an opinion on everything and it's usually the least popular one if he can help it.

"How was class?" Sara-Kate turns to me almost gratefully. Phil's impassioned rants are too much for even her sometimes.

"Fine. Except—"

"Except what?" She moves a strand of lilac-colored hair behind her ear and reaches for the menus tucked behind the ketchup and mustard bottles.

"Except . . . I was late because of the stupid train," I say as I stack my bag and coat on the empty seat next to Phil.

He stops pulling his trig textbook from his bag to look at me, his dark eyes narrowed behind the clear lenses of his aviator eyeglasses. The thin gold frames almost blend into his light brown skin when I look at him from a certain angle. "Good story, Theo."

I make a face at Phil. Then: "I have a question."

"The answer is probably no."

"I'll take my chances." I lower my voice a little. "Do you still get your pot from Hosea Roth?"

"Of course." Phil looks at me carefully. "You in the market?"

"No way." Sara-Kate shakes her head emphatically across the table, her silver lip ring glinting in the light. "Half the fun is freeloading from Phil. You can't buy your own."

"I'm not," I say, laughing at the look Phil shoots her. "But a friend might be. In the market, that is."

"Pills or grass?"

"Shrooms," I say, just to throw him off his game.

His face creases. "That's random. What friend is this? Everyone at school goes through Hosea."

"A friend from dance. She doesn't go to school here."

"I can check and get back to you."

"No, it's okay." God, what would Hosea do if he knew I was asking about him? "She said all the guys in the city are flakes or creeps, so she was looking for someone chill."

"Hosea's the most chill dude I know." Phil raises an eyebrow at me like this is common knowledge. "If he can't get them, he'll find someone who can."

"No, it's fine." I pretend to search for something in my bag so Phil can't see my lying eyes. "She probably wasn't serious anyway."

Sara-Kate twirls a straw among the ice cubes in her cup. "I don't think I've heard Hosea say more than twenty words the whole time I've known him."

"Probably because he can't get a word in around Klein." Phil opens his book to the study guide section.

"Why are they friends anyway?" I ask, buttoning my cardigan all the way to the top. It's pilled from too many washings and the once-vibrant green has faded to a murky olive, but I keep it in my bag for trips to Casablanca's because it is *always* freezing in here. Too much A/C in the summer, not enough heat in the winter.

"It's not that complicated." Phil shrugs, flips a piece of dark hair out of his eyes. "Hosea has the drugs. Klein has the money."

"Hosea is cute," Sara-Kate says thoughtfully before she sips from her straw. "But I do not like his big black boots. They're oppressive."

The sixtysomething waitress who's been giving us the stinkeye since I got here trudges over from behind the counter to take our order. Jana. She hates us and is here every time we are. Or maybe that's why she hates us. She taps the sole of her dingy canvas sneaker against the floor as she recites the daily specials, sighs when Sara-Kate takes too long to decide between fried pickles and onion rings to accompany her grilled cheese. Phil orders a bowl of chili.

Everyone bitches that the lentil soup here is bland but I choose it because I know exactly what I'm getting. They put it on the menu after someone complained about the lack of vegetarian options, and the cooks either don't know or don't care how to prepare it well. So it's kind of mushy and virtually tasteless, but at least I don't have to worry about creams or cheeses in my soup.

Someone asks Jana to turn up the television when she walks back behind the counter, and that's when I notice. That every person on a stool and in a booth, every server and busboy and fry cook is staring at the television hung in the corner of the diner. Usually it's tuned to soap operas or Bears games or crappy made-for-TV movies.

But today, everyone's eyes are glued to the breaking news report on the screen, and our eyes follow. At first I think it's the exhaustion from class catching up to me now that I'm able to relax. Because as I look at the news anchor, the camera flickers from her face to a picture of my old best friend.

My dead best friend.

I'm standing and then I'm walking toward the counter without thinking, oblivious to Sara-Kate and Phil, who are close behind.

Donovan's name comes up once or twice a year—on the anniversary of his disappearance or when someone submits a false lead. Like, someone saw him in a Burger King in Vermont, or he was spotted in line at an amusement park in Utah. I figured out a long time ago to stop believing I would see him again. He was my best friend, but everyone knows kids missing longer than twenty-four hours were sexually abused or killed or both.

But this time is different. The news anchor's glossy lips are stretched into a smile and she stumbles over her words, trips over the last-minute script. She's telling us that he's alive. Donovan's been found.

My ears are the first thing to go. I can no longer hear voices, just this buzzing. Raw and unstoppable and I can't tell if Sara-Kate and Phil and the rest of the diner hear it, too, because then my eyes get stuck on the school picture that was taken the last year I saw him. I used to keep that picture in my nightstand, separate from the photos of my other classmates. Seeing it on-screen, I feel like someone has stolen my journal and displayed it for the world to see.

I am somewhat aware of the silence as I take in that for the

14

first time ever, no one in this greasy spoon is saying a word. That they're all looking from the television to one another, slack-jawed. That Sara-Kate is stepping forward for a closer look, and Phil is rubbing my back, searching my face with his huge, dark eyes.

*Donovan is alive.*

"They found that boy," Jana says, her hands gripping the black handle of a coffeepot.

I try to hold myself up, but these legs, these same legs that will dance me all the way to New York—they can't. They are made of jelly and I would fall to the ground if Phil didn't catch me. This particular combination of relief and confusion and elation is too big to comprehend, too big to do anything but lean on Phil in front of the counter, tears streaming down the hills of my cheeks until he and Sara-Kate lead me out on my jelly legs.

Outside into the brisk autumn air, where I catch my breath for the first time in minutes, where I say it aloud to convince myself it's true:

"Donovan's alive."

Donovan came back to us.

# CHAPTER TWO

MY NEIGHBORHOOD IS A SHITSHOW.

The Pratts' house—Donovan's house—is two doors down from us, so our street is blocked off. I stop at the corner and show the policemen who I am, pull out my ID with unsteady hands as I try to look down the street to see what's happening. I've dreamed about this day plenty of times, but in my version, Donovan was standing outside on his porch—waiting for me like I've been waiting for him all these years. My version didn't look like this.

I receive an escort to my driveway and a couple of officers hold back the reporters while another walks me to my front door, smiles, and makes sure I'm safely inside before heading back down the porch steps.

The house is quiet and calm, the antithesis of the clicking shutters and shouted questions and hum of too many people on the other side of the door. I breathe in the silence.

"Mom?" I call out.

But I know she's not here. She works part-time in the research department of the library and today is her late day. Dad won't be home for another half hour, either. And I don't know what to do with myself, so I sit on the couch with my coat buttoned up to my neck and I wait.

Exactly thirty minutes later, I hear the slow crank of the garage door, my father's car pulling in, the creak of the door as it shudders to the ground. Then I hear his urgent footsteps, the flipping of light switches as he navigates his way through the dark house, looking for me.

"In here," I say when he rushes past the living room doorway.

He loops back down the hallway and into the room, stands in front of me while he scratches the back of his head. "Did you get my messages? Mom and I both called you a few times."

His eyes are slightly dazed, his silver tie with teeny black polka dots askew. I gave him that tie for Father's Day last year. He uses everything I give him. Even the misshapen ceramic pencil cup I made in third-grade art class sits on the desk at his accounting firm in the city.

"Oh, yeah." I looked at my phone once, I think, to check the time. I don't remember hearing it ring or seeing the missed calls. "Sorry. I got distracted." I gesture toward the commotion on the other side of the curtains.

He smiles a bit. "Right. It's kind of a zoo out there. But what do you say we brave the paparazzi and go out to dinner when your mother gets home? We should celebrate."

"I already ate," I say, digging my fingers into the empty cushions on either side of me.

I don't realize this is a lie until I think about the cup of lentil soup that never came to the table. I wonder if Jana ever brought out our food, if she was pissed that we left without canceling our order.

"Could I stay here instead?" I twist my hands in my lap as I look at him. "I want to watch the news."

Dad has too much energy. He wants to get out. He can't stop fiddling with his collar and glancing toward the windows. But he smiles again, bigger this time. He says, "Of course, babygirl. You're right. It's probably best if we all stay in."

So that's how Mom finds us, side by side on the sofa in the den, watching the same story play out on different channels. She settles on the other side of me, and when our eyes meet, I have to look away because I see the happy tears in hers and if she starts crying, mine will spill over again. She puts her hand on top of mine as I turn back to the television.

*Donovan Pratt, 17, returned to his home in Illinois after four years in captivity*

*Breaking News: Chicagoland teen rescued from years-long abduction*

*Locals call missing teen's return a miracle*

The news is the type of nonstop coverage that makes people turn away after a while, say they no longer care. I absorb it all, find a little pocket to store each new piece of information. The reports are vague. Every news anchor alludes to the abuse, brings up old long-term abduction cases and some that were never solved. They talk about where Donovan was found: a Las Vegas breakfast buffet, with the person they believe had him all these years. A few minutes past nine, the thick-haired anchor with the tired eyes says.

I was in second period. Chem. My throat tightens as I try to remember if I felt anything during class. But no. I was zoning out, same as any other day of the week.

Some of the channels show timelines to illustrate his life. They use fancy graphics and bold colors, but it all adds up to the same conclusion: thirteen years as a normal kid in Ashland Hills, four years at the mercy of a stranger. I wait and I wait, but they haven't revealed the identity of the abductor. All we know is there's a suspect in custody.

"You should get ready for bed," my mother says gently, around eleven.

The coverage has slowed except for the major cable news channels. There's nothing new to be learned at this point, but I'm afraid I'll miss something if I go to bed. I want to know who took him. What they did to him.

"He'll still be here in the morning," my mother says, as if she can read my mind.

Somehow I float up to my room and then I'm under the covers. But I can't sleep. How can someone be here every day for years, then disappear? How can they be gone so long and just come back on a Thursday, like that was the plan the whole time? I won't believe he's really here until I see him.

Donovan was brave. In a speak-first-think-later sort of way, but there was always truth behind his words. Like that day during our sixth-grade history lesson. I'd been dreading it all week because we were studying the Civil War and there's nothing worse than being the only black kid in class on the day your teacher talks about slavery.

Most days, I don't think too much about being a novelty in this town. Chicago is really segregated, and my suburb is almost all white, but people don't treat me like there's a big divide or anything. We've been in school together for so long, it's like they forget my skin is darker until someone or something reminds them. And the slavery discussion is one of those instances. It goes one of two ways: either the teacher calls on you because you must be the expert, or they avoid you and look all around the room at your blond-haired, blue-eyed classmates.

Mr. Hammond was old-school, so he jumped right in. Something about the modern-day effects of Jim Crow laws, and as soon as he finished his question, he looked right at me and said, "Theo, maybe you have an example of how Jim Crow laws have affected you or your family so many decades later."

I felt eyes on me and I felt eyes trying *not* to be on me. The room was so silent, I heard Macy Wilkins's stomach growling in the next row. And no matter how hard I wished it, Mr. Hammond did *not* get swallowed up by the floor and whisked away to a hell built for insensitive teachers.

I was just sitting there, trying to figure out how to answer him without being exceptionally rude, when I remembered that this year I *wasn't* the only black kid in this class. Donovan sat on the other side of the room and I didn't have to look over to know he was seething.

But I didn't expect him to say anything.

Before I could open my mouth: "Why did you call on Theo, Mr. Hammond?"

Our teacher looked away from me, confused. "Excuse me, Donovan?"

I peeked at him. He was sitting straight up in his chair, forearms placed calmly on the desk in front of him. Palms flat. His brown eyes were narrowed and his cleft chin jutted out so far, it nearly pointed at the whiteboard.

"I said, why did you call on Theo? Her hand wasn't up."

Mr. Hammond's face puckered. "Would *you* like to answer the question?"

"No. I don't think either of us should have to answer." Donovan's voice was calm but his eyes were shooting poison.

"Well, Donovan," he said slowly, as his neck then jowls then forehead burned an intriguing shade of red. "I'm asking because perhaps you could offer a . . . unique perspective, as your ancestors were so closely involved."

And that's when Donovan lost his cool. "That's *bull*. Why don't you ask Joey or Leo or anyone else in this class about *their* perspective?" He was leaning forward over his desk then, his fingers gripping the edge like it was the only thing holding him back from a full-on fit of rage. "Last time I checked, their ancestors were closely involved. Yours, too!"

He was sent to the principal's office for talking back but the smirk he shot me on the way out of the room told me it was all worth it. I blinked a quick thank-you back at him. Mr. Hammond never called on either one of us again during the Civil War lessons.

Donovan was brave, but you can be brave for only so long, and as I lie under my covers staring up at the ceiling, I can't stop wondering if four years was long enough to break him.

I had a hard time sleeping after the abduction. I would slip into my parents' room in the middle of the night and ask if I could stay with them.

"What's wrong, honey?" Mom would ask as she sat up in bed, the silk headscarf she slept in wrapped tightly around her hair.

I was thirteen. Much too old to run to my parents' bed for comfort. I couldn't tell them that in the back of my mind, I thought that if this could happen to someone as good and kind as Donovan, it could happen to me, too.

But they never made me feel bad about it. Dad would say, "Can't shut off your brain?" and I'd nod and crawl into bed between them, instantly soothed by the rhythmic patterns of their breathing, the familiar smell of their room, the warmth of their sheets.

But that was four years ago, and Donovan is back. There's no reason to be scared unless I think about who took him, and still, it doesn't matter because that person is in custody. I've thought about that person often over the years. Man or woman? Old or young? Black like Donovan and me, or white like most everyone else in this town? I think about the pages and pages of sex offenders registered online in Chicago, how most of them have nothing in common except their desire to hurt people.

I fall asleep for a bit but I wake around two in the morning. I have to pee. I sit on the toilet for a while, wondering if the last few hours were a dream. Maybe I sat in the back booth at Casablanca's and finished my chemistry homework while Phil studied for trig and Sara-Kate worked on her poem for English. Maybe I ate that cup of mushy lentil soup and maybe Donovan isn't just two houses away from me after all.

My mother is in the hallway when I come out.

"Mama." I haven't called her that since I was a little girl. "Mama, did they really find him?"

She reaches out to me and we mold into each other. My nose is pressed into the crease of her armpit. She rests her cheek on top of my head.

"Yes," she says into my ear. Her voice is tinged with sleep, but most of all, it is content. "He's home."

## CHAPTER THREE

MOST EVERYONE AT SCHOOL TREATS FRIDAY LIKE A free day anyway, but the news of Donovan's return means it's worse than usual, so the principal cancels second period and holds an assembly instead.

Before it starts, I duck outside to meet Sara-Kate and Phil behind the athletic field for a smoke.

They're standing in a little circle between the bleachers and the fence that marks the end of school grounds, next to Klein and Hosea. Klein can be found out here most mornings. I bet even he couldn't tell you the last time he made it through a school day sober.

He sees me before everyone else does. It's subtle, but he stands a little taller, holds his jaw a little higher.

"What's up, Legs?" he says, making room for me, his green eyes taking in my every move.

He smells like a cologne factory, and I'm sure whatever brand it is, it's wildly expensive. Just like every stitch of clothing on his body and the shiny car he parked in the lot this morning.

"Don't objectify my best friend like that," Sara-Kate says with a lazy grin. A breeze slices through the air and she wraps her arms around the black lace of her vintage party dress. It's thin and stylishly tattered and she must be beyond cold. But Sara-Kate doesn't believe in coats until the temp drops down to freezing, and even then only sometimes.

She passes me a half-smoked joint. I can immediately tell that Phil rolled it. He's an expert. Phil doesn't half-ass anything. If he's going to be a stoner he's going to be a damn good one, with perfectly rolled joints and lighters that never burn out on you.

"I'm not objectifying her," Klein says easily. "I can't help it if Theo has nice attributes."

His eyes slip from my neck down the length of me, hovering on my pink silk top with the Peter Pan collar. Sara-Kate gave me this shirt for my birthday; I love it but it sort of makes me look like I'm five, and I'm flat to boot, so Klein seems extra-pervy, staring at me like he wants to rip it off. I button my coat the rest of the way.

"Can we not talk about Theo like Theo's not standing next to you?" I take a long drag and look around the circle as I let out the smoke, trying to figure out who to pass it to next. I catch Hosea's eye and we both look away this time.

I wonder if he thinks I told Sara-Kate and Phil that he works at the studio.

The smoke courses through me in its hazy, familiar way, coasts through my chest and relaxes my shoulders. I close my eyes for a moment, want to remember this blissed-out state before we're subjected to Crumbaugh at the assembly. She'll be up there because she's forever front and center when anything big goes down. She's the world's worst guidance counselor—devoid of any useful advice, but always ready for the spotlight.

Klein nudges Hosea, though his eyes follow the joint between my fingers. "So what's this bullshit assembly about?" Because seriously, he never shuts up.

"Not bullshit," Phil says. He pushes a piece of hair from his forehead. It's getting kind of long now, curling over his collar in a shaggy, old-rock-star sort of cut. I swear to God, Phil could time-travel back to 1972 on any given day and no one would know the difference. "It's necessary. I heard some little freshman asking who 'this Donovan kid' is. I wanted to punch him."

"Maybe he's new in town." Even stoned, Sara-Kate likes to give the benefit of the doubt.

"That's no excuse for being uninformed," Phil counters. "It's national news."

He takes what's left of the joint and sucks on the end of the roach, brooding. For once, he isn't being testy just for the sake of it. He was Donovan's friend, too. It was the three of us for a while. We formed a little trio and started calling ourselves the Brown Brigade because there aren't a lot of people around here who look like us. When we met in kindergarten, I didn't know Phil was Mexican until I heard his mother scolding him in Spanish. His skin was only a bit lighter than mine, so I didn't understand that the history of brown skin is as varied as its shades, just that we were different.

Klein sighs. "Let's get outta here. I gotta take a piss."

He leads the way back to the two-story, stone-colored building, followed by Phil in his kelly-green corduroys and Sara-Kate in her bright red fishnets, shivering as she walks. If the administration ever proposes uniforms or actually enforces the dress code, it's no secret who'll be screwed the hardest.

Hosea takes the last drag of his clove, exhales away from me, and tosses it to the ground with all the other butts, stomping it out with his boot. "Heard you were looking for some boomers."

"What?"

"Mushrooms?" The corners of his lips lift a tiny bit.

I open my mouth and close it again without a word. Fucking Phil.

"No, it was a friend . . . She doesn't go here. She was just asking around, though."

He appraises me. Up close, his eyes startle me. They're a deep, pure gray. Like steel, but softer. He sticks his hands in the front pocket of his hoodie and says, "Let me know if she changes her mind. I can help."

"Oh. Okay, yeah. Thanks."

He starts walking toward school but I stand in place, watching him. He has a steady gait and long hair that looks impossibly soft and messy at the same time. He's taller than I realized. At least six two, maybe six three—with broad shoulders that hunch down as he walks, almost like he'd curl in on himself if he could. I stand looking at him for so long that he turns back to me. "You coming?"

We don't talk on the way inside. We walk beside each other but not really beside each other, because he has a girlfriend. Ellie Harris. She's always around. In fact, I wonder where she and Trisha are right now. I can't tell if they're best friends by default, since they're dating Hosea and Klein, or if they actually like each other.

Once we're inside I let him get a few feet ahead of me. I'm totally stoned and everyone is rushing around me too quickly, all heading in the same direction. The teachers are trying to keep some control over the crowd but we outnumber them. My reflexes are shit and I get turned around as a couple of sophomores run by me on either side, racing to break through the throng of students. I start to lose my balance but someone rights me with a steady hand just as I stumble.

"Theo! Are you okay?"

Bryn Davenport. Cardigans and khaki skirts during the day, most likely to vomit up a fifth of vodka on any given weekend. I held her hair once. It wasn't so bad. She's a polite drunk. She must have thanked me fifteen times while we sat on the floor of Victoria Martino's bathroom.

"I'm fine," I say. "Just a little slow this morning."

"God, can you believe Donovan's back?" Bryn absently runs a hand through her bobbed black locks. "I never thought we'd see him again."

"Yeah," I say. Molasses-slow. Fog city. High as shit. "I guess I never did, either."

Donovan and I used to talk about going to high school before we'd even made it to sixth grade. We vowed to never become those friends who stopped talking when they got to a new school and found new people.

"What if we're sick of each other by then?" I was hanging upside down on his bed, my head near the floor, my hand wrapped around a waxy stick of strawberry licorice.

"We won't be sick of each other, T," he said from the other side of the bed. My feet were near his head and vice versa. "We've known each other our whole lives. Almost. What's gonna change?"

"I don't know." I looked around his room: the blue-and-gray wallpaper border along the top of the walls with fat white baseballs dancing through the middle; the matching, pilled bedspread and sun-bleached curtains; the bookshelf of comics across the room, next to his desk. He was getting too old for it—except the comics; I was sure he'd never outgrow those—but I think a part of him was reluctant to ask for a new, more mature bedroom. Just like I hated to think about how it was probably the last year I could admit I still played with dolls.

"What if you get a girlfriend and she doesn't like me?" I said, cracking my toes next to his ears. "Or you stop talking to me because you don't want her to know you sucked your thumb until third grade?"

"Only when no one else was around!" he said too loudly as

he shoved my legs hard, almost pushing me off the bed sideways. "And I know things about you."

"Oh, yeah? Mr. Frog?" I gnawed on the end of the licorice. "So what. He sits on my bed. It's not like I still have tea parties with him."

"No, I'll tell them how you snore when you sleep."

"I do not!" I pushed myself up on my elbows, but all I could see was his torso spread out on my right side, covered in a navy-and-orange Bears T-shirt. "You're the one who snores. And *drools*."

"At least my parents don't keep a night-light in my room *just in case*." He laughed and I smacked him on the thigh and then we got over it because I had to ask him for the package of Twizzlers that was out of my reach.

"But T, seriously, we'll be cool, right? High school, girl-friends, boyfriends, whatever. Right?" His voice was faint, like he wasn't sure he should have said anything. Like it was too earnest and he thought I would make fun of him.

"Of course," I said, and it hung heavy in the air for a few seconds, like a verbal contract. And then: "Who else is going to put up with you?"

Donovan was around until the first part of middle school, so the students who moved here after seventh grade or transferred from private school—like Sara-Kate and Klein—know about him only through other kids' stories and the news. It's strange to think that Sara-Kate knows so little about such a huge part of my past, that even Bryn Davenport is closer to this situation than she is.

High school seemed so far away back then, it's hard to believe I'm here now and Donovan never made it. I wonder if he went to school while he was gone . . . or if he was imprisoned 24/7, secured to a piece of furniture when his kidnapper left the house.

"Sorry," Bryn says, her eyes clouded with worry as she looks into mine. "Too heavy for a Friday morning?"

"No, no." I shake my hazy head. Pull lazily at the hem of my top. "I was just thinking of our quiz in world gov later. Totally forgot."

"Well, it's Jacobsen." Bryn gives me a faint smile and lightly touches my arm again, leaving her hand there for a moment, as if she's afraid I can't hold myself up on my own. Do I really look that high? I need a mirror. "He'll give you another chance if you screw up. See you in fifth."

She scoots away from me and into the crowd, elbowing her way through two meaty football players. Small and fearless, that one.

We all pile into the musty, cavernous gym, our shoes squeaking on the shiny basketball court. I gaze around for what seems like ten minutes before I find Sara-Kate and Phil. Then I take a deep breath and climb to the top of the wooden bleachers, only stopping once to wobble. I brace myself on Joey Thompson, but his shoulders are so thick I'm not sure he notices.

I try to slide onto the end next to Phil, but he won't budge. He stops talking to Sara-Kate long enough to point to the open space on the other side of her. Great. I step over Phil's feet and then Sara-Kate's before I plunk down next to Klein. Hosea is on the other side of him. His eyes are on me and then they're not, and somehow that feels like a much bigger loss than it is.

Klein leans in and I swear to God his cologne almost chokes me, but I concentrate on breathing through my mouth so he doesn't notice. What I really want to do is look past him, talk to Hosea, ask him how he got to be so good at piano.

Klein grins at me. "You're coming to my party tonight, yeah?"

A few vodka shots and a pill or two and it would most definitely be a leer.

I stop myself from recoiling, say, "I think so" as I crack my knuckles one by one.

I look to Sara-Kate and Phil but they're no help. Phil is complaining about all the time he spent worrying over his trig test only to have it postponed for the assembly. Sara-Kate has one fishnet-stockinged leg crossed over the other as she nods. She's good; it almost looks like she cares about what he's saying.

"We'll celebrate your friend being back." Klein leans even closer and says in a low voice, "Don't *think*, Legs. Do."

"How's Trisha?" I ask in a voice that carries.

I hear a quiet laugh from the other side of Klein and I can't hide my smile, but I also can't bring myself to look at Hosea. Instead, I turn my head to the front, where the principal and guidance counselor are trying to get everyone to shut up so they can start this thing.

Principal Detz talks about the miracle of Donovan's return and how even though not everyone knew him, he's one of Ashland Hills High School's own, because he would have been a member of the junior class this year if he hadn't been abducted.

Crumbaugh stands next to Detz with her hands clasped, looking like autumn exploded all over her. It's kind of ironic that she's dedicated her life to preparing kids for their future when she still dresses like a child. Her wardrobe coordinates with seasons and holidays: pumpkin sweaters in October and red hearts from head to toe in February.

"This is a happy time," she says now in her nasal voice. "But I understand that some of you may be confused by the *feelings* brought up by Donovan's return, so I'll be holding extended hours over the next few weeks as we learn more about his story."

I lean in to Sara-Kate. "Seriously? She's making this about us right now?"

She shakes her head, brings a hand up to touch the tiny silver hoop at the edge of her bottom lip. "Totally clueless."

Nobody in this room knows what Donovan went through, can even begin to fathom what his life has been like since seventh grade. Even if he wasn't chained to a bed, his day-to-day looked nothing like ours. The more I think about it, the more positive I am he's never seen the inside of a high school. Kidnappers don't care about education or extracurricular activities or well-balanced meals.

"Thank you, Mrs. Crumbaugh." Detz smiles like she's the most gracious being on the planet before they tag-team a series of stranger danger warnings better suited for a kindergarten class.

Sara-Kate says my name, and when I look up she's standing, holding out her hand to help me up. The assembly is over and I feel worse than when it began.

Talking about Donovan won't make me forget how I'd step out my front door and hear his voice for months, even years after he'd been gone—teasing me about the way I stand in first position when I'm not in ballet class: heels together, toes pointed to opposite corners. Or inviting me over for dessert because the Pratts had pie or cake or ice cream every night and not just for holidays and special occasions.

A sit-down with Crumbaugh may help other students, the ones who don't have the memories or connection I do. The ones who haven't logged years of sleepovers and countless carpools with Donovan, who don't know that he completely understood me without even trying.

But talking about Donovan won't make me forget the last day I saw him. It won't make me forget how the last minutes between us were so filled with tension and secrets that for the first time in my life, I questioned whether we were still best friends.

# CHAPTER FOUR

THE THING ABOUT KLEIN ANDERSON'S PARTIES IS THAT they really are the best.

Most families in Ashland Hills do pretty well for themselves, but the Andersons are Old Money, which sets them apart. It also means Klein has access to any kind of liquor and drugs he wants. Girls, too, if Trisha Dove weren't around to keep him in check.

I eat dinner with my parents, change out of my school clothes, and wait for Phil. Sara-Kate is coming, too, but he swings by to get me first since I live three blocks over. My parents are parked at the dining room table, involved in a hot and heavy game of Scrabble. When I walk in wearing my jacket, they take a break to issue the standard weekend warnings: be careful, home by midnight, don't get in the car with anyone who's been drinking, and I stop listening after that.

I look over at Donovan's house as I walk out to Phil's car. Déjà vu. Just like four years before, the porch and front steps are covered in signs. Only this time, instead of hopeful, almost pleading messages, they are happy! And grateful! And heavily punctuated! WELCOME HOME, DONOVAN!, and GOD IS GOOD ALL THE TIME, and WE MISSED YOU!!!! Stuffed animals are everywhere, like plush dolphins will make up for all the time he didn't get to be a kid. And the candles—they're propped up on every available flat surface. Tea lights and pillars and scented. I know the people who left all this stuff mean well, but they've only succeeded in making the Pratts' lawn look like a shrine . . . or a junkyard.

Phil is staring at it, too, when I slide into the passenger seat.

"So, I guess you haven't seen him?" he asks, chewing on his bottom lip as he turns to me.

"We've called a few times but they're not answering." I take a deep breath, thinking of how hopeful I was this afternoon when my mother and I sat next to each other on the couch, the phone between our ears. "I think they unplugged their answering machine. And my mom says we can't go over without talking to someone first."

"What do you think he's doing? Besides feeling really fucking happy that he's back?"

"Maybe that's all." I strap my seat belt across my chest, click it into place. "Maybe being happy is enough."

I look along our street as Phil reverses down my driveway. Our neighborhood looks like any other neighborhood in Midwest, suburban America. The same brick houses, the same long, wide driveways, the same tastefully landscaped yards and seasonal porch decorations. This time of year, it's colorful gourds displayed in groups of three and four, and harvest wreaths hung on front doors.

"Phil, where do you think he was?" I ask, glancing at Donovan's house once more before we head in the opposite direction. "I know the cops found him in Vegas, but where do you think he was actually *living*?"

"I don't know." Phil looks both ways before he continues through a four-way stop. "I didn't really think about it. I mean, I did, but it felt wrong. Like, here I am living this normal life in a normal house and he's out there being forced to do God knows—"

I put my hand on his arm when he doesn't continue, gently squeeze right above his elbow. "Yeah. Me too." Then, "Do you think he's the same at all? I mean . . . what will we talk about when we finally see him? I can't picture it. I can't . . . I won't know what to say."

Phil is quiet for a few moments as we coast through town on the way to Sara-Kate's, and I wonder what Ashland Hills would look like to Donovan now—*will* look like, once he leaves his house. It's changed some since he's been gone. Not a ton but enough to notice if you haven't been around for four years. Like the big-name coffee chains that have cropped up, trying to put Coffee & Jam out of business. Or the new barbecue place down the street from Casablanca's where every day around noon it smells like someone's shooting off a pulled-pork cannon. There's Ashland Hills Elementary and the organic foods/hippie store that's always empty, and we don't think about what it would be like to suddenly stop seeing them every day.

"Do you remember that time we went to Great America?" Phil rolls to a stop at a yellow light instead of cruising right through like I would. He drives like a model in a student driving handbook—hands at ten and two, never more than two miles above the speed limit.

"Oh. With all our parents?" I haven't thought about that day in years.

"Yeah." When I look over, Phil grins. "We were eight, right?"

"Nine. And Glenn was with us and started crying because he was too short for that roller coaster we rode over and over again until you puked."

"Weak stomach. It's genetic." His grin widens, showing his perfect white teeth. They should be, considering they were caged under braces for three and a half years. "I wasn't the only one. Remember my dare?"

"God." I groan, clutching my stomach at the memory. "How could I forget? I still can't touch hot dogs."

Great America food patio. Phil dared Donovan to eat three foot-long dogs in one sitting. Paid for them with his allowance and everything. Donovan did it, but ended up vomiting his accomplishment at the edge of the patio five minutes later. Phil sympathy-puked shortly after that and needless to say, the park employees and our parents were not amused.

"Ma wants to have Donovan's family and you guys over for

dinner," Phil says. "We haven't even talked to them and she's already planning the menu. She'd probably feed me to death if we were separated as long as Donovan and his mom."

"Your mom would try to feed the entire neighborhood to death." I pull out my phone to text Sara-Kate, let her know we're only a few blocks away.

She's waiting outside, smoking on the front porch of her darkened house. She strides toward us in a body-hugging tunic, leggings, and knee-high suede boots and I can't imagine what it would be like to have curves like that and not want to hide them.

She'd kill me if I ever said this out loud, but Sara-Kate is kind of a cartoon character. Her features are just so exaggeratedly perfect that if you stare at her too long it looks as if someone drew her. Bow-shaped lips and brown eyes so big and sincere you could drown in them. She knows her way around a makeup bag, but I'd never put anything on my face if I was her. She's just as pretty without it.

"Hey, doll." She kisses my cheek, wipes away the lipstick print with her thumb, then crawls behind me to sit in back.

"Where are your parents?" I ask, looking pointedly at the cigarette dangling between her index and middle fingers. I keep the window cracked.

"My mom has a show in the city tonight."

"You'd better be careful with that thing," Phil says in his dad voice as he turns to eye Sara-Kate and her cigarette.

"Have I ever burned or otherwise desecrated your precious

car?" she says, holding it just outside the window so the smoke and ash will blow behind us in the wind.

"Just watch where you hold it, okay?" Phil heads toward Klein's, which means the houses grow larger with each street we cross. The yards become more spacious, the cars in the driveways more luxurious.

Sara-Kate blows two perfectly circular smoke rings out the window, then pushes her round face between the seats. "Thanks for driving, Philip."

"No problem, Sara-Katherine." He turns his head slightly to give her the side-eye.

"But it's not Katherine." Her perpetually sunny face twists into a pout.

"And it's not Philip." He pauses as we drive by my favorite house in Ashland Hills: all white and three stories high with a flat roof, sturdy columns, and a long balcony off the second level. "Not unless you're my mother."

But he doesn't hide his grin fast enough when I look over.

Klein's parents are always on some type of vacation or business trip, and his parties have become an institution. He hires actual DJs from Chicago and these things generally last all night and the cops never break them up because his family has more money than anyone in Ashland Hills.

His street is already lined with cars, so we have to park on the next one over. My parents would flip their shit if it ever got back to them that I'd thrown a party this size. Not that I ever would. Mom and Dad are pretty chill on a day-to-day basis, but when something big goes down, they take action *fast*. Attempting to pull off a party like Klein's would land me at least a monthlong grounding. Probably more.

Ellie Harris is sitting on the front steps as we walk up. She leans her head close to Lark Pearson, looks at us, and throws her head back in laughter. I don't know what Hosea likes about her, because I haven't found much. She's pretty enough, I guess, in a manufactured sort of way. Good highlights and perfectly glossed lips; the kind of girl who's never in public without full makeup. I wonder if Hosea has seen her without makeup.

She takes a delicate sip from a bottle of hard cider. "Hi, Phil."

"Yeah, hi, Phil," echoes Lark. Her eyes are rimmed with so much liner, it looks like someone punched her.

Phil pauses for a couple of beats to see if they'll acknowledge me or Sara-Kate. They don't. Lark whispers something to Ellie and this time they both laugh. Ellie giggles as she tips the bottle back for another drink.

"Excuse us, *ladies*," Phil says, and damn does he know how to make a polite word sound like something he found in a toilet.

He holds the heavy front door open for us and closes it firmly behind him.

We step into the room off the foyer where everyone dumps their coats. It's the maid's sitting room, small and plain but comfortable, with a cream-colored suede couch and matching love seat, a bookshelf of hardcover classics, and a sleek television mounted on the far wall. Phil stows our coats in the closet on wooden hangers instead of draping them over the couches like everyone else. "We don't know where their shit has been," he mumbles as he hangs his thrifted brown leather jacket.

"You know, Lark was in my study hall last year and she was really nice to me," Sara-Kate says, her eyebrows furrowed in confusion. "She'd always tell me about the big makeup sales."

"Blame Ellie Harris." I shrug off my black peacoat and hand it to Phil, who's waiting, hanger in hand. "Everything she touches turns to bitch."

"And the first round goes to Theo," Phil says, nodding with an eyebrow raised in appreciation.

Klein is one of the first people we see as we walk back out to the foyer. He's standing near the bottom of the spiral staircase with a drink in one hand as he surveys the crowd, practically holding court. Just in case anyone forgets this is his house and all. Phil rolls his eyes.

"I still can't believe you fucked him," he says as he tugs at his denim vest with the frayed edges.

"I didn't." I give his vest the once-over. It's actually an old denim jacket with the sleeves cut off, but whatever. "And you're *friends* with him."

"We're tangential friends." We step into the living room. Sara-Kate by my side, Phil facing us. "Like, one step beyond acquaintances."

Leo Watson squeezes by us in his Wranglers and signature brown Stetson, pauses for a second to make a face at Phil's black skinny jeans. I don't think he has much room for judgment, considering he dresses like he works on somebody's ranch.

"I think the number of times you've gotten high with someone directly correlates to your level of friendship," I say to Phil. "You and Klein are one hit away from buying matching bongs."

"Bullshit." But he takes off his glasses to wipe them on his shirt and he only does that when he doesn't know what to say.

I tilt my head to the side as I look at him. "Three words: winter formal afterparty."

Sara-Kate bursts into giggles and I'm next. We'll use any excuse to bring up what happened.

Winter formal is *the* dance at our school. Few people take homecoming seriously besides the athletes and student council, and prom is so overhyped that I wonder how it ever meets anyone's expectations. But winter formal is smack in the middle of the school year, a couple of weeks after we return from break, when everyone is looking for something to beat the post-holiday slump that falls in the dead of winter. Plainly put, it's the night when the entire school gets dressed up and shit-faced, all under one roof. I've been with a date only once, and that was with Klein, my freshman year. I went stag with Sara-Kate and Phil when we were sophomores, but it would be fun to switch it up this year, if there was actually someone I wanted to ask me. Someone available.

Last year, Phil got wasted on airplane bottles of gin and

we found him in the Andersons' game room with Klein: arms around each other, straight-up kumbaya bro-love in front of the Indiana Jones pinball machine, and we couldn't tell how long they'd been in there. Seeing the two of them get along so well would have been disturbing if it hadn't been so funny. I swear I heard the words *best buddy* slurred back and forth a few times. Of course Phil denies it and I honestly don't think Klein remembers any part of that night, let alone the end.

"Whatever, Theo. It's still not the same as hooking up with him."

"It was a couple of times. There was no sex. And it was, like, a million years ago, so I'd appreciate it if you'd stop bringing it up."

I glare at him, but it's not my full-on death stare. Murderous looks don't go with my new sweater. I'm so flat that most sweaters look ridiculous on me, but my mother brought this one home last week and it's perfect. Fitted with a deep scoop neck and made from soft cashmere the color of eggplant.

"Not a million." Phil won't let it go. "Freshman year. Two."

"Maybe *you* need to get laid and stop fixating on who *I* didn't sleep with two years ago." I look to Sara-Kate for support. "Right?"

She holds up her hands, shakes her pale purple head at us. "I am *so* not getting into this. Now let's go find some booze. Mama's thirsty."

Next stop: the kitchen. Nearly every brand and type of liquor imaginable is spread out on the granite counters—some

44

uncapped, some half empty, and others completely untouched, like the monstrous bottle of butterscotch schnapps. The door at the back of the room opens out to a terrace, where people are gathered around three kegs. Music pulsates through the house at such a deafening volume that even the bottles clink to the beat.

Phil and Sara-Kate go outside to check on the keg situation while I peruse my options on the counter. I'm inspecting the label on a bottle of vodka when Klein walks in. He hasn't changed much since we used to hang out. He shaved off his curls so that his hair is nothing more than black prickles, but it only accentuates his remarkable bone structure.

He stands so close to me, I can smell the soap from his shower. And the liquor on his breath. Better than cologne, I guess.

"Legs. You made it."

I smile and say hello. I guess I'll always be grateful to Klein in some way. He's not my type, but he's exactly what I needed two years ago. He made me forget what had happened to Donovan and also those months at Juniper Hill. But most importantly, he made me forget about Trent.

Trent, who was five years older, eighteen to my thirteen. Trent Miller, who told me he loved me and wanted to be with me and made me believe every word he said about us. Trent Ryan Miller, who just up and left one day, who was never to be heard from again, who the shrinks decided was a big part of the reason I ended up at Juniper Hill in the first place. That is, when they weren't busy blaming ballet.

Klein was sloppy, but he was sweet and always treated me like I was the best-looking girl in the room. He still does, so long as his girlfriend's not around. As if she knows I'm thinking about her, Trisha wanders in a few moments later, all glassy eyes and fashionably unbrushed hair. Trisha is tall and thin, but not the type of thin that makes people want to send you away.

"Hi, Theo," she says in this faraway voice. "It's really amazing about Donovan. I sat behind him in fourth grade. Remember? We did that science fair project with the rain gauge."

I don't, but I nod and start backing up, slowly so she won't notice I'm trying to get away.

But Klein sees everything.

"Wait." He pulls a red cup from one of the upside-down stacks, all lined up like those hats the Shriners wear. "Let me make you a drink."

"No, thanks." I point toward the patio. "Beer."

"Okay." He wraps an arm around Trisha's teeny waist. "Well, we're gonna roll later. You in?"

I choke down a "no fucking way" and say that I have to be up early for ballet tomorrow. Which is true. But also? Doing E with Klein Anderson and his girlfriend is about the last thing to check off of my list tonight. They hooked up with Mallory Frank at a pool party last summer. I wasn't there but I'd believe it even if there hadn't been witnesses. Mallory is on the fringe, one of those girls who will do anything to make her way into the circle.

He looks at me now and shrugs. "Your choice. Hey, if you see Hosea out there, tell him I'm looking for him. Dude has no fucking concept of time."

He and Trisha start fumbling with a bottle of rum and a two-liter of Coke and that's my cue to leave. My friends are no longer on the patio, but the kegs are getting plenty of action from the fringe people—like Mallory. People who are cool enough to be invited, but awkward enough to feel like they have to kiss everyone's ass for their next invitation. I don't know if anyone would call me, Sara-Kate, and Phil popular, but we're cool with the people who *do* hold most of the power in our class—particularly the two messy people I just left in the kitchen.

"You look like you could use a beer," says a friendly voice to my left.

Eddie Corteen. We've gone to school together our whole lives but I don't know anything about him. He shows up to class every day, he comes to all the parties, and he's so *nice,* it seems like an act until you realize no one could keep that up for so long. But I can't remember having an actual conversation with him, nothing more than hello in passing or asking him for his notes if I missed English class.

"I *could* use a beer," I say since he's already pumping the keg. "Thanks, Eddie."

"No problem," he says, sort of ducking his head as he reaches into a plastic bag near the base of the keg and fills a red cup. "So how's it going? I've been thinking about you."

Eddie flushes so quickly, I wonder how his mind had time to communicate with his body. His white-blond eyebrows get lost in his pinkened skin. "I mean, not like that. I just—Donovan. You know?"

Right. He knew him, too.

He hands me the cup and I sip. Ice-cold, hasn't gone flat, and hardly any head. Normally I'd forgo the beer on a Friday night since I have ballet early the next morning, but after the past couple of days I deserve this. Except . . . thinking about Donovan mars the perfection of this beer.

"I feel like I shouldn't be out right now," I say, spilling my fears to the person I probably know the least at this party, as if that makes any kind of sense. The words are out before I can stop them. "Like it's wrong because he's at home with his mom . . . recovering."

*Recovering.* Such a crap word, but I don't know what else to say. He was hurt and suffering and now he's home and trying to heal. Maybe he can't close his eyes without launching a thousand nightmares.

So what am I doing? It never occurred to me to skip Klein's party until now, but guilt coats my insides as I think of Donovan while I stand on the terrace, holding a beer and talking to people who used to be his classmates.

"You can't think about it that way," Eddie says in a careful voice. "I used to sit behind you guys on the bus sometimes and you . . . well, you two seemed real tight. You were a good friend to him when he was here, Theo."

"Thanks, Eddie," I say, staring down at the toes of my black riding boots. Surprised that he remembers how we used to be.

But four years apart have turned Donovan's life upside down, and now even the familiar pieces of his former existence—his mother, his house, his bedroom—must seem so far removed from who he is today.

"Try not to think about it," Eddie says, his hair winking silvery blond in the bright lights shining over the patio. "We're gonna get a game of flip cup going later, if you're up for it. You could be on my team."

He gives me a smile so wide and genuine, I smile, too. And for a moment, it makes me feel a little less stupid for confiding in him.

"Maybe," I say, glancing behind him, where the two guys I always see him with are hanging back, watching us. I don't know their names. They turn their heads as soon as I make eye contact. I look at Eddie again. "But thank you."

"Anytime, Theo." He tips an imaginary hat to me in such a nerdily endearing way, I can practically hear his friends teasing him already.

I turn toward the lawn and start across the perfectly manicured grass toward the Andersons' gazebo. I navigate my way up the steps and sit cross-legged on the floor. I sip my beer and close my eyes but I can't shake this. Him. Donovan.

Footsteps are crossing the yard, crackling through the layers of fallen leaves. I open my eyes to Hosea Roth's dark figure silhouetted against the autumn night sky. I stand, hold carefully to my beer.

He stops.

"Oh. I didn't know anyone was out here. Sorry."

"Wait," I say. "It's Theo."

I step out of the shadows; he squints up at me.

"Well. I guess it is." He pushes a few loose strands of hair behind his ear. "Twice in one day."

Which is strange, considering he always blended into the background before. This morning seems so long ago, though I remember every second we were alone together.

We stare at each other. He says, "I can leave . . ." just as I ask, "Do you have a cigarette?"

He laughs, then pulls a packet from the front pocket of his hoodie. "Cloves okay?"

I nod and sit down on the steps. Hosea sits next to me and leans against the cool, painted wood. His usual black T-shirt has been replaced by a thick cotton hoodie, the kind you have to pull on over your head. Or maybe the shirt is underneath. My face goes warm when I think of this, as if I were undressing him in my mind.

He knocks loose a clove, holds it out to me. He lights mine first, cups his hand around the flame until it sparks on the tobacco. Then he leans back and lights his own, takes a long drag. His face is defined by a square jaw, hard lines that make him look angry even when he's not. I wonder if he ever wears his hair down, if it makes him seem softer. Less stoic.

"What does Marisa think about this?" he asks, moving his clove around in lazy circles, sending tendrils of smoke curling out from the end.

"About the smoking? It's more of a don't ask, don't tell situation."

"And the beer?" He grins and even in the dark I can tell it's a nice grin.

"A girl can't live on ballet alone." I smile at him and look away and I wonder how this snuck up on me.

Hosea Roth. He's always just been there. I was in eighth grade when he moved from Nebraska, started at Ashland Hills High, but even when we were at the same school the next year, he never stood out to me. Not for more than what he was already known for. Now I don't know how I ever could have missed it, that something deeper was lurking behind his image.

"You look like you could," he says as he returns the lighter to his pocket. "Live on ballet."

"I do?" His words make me feel shy but understood. Happy but nervous. I take a sip of my beer as I process this.

"You're so in your own world at that place. Like nothing could ever bother you."

"Oh." My skin burns again as I think of him watching me dance. I was practically in my underwear in front of him, slick with sweat and stretching my muscles to their limit. Maybe it doesn't seem like a big deal in the moment, when we're all in a room together, when he's there for the strict purpose of musical accompaniment. But now, thinking about it like that . . . I know he's not playing specifically for *me* but it seems so intimate, dancing to the music he makes.

"I didn't know that was your . . . I wouldn't have just shown up like that if I'd known you go there. You looked like you wanted me to get the hell out."

"Maybe a little," I say slowly. "But only at first."

I sort of laugh and it makes him laugh, too, and there it is again. I could listen to that sound for the rest of the night.

"What do you think about?" he asks. "When you're dancing." And when I look up, his eyes are already on me. Mine sweep across his face and I wonder why I never noticed how much I *like* his face. Even parts I never thought I could care about. Like his nose. It's a good nose. A strong nose that fits the rest of his strong features.

I hesitate, but his voice is softer and I don't think he's making fun of me.

Still, I can't quite say it. Not yet. I've never talked to anyone outside of dance about ballet. Not beyond the basics. No one else understands that when my feet are laced into pointe shoes I feel like I can do damn near anything. And I'm embarrassed to say I have no clue what I'd be doing if I didn't have dance.

I clear my throat and take a drag so I can stall some more. Finally, I say, "It's dumb."

He taps his long fingers against his knee, then looks at me with his clear gray eyes. "When I lived in Nebraska, I worked on this Rachmaninoff piece until I could play it with my eyes closed, play it backward, whatever. My piano teacher loved it.

She stared at me like a goddamn groupie. And then I played it for my mom and she cried. Through the whole thing."

Rachmaninoff. So he knows his shit. I wonder how people would look at Hosea if they knew music is such an important part of his life. *Real* music, not the crap like Donnie Kenealy and his garage band play. It makes *me* look at him differently, now that I know we really have something in common.

"How old were you?" I ask.

"I don't know. Maybe eight? But I guess . . . when I play, I wonder what people are thinking. How they're interpreting the song." He points his clove toward me. "Your turn."

"I think about my future . . ." I pretend that Hosea is Ruthie or Josh or Marisa, the people who get how much ballet means to me. If I think about him like everyone else, even like Sara-Kate or Phil, I won't be able to finish. "Dancing on a real stage in front of a real audience. With a real company. How different it will feel."

"That's what you've been working for this whole time?" He stretches his long legs down the steps of the gazebo, his feet pointing toward the enormous, shedding sycamore tree across the yard.

I nod because I don't know how to say ballet is the only thing in this world that makes me feel alive, that doesn't disappoint me.

"Then it's not dumb." He gives me a small smile. Similar to the one he flashed us his first day at the studio, but this one lingers.

And perhaps it is the cool air passing through the night, but deep down I know the shiver travels down my spine because that smile was just for me.

He taps his clove against the gazebo, spills ashes through the rails and onto the ground. I inhale and hold mine out in front of me, see how long I can go without breaking the long tube of ash that has grown on the end. I let out a stream of smoke and lick my lips. Nobody I know smokes cloves besides Hosea. I've only smoked them once, a long time ago, but I've never forgotten how they make your lips taste like sugar.

Our gazes gradually shift to the house in the distance. Joey Thompson has muscled his way into the crowd of fringe people and is lording over a keg with one of his football cronies, David Tulip. There's a ripple in the crowd and Lark Pearson breaks through, grabs Joey by the forearms, and shouts something incoherent in his face. Everyone on the patio cheers, then Joey and David each grab one of her legs and up she goes. Kegstand time.

I tried it once and lasted about two seconds. Something about the unique combination of being upside down and chugging beer doesn't mix for me.

Lark makes me think of Ellie, which makes me think of Trisha, which makes me think of what I was supposed to tell Hosea when I first saw him.

"Klein was looking for you."

"Yeah, I know." Hosea shakes his head. "He's been texting me all fucking night."

I don't know how he deals with basically being at Klein's beck and call. I guess you're supposed to bend over backward for your customers, but Klein gets off on pushing people to their limit. Even his best friend.

The color in his face deepens in the light cast down from the moon. "Listen, would you mind not saying anything to Klein or Phil or . . . anyone about my gig at the studio?"

I bite my tongue against asking him why he doesn't want people to know one of the best parts about him. "Sure."

"Cool," he says, his eyes moving back out to the lawn.

The lawn, where another person is walking in our direction. A girl this time. Short, with legs that travel very fast. Ellie Harris.

I should have known she wouldn't be far behind Lark. Who has been released from the kegstand and is now wiping her mouth, burping into her forearm before she goes up for round two.

Ellie plants herself in front of Hosea, one French-manicured hand holding on to a bottle at her side, the other smoothing down the fabric on her hip.

"Klein's been looking for you everywhere," she says in one of those false-bright voices that makes it apparent nothing about the situation in front of her is okay.

"So I've heard." Hosea stands and stubs out the clove on the bottom of his boot. "I needed some air."

My phone buzzes in my pocket. A text from Sara-Kate: *Where are you?* I write back that I'm in the gazebo, put out my clove, and stand up, too.

"You guys know each other?" Hosea motions in my direction as if Ellie's stare was not already boring into me like hot fire.

"Mmm. Thea, right?" She turns away before we can make eye contact and pulls on the bottom of her skirt, trying to tug it down to cover more of her bare legs. The fabric hardly budges and she gives up after a while, takes a long drink of cider as she looks at Hosea. She lowers the bottle and rakes her fingers through her chunky blond highlights. "Babe, we should go see what Klein wants."

He takes her hand and I stare too long. At their intertwined fingers, how things are so easy between them. I wonder if I could have that, too.

They start to walk away but I don't want Hosea to leave without a goodbye, so I blurt out, "Thanks for the clove."

I'm not talking to her but Ellie turns her suspicious eyes on me and I don't care. Trisha may be a burnout but at least she never pretends she doesn't know who I am when we've been going to school together our entire lives. One day, I'll leave girls like Ellie and Lark behind, and then they can't say shit because I'll be touring the world with a professional company. Lark is smart—National Honor Society, academic scholarships, the whole deal—so maybe she'll do something worthwhile with her life when she leaves the kegstand phase behind.

But I don't think Ellie has a whole lot going on behind the makeup. She coasts by on her looks and Trisha's popularity and one of these days that has to catch up to her, right?

Hosea glances back at me and kind of nods. "Yeah, sure. Later, Theo."

I sit down again to wait for Sara-Kate, pulling my knees up to my chest and wrapping my arms around myself as I inhale the sweet smoke that clings to my jacket. And for the tiniest moment, I let myself imagine Hosea's arms are wrapped around me instead of my own.

## CHAPTER FIVE

I WALK DOWNSTAIRS IN MY PAJAMAS THE NEXT morning to find my father sitting at the kitchen table, drinking coffee and reading the newspaper. He used to bring work to the table sometimes until Mom forbid it. He's good about sticking to her rule. Even if it means that some days he eats breakfast in record time or goes into the office absurdly early so he can work on spreadsheets over a doughnut and coffee.

He looks up as I approach, pushes his wire-rimmed glasses up his nose. He looks cozy in his green-and-navy flannel robe with the cuffs rolled up. "Morning, babygirl. Ready for ballet?"

I nod as I stifle a yawn. Saturday mornings always come too early, whether or not I went out the night before. And I'm never hungry for breakfast. I know it's important because it sets the tone for the day and blah blah blah. But most days, the thought of food before 11:00 a.m. literally turns my stomach. Especially rich breakfast foods like fatty bacon and runny eggs and the worst of it all: syrupy French toast.

But I can't skip it. That's a promise I can't break or even bend, because one slip-up and they'll be on the phone with Marisa, who could help them decide it's time for me to go back to Juniper Hill. And I can't go back there. I won't.

So I make my way to the refrigerator and push aside the leftover baked spaghetti, reach for a carton of plain yogurt. I dump a few large spoonfuls into a bowl and sprinkle fat-free granola on top. Leaning against the island is my favorite way to eat. Standing up, taking in slow, deliberate spoonfuls so no one can accuse me of cheating.

Dad looks up in my direction, but not really *at* me. He does this for a while and I've opened my mouth to ask him what's wrong when he says, "There's news about Donovan."

I almost drop my spoonful of yogurt on the floor. "More news? Is it bad?"

He looks right at me now. "He's not talking, Theodora."

My father is the only one who calls me that. His mother was Theodora, too, but I never met her. Usually my full name is attached to fairly innocuous sentences (*How was your day, Theodora? Isn't your mother's tomato sauce delicious, Theodora?*), so it takes a bit for the weight of this one to sink in.

"Not talking?" I set my bowl down on the counter. "Like, at all?"

"Not at all," he says to me with sad eyes. Then: "And they've released information about the suspect." He rubs a hand over the thinning hair at the back of his head before he folds the front page of the paper in half, highlighting the mug shot on the front. "The person who took him is . . . a man. Thirty years old. His name is Christopher Fenner."

I take the paper from my father, scan the story in front of me. Christopher Fenner's name floats across the page, along with the kidnapping and child endangerment charges. My eyes travel to the picture that accompanies the article.

Fuck.

Christopher Fenner has bright eyes and a defiant mouth and dark hair that curls over his collar. Even with a scruffy beard, he doesn't look thirty. He seems like the kind of guy whose worst offense would be pounding too many Bud Lights and passing out in his truck, not someone who would kidnap a child and drag him thousands of miles from his home so he could—

No. I can't think about the images that have been swimming through my mind for so many years. He's only a suspect. Maybe there was a mistake. Or maybe that's what I'll tell myself until we know more, because it's easier than putting a face to all the abuse I've imagined that Donovan endured.

Donovan was—

No match for someone like this.

The suspect's flat, still eyes stare into mine until I can't take it.
*Fuck.*

"They say he worked at the convenience store a few months before the abduction, that Donovan probably knew him." Dad is talking again but I can't look at him.

I try to swallow the bile in my throat but seconds later I'm rushing toward the sink, leaning over, vomiting what little breakfast I've had into the basin. I stay hunched over for a while, rasping out breaths and wiping my eyes, even after Dad jumps up to stand behind me. He sort of pats my back and says, "Oh, Theodora" over and over in this sad voice.

A couple of moments pass before he adds, "I didn't mean to upset you. I wouldn't have shown it to you if—"

If he'd thought I couldn't handle it.

I turn on the faucet to wash away the mess, then cup my hands under the water, rinse out my mouth.

"No, it's okay. I wanted to know." My voice echoes back up from the sink. I straighten up and wipe my lips with the striped dish towel sitting on the counter. "I needed to know."

"Why don't you stay home today?" He says it like he's doing me a favor, like he's suggesting I skip school on the day we're scheduled to dissect fetal pigs.

"I can't." I haven't missed a dance class in three years, and the times before that weren't by choice. He knows this, which is why he doesn't challenge me.

I dump out the rest of my breakfast because I don't think I could get down another bite.

"You're sure you don't want to take the morning off?" Dad removes his glasses to look at me. He only needs them when he's working or reading. "I could call Marisa and explain. I'm sure she'd understand if you need to stay home today."

"I should go," I say. Throat burning. Tongue sour. "I'll miss the train if I don't leave soon."

"Theodora, you know you can always talk to me, right?" He's standing next to the island and he could be the father in one of those feel-good coffee commercials right now if he didn't look so *sad*. His eyes, they kill me.

"Of course, Dad." I start making my way to the door. Hoping he'll get the hint. Hoping he'll drop it.

He doesn't.

"Or you can talk to your mother. Or someone . . . professional, if that's more comfortable for you." He clears his throat once, twice. "I know this is hard, Donovan coming home after all this time when we thought . . . And now this. It's . . . it's really hard and I want you to know you can talk to us, babygirl. Anytime."

"Sure. I mean, I know." I've almost got one foot out of the room now. "I do. Thanks, Dad. I'm going to class now, okay? I'll come home right after and rest."

He nods. "Have a good class. *Merde.*"

I've told him dozens of times that dancers say that to each other only before they go onstage—the ballet world's answer to "break a leg"—and that if there's no performance, he's simply saying "shit" in a poor French accent.

But as I walk up the stairs, I can't help thinking he's inadvertently described how I feel about this day.

# CHAPTER SIX

BALLET IS SUCH A UNIVERSAL, RECOGNIZABLE ART form that people always think they know more about it than they do. I've endured more than my fair share of goofy fathers pirouetting in place as they pretend to be me. And the guys who don't realize that they're the millionth person to ask where I've hidden my tutu. Or girls who say, with such *authority,* that they used to dance and then sheepishly admit to only taking classes for three or four years.

Ballet is my life. I'm powerful, untouchable when I'm out on the floor, and one day I'll hold the titles I've dreamed of since I was a little girl: Soloist, then Principal Dancer. The Misty Copelands and Julie Kents and Polina Semionovas. The cream of the crop, the best of the best, the dancers *nobody* can fuck with. I started to think seriously about a professional career when I went on pointe five years ago, and that's when I truly realized just how few black dancers are performing in classical ballet companies. Sure, sometimes you can find them in the corps, but that's not the same as having your talent highlighted for everyone to see. I can't let that stop me, though. I'll keep training as hard as I can, become such an amazing dancer that the companies will *have* to judge me based on my talent instead of my skin color. I want to be the best, plain and simple.

But today, I feel like a beginner. I'm sluggish and the taste of bile coats my mouth and it's affecting my dancing. Not to mention the face of Donovan's kidnapper is everywhere I turn.

His smirk dances across the top of the barre as I stand in first position and bend my knees into a grand plié, my heels rising off the floor. I see his eyes in the mirror as I extend my leg straight behind me; they follow me around the room as I promenade in arabesque, daring me to break my slow, controlled balance. Usually, dancing calms me when I'm upset, but those goddamned eyes won't let me go, and I'm starting to wish I'd never left my bed this morning.

Donovan was found nearly 2,000 miles away with an older man, and that's reason enough to believe he could've been abused. But I can't stop thinking about how inexperienced he was when he disappeared. How scared he must have been. I'd had sex by the time he was abducted, but neither of us knew much about anything until he found that book a few years before he was taken. We were aware of the mechanics, of course. How babies got here. We knew that kissing led to touching, which led to sex. We knew that people in our class had kissed, though having a boyfriend or girlfriend back then mostly meant holding hands at recess for a couple of days and sharing your lunch without complaining. We just didn't know about the whole "touching" part and certainly nothing about how sex actually worked—not beyond the occasional glimpse of a watered-down scene on one of the shows our parents watched when we were supposed to be in bed.

But all that changed the day Donovan told me he'd found something I had to see. It was the winter of our fourth-grade year and we were in his room on a Saturday afternoon, forced indoors because of a snowstorm. I was bored at home, so I'd bundled up in my boots and coat and walked two houses down to be bored with Donovan.

I was sitting cross-legged on the rug, paging through one of his Avengers comics, when he said, "T, I have to show you something" in a low voice that promised secrets.

His door was closed, but his eyes kept darting toward it, as if someone would burst into his room at any second. We were safe. His sister, Julia, was just a baby, and she was down for her afternoon nap. Mr. Pratt was kicked back in the den with a tumbler of scotch, watching the Bulls shoot for victory, and Mrs. Pratt was in the kitchen, slicing apples for a cobbler.

Still, Donovan put a finger to his lips as he reached behind his bookshelf and pulled out a heavy-looking book with strange writing on the cover and an illustration of a man and woman facing each other. Bodies intertwined, the man's hand cupping her naked breast.

I gasped. The people weren't real, but I was nine years old and it was the most explicit thing I'd ever seen. And from the look on Donovan's face, I knew the pages inside had to be even worse. He sat down next to me, placed it on the floor between us.

"What is that?" I brushed my hand across the title and the people, then snatched my fingers away as if someone would go dusting for prints later.

"The *Kama Sutra*?" He said the beginning of *Kama* like "cam" and I thought that was how it was pronounced for years. Not that I ever advertised I'd been up close and personal with a copy.

"Where'd you get it?" Now *I* was looking at the door, listening for footsteps, plunging my fingers into the carpet to keep from opening the book.

"I found it in the garage last night," Donovan said. His jeans-clad knees were drawn up to his chest, his chin resting on top. He eyed the book warily, like it was going to stand up on legs, walk downstairs, and announce its presence. "I was looking for my old glove and there was a box . . . It looked really old, like they hadn't opened it for a long time." He paused to scratch his nose. Maybe to stall. "Do your parents have books like this?"

"Um, I don't think so." My parents were sweet to each other; they snuck kisses when they thought I wasn't looking and shared glances that made me know they were very much in love. But I'd never come across anything like *that* in our house. I pushed away the Avengers comic. "Have you looked in it?"

He nodded, and it's like that was the permission I needed, because I inhaled long and deep and then I opened the book to the middle and began to flip through it. More soft, full bodies. More illustrations that made me do double, triple takes. Some of them I just stared at, sure there was no way two humans could possibly put themselves in those positions. Or that they'd actually like it once they got there.

I could feel Donovan looking over my shoulder, but he didn't touch the book again. All he said was, "Pretty gross, right?"

"It's just . . . weird." I didn't know how else to put it.

I noticed boys, but every time one of my friends mentioned kissing or even holding hands, I felt like that was so far away for me, it was beyond comprehension. And clearly, Donovan was even less interested at that point. He'd much rather toss around a baseball with the other boys in class than spend time worrying about girls.

I looked away from the book after a couple of minutes. I felt warm all over, though I'd barely moved except to turn pages with the very tips of my fingers. It all seemed weird and a bit wrong, but I also felt a sense of relief. At least now I'd know what people were talking about whenever sex came up. Sort of.

That was the last time we looked at that book. The last time we discussed it, too, but sometimes over the next few weeks I'd notice Donovan zoning out and I didn't know how to explain it but the look on his face was how I felt when I was paging through the book, and I was sure he was thinking about it. Every time.

I need to get my shit together now because I swear, Marisa seems to be watching me more closely than usual in class. She knows our bodies almost as well as we do, what each of us is capable of doing. But the more I worry about disappointing her, the harder it is to concentrate. To stop thinking about the guy who took Donovan.

I use the extra seconds between combinations to close my eyes and breathe in deeply, and then, just when I think I'm safe, the memories of my ex-boyfriend come flooding in.

I remember how we used to drive out to the abandoned park because nobody would think to look for us among the overgrown paths and rusted swing sets. He'd always bring something for us to share—a small, flat bottle of whiskey, a fresh pack of Camel Reds. Anything that might relax me, make me feel better about the things we did when we were alone.

So many firsts happened in that park. My first taste of strong liquor. The first time I was touched between my legs, the first time a long, slow path was kissed along my breasts. The first time I saw a guy completely naked and held him in my hand.

It was also the first time I told someone "I love you."

It was easy to believe he felt the same way. Especially when his mouth curved into a small smile, when he kissed me long and deep. Those times, the sex was sweet. Slow. *Making love,* he'd say as he held my stare. *I love making love to you, Theo.*

Then there was fucking. Hard and fast and no time for kissing. Just grunting and grabbing. Eyes squeezed into slivers, lips tense with effort. I was surprised the first time because I still responded to him. My body didn't mind the new way of doing it. But I felt used afterward. Disposable. He never looked in my eyes when we were fucking.

I yearned for him to look at me, to make that connection. His eyes were hypnotic enough to captivate me, even as he lay on top of me, sweating and drowsy after I'd given him what he wanted.

It's those eyes that cause me to stumble on a double pirouette a few moments later. Marisa notices. So does Ruthie.

It doesn't help that she's a machine, Ruthie Pathman. She barely seems to break a sweat during class, but she always works her ass off. She may roll her eyes when Josh and I talk about our careers and she may pretend like she doesn't want it as much as we do, but she *does.* If I wasn't sure before, the determined set of her jaw, the spark in her eyes lets me know how true it is now.

At the end of class, Marisa asks me to stay behind and I'm cursing myself for practically falling apart until she calls Ruthie and Josh's names, too.

I glance at the piano, where Hosea slides the day's sheet music into a single stack, slings his backpack over one shoulder, and nods in our general direction before filing out of the room behind the rest of the company. I feel Ruthie's eyes on me as he leaves, but I look down at the floor, stare at the scuff marks that swoop across my pointe shoes.

Marisa closes the door behind Hosea, stands in front of the mirrored wall, and gestures for us to sit down in front of her.

She's wearing her standard outfit—a black long-sleeved leotard under a thin white wrap skirt, black leggings, and plain ballet slippers.

"I don't think I have to tell you why you're here. But just in case . . . Well, you're my best." She smiles big, stops to look at each of us. "You have my full support if you'd like to audition for next year's summer intensives."

A professional career has always seemed so far away, but one day, Josh, Ruthie, and I will headline our favorite ballets. *Coppélia. Giselle. Sleeping Beauty. Swan Lake.* Josh was damn near tailor-made for the role of Prince Siegfried and every little girl pictures herself dancing Odile at least once in her lifetime. We don't kill ourselves practicing all those fouettés for nothing.

But first, our sights are set on summer programs, at one of the best schools in the country. It's the next logical step if you're on our path. The word is that Marisa recommends summer intensive auditions to only a couple of her students each year, if that. And we don't need her permission to audition, but Marisa doesn't make mistakes.

I try to bite back a smile, but I can't help it. Even my sick stomach and weak legs can't ruin this moment. These are the words I've wanted to hear from Marisa since I first went on pointe.

"I'm afraid this is also where it becomes more of a job." Marisa's smile fades just a bit as she paces in front of the mirror, the piano to her left, the door on her right side. "If you decide to audition, it will be a huge commitment. Less time with friends, more days and nights here at the studio."

We nod in unison, our faces turned up to her like we're three years old again. Josh, especially, looks nearly the same as he did back then, with his wide eyes and the dusting of freckles across the bridge of his nose. I cross my legs and lean forward with my elbows on my thighs, catch a quick glance in the mirror to evaluate how much of me has changed and how much has stayed the same. I can't see a big difference and I wonder if I've changed more on the inside or the outside over the years.

"You'll have to make some difficult decisions, but I won't waste my time working with anyone who doesn't want this, so think hard before you decide to audition. Professional ballet is incredibly difficult. It's physically and mentally taxing, and this is just the start." She hesitates and then slowly, her smile returns. "But I know all of you can handle it and then some. You wouldn't be sitting in front of me if I didn't believe it."

She says our training will increase and we'll need to list the pros and cons of each program, from type of instruction to tuition payments. It's strange to think we may not be auditioning for an identical list of schools, that there will be a day I won't dance next to Ruthie and Josh. But it's even weirder that the only reason we're friends at all is that we've been training for a career in which we'll compete against one another for as long as we're dancing. We haven't discussed it outright but I know we'll end up auditioning for some of the same programs.

Josh will be all, "This doesn't change anything between us, Cartwright," because he's sweet and earnest like that and it's true—it wouldn't change us. But I don't know about Ruthie. She's talented *and* competitive, and there's not always room for friendship when those two come into play.

"I want to see you all push yourselves," Marisa says before we go to the dressing rooms. "Think beyond the summer. If you're admitted to a summer intensive that has an affiliated school and dance for them the way you've been dancing for me all this time, you could very well be invited to attend their preprofessional program."

Year-round ballet school—which could lead to a contract at a major company someday.

I'd be away from home but it would be nothing like Juniper Hill, with its drawn-out therapy sessions and ridiculous art shed. They would understand why you can't throw everything away just because some woman in a caftan doesn't like the number on your scale.

My skin is peppered with goose bumps. The last time I got them like this, I was being fitted for my first pair of pointe shoes. If I were in a professional company, I don't think they'd ever go away when I was performing. Not even if I were only in the corps.

Josh gives me a look, the same one I am already giving Ruthie.

We had faith in ourselves, but now it's official. We're ready to move on.

Ready to move up.

The house is empty when I get home. Mom left a note on the kitchen island in her loopy cursive. They went to a matinee.

The paper lies on the kitchen table next to Dad's empty coffee cup but it's been turned over so Chris Fenner's mug shot is facedown. My hands shake as I pick up the paper, slowly turn it over so I can see his face again.

I don't know why I want to look at him. Once was all I needed and it doesn't change anything. Not the fact that his face is deceptively friendly or that his smirk is playful. Almost cute. It doesn't matter that he looks young and normal and maybe even charming.

His eyes peer at me, like he's alone with me in this room. The twist of his lips is so bold.

His *eyes*.

I leave the *Tribune* lying on the kitchen floor, pages tented haphazardly over the tiles. I take the stairs two at a time until I reach my room and flip open my laptop, type Chris Fenner's name into a search engine. I don't know how my hands stop shaking long enough to pull up the associated images.

His hair is longer now, his face a bit older, his jaw concealed by the beard.

But it's him.

He told me he was eighteen. But if he's thirty now and we

were together four years ago—that means he was twenty-six then.

My boyfriend was Trent and Trent is Chris and Chris is the person they think kidnapped Donovan.

Abducted him. Drove him across the country. *Violated* him.

But would he do that? *Could* he do that? He was my boyfriend, but Donovan knew him, too.

They were *friends*.

Or maybe they were more. Donovan had a good family and a nice house and friends who cared about him. I don't think he'd have run away to live with Chris if he didn't want to *be* with him.

I squeeze my eyes shut, try to think about this with a clear head, but it doesn't help. Nothing can help. There are only two options, and I have to find out the truth as soon as possible.

Because either Donovan ran away with my boyfriend after he abandoned me, or I was charmed by the scum of the fucking earth.

# CHAPTER SEVEN

MY ROOM AT JUNIPER HILL WAS PAINTED THE COLOR of celery, which is funny because that was a safe food for my roommate, Vivian. Sometimes I'd catch her staring at the walls almost dreamily, like she was fantasizing about her old meals of celery and rice cakes and apple slices.

Juniper Hill accepts only a few patients at a time and costs a lot of money. I didn't know this when my parents dropped me off, and the counselors and Dr. Bender wouldn't discuss money with me. Once I came home, I snooped until I found the bills and felt bad that they'd spent so much on me. Especially when all I'd needed was some time. It's not like things were easy back then. Trent stopped showing up to his job, stopped answering his phone, stopped loving me. Then Donovan disappeared.

They said I was a restrictor—that I was trying to lose weight by severely limiting my diet. All I know is that Donovan consumed all of my thoughts and I lost my appetite each time I imagined him dead in a ditch somewhere—or being abused.

And I thought about those things every single day. Multiple times a day.

And Trent. Was he with another girl, telling her all the things she wanted to hear? His favorite food to steal from the convenience store was packaged snack cakes, the sticky, chocolate kind loaded with preservatives. We'd shared them as we sat on the hood of his car and the taste reminded me of his kisses, so I couldn't eat them after he left. Then chocolate was banned altogether because it reminded me of him, too. Same with foods that were baked or sweet or wrapped in cellophane. Soon I could hardly eat anything without thinking of him, and by the time Marisa forced me onto her office scale in front of my parents, I was finally down to double digits and that much freer of Trent.

I was thinner than anyone else in the junior company. Even Ruthie, who'd been more or less the same size as me since we were toddlers. I was probably thinner than every student in my class at school, too. Sometimes I caught the other girls glancing at me too long when we changed before gym class, and I wondered if they knew how marvelous it felt to truly take control of your body, to possess the kind of daily discipline most people won't know in a lifetime.

But Mom and Dad trusted a bunch of Middle America hippies over me telling them I was fine, so I spent the summer before my eighth-grade year at a yellow Victorian house in Wisconsin. The director of the program was named Dr. Lorraine Bender, but she didn't look like any doctor I'd ever seen. None of them looked even remotely like they worked in a place that treated medical issues. They wore flowing linen pants and ratty overalls and Jesus sandals. They harvested their own fruits and vegetables and purchased milk, meat, and eggs from local farmers because they wanted to show us how beautiful food can be when it's lovingly produced.

We were greeted with patience and soft smiles in the hallways, in the garden, or when we were throwing clay in the art shed. But when it came to eating and talking, they never let us forget who was in charge.

"Who's your counselor?" Vivian had asked as she sat on her bed watching me unpack on my first day. Her side of the room was a mirror image of mine: a twin bed, a small desk, and a dresser.

We weren't allowed to bring much—not even cell phones— but I had my pointe shoes. There was a huge discussion about whether or not I should be able to keep them. The woman who admitted me thought they could be considered a trigger. In the end, Dr. Bender decided against confiscation but said I was not to put them on, under any circumstances. She claimed I was too malnourished and weak to even think about dancing.

I'd shrugged at Vivian as I placed the shoes neatly on top of my bureau, ribbons dangling over the sides. "I think her name starts with a *D* or something."

The name of my primary counselor was written in my welcome packet, which included my daily schedule, the rules of the facility, a map of downtown Milwaukee for the days we went into town, and a sheet of paper with a layout of the house. Which seemed unnecessary. The place was big but it wasn't *that* big. It's not like I was going to mistake the dining room for Dr. Bender's office.

"Oh, Diana." Vivian nodded and kind of smiled and I didn't know if that was good or bad, so I stared at her until she said, "She's okay. Better than Pete or Ivy or Dr. Bender." She shuddered.

"But?" I turned away from her to place a stack of underwear in the top drawer.

Vivian appraised me with her kohl-rimmed eyes. They were big and blue and so serious.

"But Diana's tough." Vivian ran a hand through her stringy blond hair. Later, I'd notice the bald patches when she was carefully brushing it out before bed. "She won't let you off easy. Not even if you cry, so don't waste your time. It works on Pete . . . and Ivy, when she's in a good mood."

"What about Dr. Bender?" I stopped to wrap my sky-blue cardigan tighter around my shoulders, but it was useless. All my clothes were falling off by then. It had been that way for a while, months before anyone noticed. And it was hot. Stifling, but I didn't want anyone to see how skinny I was that first day—*really* see—or I thought they might do something even more drastic. Like, send me to a real hospital with doctors and nurses who looked like what they were. Who put tubes down your nose and held therapy sessions in cold rooms that smelled like bleach.

"I've never been brave enough to try."

I almost laughed when I first met Diana Porcella. She looked like a college student, and from what I could tell, she was the only person on staff who believed in closed-toe shoes. She smiled big when I walked into the parlor-turned-office and said it was nice to meet me as she gripped my hand in a firm shake.

Her questions started out simple enough but it was clear she already had some type of file on me. Despite the toothy grin plastered on her face that first day, I knew she was feeling me out, trying to see how far she'd be able to push me. She nodded as I told her about Ashland Hills, like she was already familiar with my life, down to the name of my best friend. I could have lied when she asked if I had a boyfriend. I didn't have to tell her about Trent.

About how he made me feel wanted. How I always felt I had to prove myself to him because he was older, because he was putting himself on the line with our relationship. ("Five years isn't a big deal to us, but other people care," he'd said to me the first time we kissed. I was still in a daze, a haze of bliss and disbelief that his lips had been on mine. "We can't tell anyone, Theo. I want to keep doing this"—he'd grinned at me, kissed my nose, caressed my cheek—"but we have to keep it a secret, or I could get into a lot of trouble.") And then, how when we started having sex, I wanted to show him he wasn't making a mistake, so I pretended I was always into it—always wanted him—so he wouldn't get bored and choose someone more experienced. Someone older, who didn't have to be a secret.

During our first couple of sessions I was too nervous to talk about Trent. The counselors were adamant about the fact that, except for cases where they were concerned our lives were in danger, everything we told them was confidential. But something changed the first time I mentioned him by name.

I felt a release so beautiful, I could have cried.

I'd never spoken to anyone about him before. Donovan knew, but we had a sort of silent agreement that he wouldn't ask what Trent and I did when he wasn't with us, and I wouldn't say anything about it at all.

I never stopped looking over my shoulder that first day, afraid someone would burst into the room and take me away now that I'd finally said Trent's name. Each day after that, it became easier to tell Diana Porcella about how he called me Pretty Theo and the tender note in his voice when he talked about growing up a half hour outside of Detroit. Or how after we had sex, he would burrow his head into my shoulder and doze off instantly, how it made me feel special that he could fall asleep so easily with me.

I couldn't tell her how old Trent was, though. If she had known he was eighteen, that would have trumped any confidentiality agreement. What if they tried to find him, tried to press charges against him because of something as stupid as a five-year age difference? Or worse, what if he came back but they'd found out and said I couldn't see him?

So to Diana Porcella, Trent was fifteen and he moved away suddenly when his father got a new job and that is the guy she thought I missed. I didn't trust Vivian, either, so I told her the same story and that is the guy she thought I was crying about when she woke in the middle of the night to my tears, when I hiccupped out how much I missed him.

The really hot nights were worse than the ones when I couldn't stop wondering why he'd left. The restlessness worked its way through the bones of the house; you could practically hear the rustling of the other patients trying to get comfortable in their rooms down the hall. I knew Vivian was awake on those nights just as she knew I was lying there staring at the ceiling. But we never said a word to each other. We simply lay on top of our covers, breathing around the *tick-tick-tick* of the rickety ceiling fan in our celery-colored room.

## CHAPTER EIGHT

WHEN I WAKE UP MONDAY MORNING I IMMEDIATELY turn on my laptop and type in Chris Fenner's name. Then I stare at his face and wait for his features to rearrange themselves so his eyes are not that gorgeous amber color, so his lips aren't the same ones that kissed me all over my body.

I did the same thing yesterday. All day. I told my parents I was studying for a big chemistry test, but instead I spent hours up in my room, covertly nursing a weak stomach and mind-numbing headache as I scoured the same articles about Donovan and Chris, trying to see if I had missed something.

Chris. Yes, Chris. I'm not going to call him Trent anymore. I'm not going to call him someone he never was.

Nothing has come out about the suspect besides his name. Maybe Chris didn't take Donovan. There could have been a misunderstanding. Maybe the lawyers and reporters and police officers were confused when they found them, jumped to conclusions because the waitress who called them was so frantic after she recognized Donovan. Maybe Donovan agreed to go with him. They used to be friends. *Friends.*

Unless there was something going on with them the whole time and I was too stupid to see it. Did Chris make me his secret so he and Donovan could keep an even bigger one?

Mom always says the most effective way to take your mind off something is to stay busy, so I convince myself that this sick, sick feeling will go away once I start getting ready and drive to school and get on with my day.

Except I puke in the shower. My stomach is knotted with shame. I'm not safe from thoughts of him, even standing in the steam with needles of water pricking my skin. It's as if he's here in this room, as if Chris Fenner can somehow see me standing here naked. No matter how hard I scrub, I still feel his fingers on me. In me.

I take too long in the shower and then too long deciding what I can choke down for breakfast without getting sick again, so by the time I pull into the student parking lot I'm already late for homeroom. It's not that big of a deal; homeroom isn't a real class. But now I'll have to stop by the office to get a late pass and that always takes forever and if I had somewhere to go I would pull right out of this lot and not look back.

I close my eyes as I think about getting out of my car and walking into school. I remind myself that only two other people in the entire world know about this; one of them is *certainly* not telling and the other one isn't talking at all.

Unless he does.

So I whip out my cell phone and before I can really think about it, I'm calling Donovan's house.

The phone rings. And rings. And with each one, my palms sweat more, slipping around the phone as I pray for someone to pick up. At first, I wish for Donovan, think maybe he'll see that it's me calling, recognize my number after all these years. But soon I'm desperate for anyone to pick up, even if it's Mrs. Pratt, even if she uses her defeated voice, the one we all heard in press conferences and interviews after Donovan had been gone too long to hope.

No one answers. Not Donovan, not Mrs. Pratt, not a voicemail telling me my call will be returned. I know they must be ignoring everyone—he's only been back three full days—but for some reason I thought Donovan might come to the phone if he saw it was me. *Talk* to me, because he must know I'm freaking out.

I remember the first time Chris pulled me into the bathroom of the convenience store for a quickie. He was working and it was risky, but the store was still empty when we came out. Except for Donovan, who was staring very hard at the comics on the shelf before him, like he wanted to be anywhere but there. When he looked at me, his eyes rested on the waistband of my skirt and I looked down, too, horrified to see it all bunched and misshapen around my middle. He looked away quickly but I felt the burn of his stare until I buried the skirt deep in the bottom of the hamper that night.

But he's not talking. He won't tell.

It takes five minutes to roll up the window and step out of my car. I spend the next ten hanging out in the science-wing bathroom before I stop in for my late pass.

And after that, I watch the clock in my classrooms for the rest of the morning, and 210 minutes later, my stomach has still not stopped turning over.


You can tell everything you need to know about a school if you poke your head into the cafeteria at noon on a Monday. Like which friends are fighting and who got too wasted over the weekend and who smoked a joint before lunch. It's no place to be invisible.

The chicken in the hot-lunch line is dry and I can't bring myself to walk over to the salad bar, so I grab a Diet Coke and a package of trail mix at the register. My hand holding the trail mix feels light and I squeeze it around the package, determined to not look down at the calories printed on the back.

Phil stares as I sit down across from him. "She lives," he says around a mouthful of mashed potatoes.

"I know I look like shit." My hair is back in a wispy ponytail, my eyes tired and red and puffy from my weekend of crying and insomnia and trying to keep my food down. I'm wearing jeans and a long-sleeved T-shirt I found on the floor, and a pair of bright red flats that don't match my outfit in the slightest.

"You don't look like shit," Sara-Kate says quickly, glancing at Phil. "We were just wondering if you were okay. We both called and texted but—"

"I know." I scoot my round plastic chair closer to the table, look down at the sophomores at the other end to see if they're watching us. They're not. "I mean, I saw."

I'm lying because once again I don't remember even looking at my phone this weekend. The first time I've really paid attention to it in the last two days was this morning, when I called Donovan.

"Trisha was talking this morning," Phil says. And his eyes move down to the table, like he's not sure whether to share this with me. I look at Sara-Kate to see if she already knows, but her face is neutral. "Her dad said if that piece of shit pleads not guilty, this trial could get huge coverage. Especially if Donovan still isn't talking when it starts."

"Yeah, because Mr. Dove is the expert on these kinds of cases?" My fingers skate across the top of my Diet Coke can until I force them to sit still while I open it with my other hand. "He's a divorce attorney."

"He's still a lawyer. He might know what he's talking about." Phil shrugs, his neck sinking into the collar of his plaid button-down. Red and black and white, rolled up to his elbows, like a skinny brown lumberjack. "And dude, if he pleads not guilty, you could help put a total scumbag in prison."

Sara-Kate looks at Phil, then tilts her head to the side, her big eyes blinking rapidly, as if she'd never thought about the possibility of a trial.

"I don't know what happened that day better than anyone else." My eyes flick to the salad bar, where people are lined up, dropping chunks of browning iceberg lettuce into their bowls. I clear my throat, try to sound normal as I say, "It's not that big of a deal."

"It's kind of a big deal. You were one of the last people to see him. My mom—"

He stops but I look at him, curious what Mrs. Muñoz had to say this time. "Your mom what?"

"Nothing." He shakes his head, presses his lips together.

I frown at him, tap the edge of his tray with my soda can. "What did she say, Phil?"

My tone must be harder than I realize. Sara-Kate's eyebrows go up as she swirls a french fry through a pool of ketchup on her plate.

He pauses again before he speaks. Not Phil's style. "She said she was glad she never let me go to that store with you guys, because it was cursed."

I brush a hand over my messy hair, wish I could brush one over my face and wipe away the bags under my eyes. "Cursed?"

Phil looks sorry he said anything at all. "You know how she is. She practically lives on superstitions. Did I ever tell you about the time she swore some lady gave me *mal de ojo* in the grocery store?"

Sara-Kate and I both stare at him.

"The evil eye," he says, shaking his head. "It's when a stranger looks at your baby the wrong way and shit starts getting out of hand. So every time I cried a lot or had a fever or whatever, she would think it was because of a woman we passed in the dairy aisle."

"That is the weirdest and best thing I've heard all day," Sara-Kate says in wonderment. She looks really cute in a pair of fitted gray suede pants and a vintage crocheted white sweater with a red tank underneath, and it makes me feel even frumpier than I already do.

And for a moment, I wonder—if it were just the two of us, would I tell her about me and Chris? What would she think about me after I confessed something like that? What would *everyone* think?

My life would never be the same if I put everything out there for the world to talk about. The paparazzi would show up at *my* house, harass *my* family. There would be no more parties at Klein's because no one invites girls like me after they learn the truth. My reputation would be ruined. My life would be over: ballet, friends, all of it.

No, I think, as Sara-Kate grills Phil about *mal de ojo*. I can't say anything before I talk to Donovan. The truth is so close, and I know he'll talk to me eventually, I just have to keep trying.

The fact that we're no longer talking about the trial seems like a small victory, so I decide to try the trail mix. I tear open the plastic bag and pop a raisin in my mouth. A raisin that is too juicy, too sweet on my tongue, but I chew and swallow so I will look like everyone else in this room.

Phil scoops up the last bite of his mashed potatoes and I'm

kind of amazed. Lunch started less than five minutes ago, so that must be some kind of record. Especially for something that looks as lumpy as those potatoes. He chews and swallows and points his fork at the patch of table in front of me.

"Is that seriously your lunch?"

"My stomach's off." I stare at the stack of thin black bracelets around his wrist. "I think I caught a bug."

Phil makes a face at me. "I don't see how eating like a woodland creature can help. Isn't it starve a cold, feed a fever?"

"Not *even,* Philip," Sara-Kate says, flashing him a smile that is equal parts sweet and defiant. "It's starve a fever, feed a cold."

"I don't think either of them are true," I say. A little too loudly. One of the sophomores at the end of the table actually looks over. "And I *don't* have a fever or a cold. Maybe I just don't feel well."

"Then you should be eating soup or bread or—"

"Back off, Phil." The frost around the edges surprises even me and I get a flash of déjà vu.

So does Phil. His face tells me so.

He looks at me for a very long time, so long that I know what he's thinking. I know exactly what he wants to say to me, exactly what he thinks I need to hear. But I'm not interested. If Phil won't stop obsessing over my old food issues, how would he react to my news about Chris? I trust Phil, I do, but not with this. Not until I know more, until I know the facts and it's not simply speculation.

Phil stabs his fork into a brick of chicken, begins sawing away at it with a butter knife. "Okay, Theo. Whatever you say."

He and Sara-Kate discuss our options for Halloween and Phil sounds normal enough, but he doesn't look at me for the rest of lunch and I wonder if we are the friends everyone can tell are fighting.

# CHAPTER NINE

THE ASHLAND HILLS HIGH SCHOOL FALL FESTIVAL IS A necessary evil.

It's not mandatory to participate, but it's easy extra credit and as long as you don't get stuck manning a super-lame booth, like the pumpkin ring toss, it's somewhat bearable.

The festival is held on the athletic field and is basically a giant clusterfuck of students and parents and young siblings nobody wants to be seen with. Student council organizes the whole thing, so I have an in. Bryn Davenport is the junior class president and being on her good side means I get to work the popcorn stand. Sara-Kate is working the face-painting stand and Phil is, unhappily, manning the football throw booth with Joey Thompson. Sports are not on Phil's radar—he thinks they're either barbaric or nonsensical—and he's been grumbling all week about the troglodytic nature of a football toss. ("I mean, why not have the guys choose a girl to club over the head as their prize? Pathetic," he scoffed when we got our assignments.)

But when I walk into the little brick concessions building at the edge of the field to start my hour-long shift, I think Bryn Davenport must hate me, because she's paired me with Klein Anderson.

The back of his dark head is facing me when I arrive. He's straddling a stool, fiddling with a radio that sits on a low shelf. He turns when the side door opens, and grins.

"About time you got here, Legs. Thought I was gonna have to run this thing myself."

I set down my bag on the back counter. "Since when are you about Fall Festival?"

"Eh." Klein turns the dial on the radio until he finds the punk station and stops. "I'm failing Earth Science."

"I thought you could talk your way out of any F," I say, moving to the service window to slide it open. The room smells like stale peanuts, but it's tidy, with containers of popcorn kernels, salt, and condiments aligned on a row of shelves along the back, and a whole cabinet full of paper cups, paper plates, and plasticware.

"Yeah, well. Doesn't really work like it did at my old school." He slides off the stool, closing some of the gap between us. "But everything happens for a reason, right? You, me, this little room."

"Do you know how to work that thing?" I ask, ignoring him as I gesture to the popcorn machine sitting in the corner.

"Yeah, McCarty came by to put in the oil and kernels. Something about liability. We just turn it on and make sure not to touch that metal thingie inside."

92

"One of us should bag and the other one should hand it out and take the tickets." I decide, because it's probably best if I take charge.

"I'll bag," he says with a shrug.

"Thanks." I'll have to talk to people if I'm manning the window but at least I won't have to touch the popcorn. I can't believe I used to eat it every single time I went to the movies. And then, for a long time, I didn't let myself think about how amazing it smells, because all that butter and salt isn't worth it.

"All the better for me to stare at your ass for the next hour, Legs," he says, his eyes sparkling like stolen emeralds as he winks at me.

I wrinkle my nose like I've smelled something bad, but he just laughs and flips the switch on the popcorn machine. And when I turn around I smile a little, too, because Klein is so fucking foul but he knows it and for some inexplicable reason, that's always been part of the small charm he possesses.

Luckily, our first customer arrives and I'm able to forget about Klein for the next thirty minutes. Klein is as lazy as they come, but he may have found his calling with this popcorn thing. He's fast and efficient and manages to keep most of it off the floor. Plus, we don't have to worry about using the soda fountain since another booth is handling drink sales.

The little kids show up first, their parents standing off to the side while they proudly hold out their tickets as if being at the Fall Festival means they belong here with all the older kids. Then come the freshmen and sophomores who showed up too early and need something to do while they stand around and decide which booths are acceptable to be seen at.

A few people stop by to say hey. David Tulip crams handfuls of popcorn in his mouth while he banters with Klein about the football game they watched last Sunday. Eddie Corteen walks up a few minutes later, his friends in tow, sweet and seeming a little unsure of whether he should be standing here. And of course Lark Pearson sidles up to the window, completely ignoring me as she bats her thickly lined eyes at Klein and asks if he'll give her a "sample."

There's a lull halfway through our shift and after a while I get tired of wondering if Klein really *has* been staring at my ass the whole time, so I turn around. He's messing with the radio again and it reminds me of the first night we made out. He'd taken over the music at the house where we were partying, and when he saw me watching he'd grinned and motioned me over. Our arms and legs were touching as we'd scrolled through songs to add to the playlist and as soon as I sat down next to him I knew I would kiss him later.

"What?" he says now, and I tune back in to find him staring at me because I was already staring at him.

"Nothing. I'm going to grab something to drink. You want anything?"

He stretches, his long arms reaching for the ceiling as his mouth opens in a yawn. "Will it have rum in it?"

"Like you don't carry your own," I say, reaching into my bag for my red leather wallet.

"Touché, Legs. Just seeing if you were paying attention."

"I'll be back," I say, and then I'm out the side door again.

There's a set of vending machines adjacent to the concessions building, housed in a compact, fenced-in square of concrete. The fence is always locked, unless we're having a game or an event on the field. I assume it will be closed off tonight, since the school is promoting its booth of Fall Festival drinks, but the gate is slightly ajar.

I slip through and I don't hear anyone walk up behind me, but right away, I know he's there. The wind carries the heady scent of cloves and when I turn around he's looking at me.

"Hey," he says almost shyly, his hands in the front pocket of his hoodie. He must be freezing, walking around without a jacket. I'm already cold and I've been outside for less than a minute.

His cheeks are chapped from the cold, but it looks cute on him. Sweet, almost. Little pink circles on such a serious face.

"You're working here tonight?" I ask, rubbing my arms for warmth.

"Not for the school." Hosea nods toward the concessions building. "But you are?"

"Popcorn duty." I wrinkle my nose.

"Ah, that would explain the butter smell."

"Fake butter."

"The best kind," he says with a smile that's lightning fast but manages to melt my insides anyway.

Fake butter makes me think of the movie theater, which

makes me think of dates. Which makes me wonder if Hosea and Ellie ever go to the movies. Or if they go on dates at all. They show up at all the parties together and they eat lunch together and I've seen her getting out of his car in the student parking lot, but do they go *out* like a real boyfriend and girl-friend?

I've never been on a date. Chris and I could never go any-where for fear of what people would say if they saw us together, and Klein and I couldn't drive at the time, so we met up at parties and made out in empty bedrooms. The closest we came to an actual date was winter formal freshman year, but we went in a group, so it didn't feel like one.

"Who's in there with you?" Hosea asks, leaning against the fence.

"Klein." My hands are starting to sweat, despite the cold. I tuck my wallet under my arm.

"No shit?" He looks as surprised as I was.

I shrug. "Desperate times, I guess."

"Really fucking desperate," he mumbles.

"He's actually been on his best behavior," I say with a straight face.

Hosea lifts an eyebrow enough to make me laugh.

"Well, for *Klein.*" A breeze whips through the field, cold and unexpectedly sharp, and I wrap my arms around myself, cup my elbows in my hands.

"What are you up to when you're done here?"

What? Is he trying to hang out with me or something? I

haven't seen her tonight, but if Ellie walked up right now and saw us talking alone—again—her head might actually explode.

"I'll go find Phil, I guess." Phil and I had the first shifts at our booths because no seniors had been assigned to them, but Sara-Kate's hour at the face-painting station doesn't start until ours ends. "Are you sticking around?"

"Yeah, I need to meet up with a few more people." He pauses, threads a couple of his fingers through a diamond-shaped space in the chain-link fence. "And I have to grab a couple of drinks for me and Ellie."

Of course she's here. I paste on a smile.

"I should get back to my popcorn duties," I say, half turning toward the brick building. "We've been pretty busy all night. Fake butter is in high demand, you know."

He's standing at the vending machine next to mine now, feeding money into the slot. "What do you want?"

"I can get my own."

"I didn't ask if you could get your own, I asked what you wanted," he says evenly as he looks over his shoulder to make eye contact.

"Diet Coke," I say quietly. Like that first day I saw him in ballet, I want to look away first, but this time I don't. I wait for him to turn back to the machine and then I let out a breath. He makes me nervous. It's exhilarating, in a what-happens-next sort of way, but I'm nervous all the same.

He pushes the button and seconds later, a can comes tumbling noisily down the machine into the bottom tray.

When he hands me the can, our fingers brush against each other and I tremble. I can't tell if he noticed, but I snatch my hand away because I'm embarrassed.

"Thanks. Now I owe you a clove *and* a soda." I smile at him as I shift my weight on the concrete square. "In case you're worried I'm not keeping track."

I almost drop the cool metal can as his soft eyes land on me and he says, "I think I know where to find you, Theo."

The way he says my name, the way his voice dips a little lower, sends heat flaming across my chest and up my neck and over both sides of my face. I want to take his hand in mine, hold it against my skin, ask him if it's normal to react to someone like this.

I'm not brave enough for that, though. "I guess you do," I finally say.

We share a long look before I head back to the concessions building, arriving lighter than when I left and a thousand times more confused. Klein looks up from his phone as I come through the door and at first, I'm worried he's mad that I was outside so long, but there's nobody at the window. He's probably just sending dirty texts to Trisha anyway.

"Mixer for your drink?" He slips the phone back into his pocket.

"I think I'm good." I look down at the soda in my hand. I kind of don't want to open it now. It's stupid, but part of me wants to save it because Hosea bought it for me.

"Hey, Legs?" He does this little waving motion with his hand, even though I'm two feet away from him.

"Hey, Klein?" I settle onto the stool in front of the window, place the soda can on the counter next to me.

"Why do you think we never got together?"

His voice is so subdued, I can barely hear him over the sounds of the carnival outside. The shrieks and subsequent splashes from the dunking booth; the chatter surrounding a group of freshman cheerleaders passing by in a cloud of vanilla body spray and cigarette smoke; a guy from my math class standing a few feet away from the service window, telling someone they can go fuck themselves.

This night is becoming more bizarre by the second. I would think Klein was screwing around if he didn't look so vulnerable. Right now, he's somewhat sober and serious and my God, are we really going to have this conversation?

"I don't know . . . You started hanging out with Trisha." My eyes dart to the window. Quickly, as if she's going to bounce over at the sound of her name.

"Because you didn't seem into it." He scratches at the back of his head with the heel of his hand. "I was into you, Legs," he says, without quite looking at me.

"I had a lot going on back then . . . I was kind of a mess."

A *total* mess. I was eating again—Juniper Hill had taken care of that—but food wasn't the same for me. I ate because people were instructed to watch my habits: teachers, counselors,

Marisa, Phil. I ate because I loved ballet and never wanted it taken from me again. But I mostly ate because my parents might have resorted to something more drastic if I didn't.

Besides that, I was adjusting to a new school, new people, a new routine—all without Donovan. And it had been two years since Chris had left without saying goodbye. Klein was a diversion—a sly, smooth-talking diversion who looked like he'd been created in a factory of beautiful people and came with instant popularity—but I knew we were short-term from the start.

"I was messed up, too," he says with a shrug, like, *hey, everyone was messed up back then.*

*You still are.*

"I guess we just weren't right for each other," I say, hoping he'll drop it.

I don't know how to answer his question any more than I know why there is something between Hosea and me. Klein was good for a while and then he wasn't. And it was pathetic to tell someone that you were still hurting from a breakup that had happened two years before.

Klein swallows hard, looks at me harder. "What about now?"

I shake my head a little as I play with the clasp on my wallet, sitting snug against the can of soda. "Dude, you're with *Trisha.*"

"What if I wasn't?" His gaze is so intense, I have to turn away.

"I don't know, Klein."

What I do know is that I never felt an ounce for him of what I feel for Hosea, and the most physical contact Hosea and I have shared is accidental finger brushes. I knew everything about Klein before I ever spoke to him, but with Hosea, there's something new to learn each time we talk. A look or a laugh that surprises me. A story I never would have expected from him.

"Well, when I give Trisha the boot, you'll be the first person I call, Legs," he says, his eyes flickering over me from top to bottom and back again.

Luckily our second rush of the evening starts up just then. A gaggle of freshmen are making their way across the field and form a line in front of the window. Total lifesaver.

Klein doesn't get another word in until Mrs. McCarty is back to refill the popcorn maker and the two sophomores taking over for us have arrived. I walk out first and Klein follows as I trek across the field to rescue Phil. The earthy, pungent scent of wood smoke drifts over from the other side of the field; Principal Detz is manning a portable fire pit so people can roast marshmallows for s'mores.

"I wasn't kidding back there," he says, his army-green coat hanging from his hand. I get a glimpse of the label. Burberry.

We're standing a few feet from the caramel-apple booth where Mr. Jacobsen whistles as he dips Granny Smiths into a slow cooker. He looks up and catches my eye, waves me over as if the allure of caramel apples is too strong to resist. I like

Mr. Jacobsen—he's the undisputed favorite among the teachers at school—so I smile at him as I shake my head.

"Okay," I say to Klein.

I feel around in the pocket of my black peacoat until I find a loose thread, roll it into a teeny ball between my thumb and forefinger. The more he talks about us being together, the more I think about Chris. About which version of him to believe. He was a liar. Of course he was a liar, but how far would he go? How far *did* he go? And did I ever mean anything to him?

"*Okay?*" Klein looks more than a little hurt but only for a second. He shakes it off as fast as I can blink.

"Klein, you have Trisha. And I'm busy with ballet and . . . we already tried once. Maybe it wasn't meant to be."

*And I like your best friend, anyway.*

He shakes his head but he's smirking and patting the pocket where he stored his flask.

"Never say never, Legs," he says as he starts walking away, backward so he can watch me as he retreats. "Never. Say. Never."

# CHAPTER TEN

THE MINUTE I STOP EXPECTING TO SEE DONOVAN IS exactly when I get my first glimpse of him.

Mom and Dad are watching the news, listening to reports about the economy and gas prices and cheating politicians. I'm pretending to give a shit about the English essay that's due tomorrow, but the news anchor's voice breaks into my thoughts about Miss Havisham, and when I look up, Donovan's face is on the television.

He's there so quickly, I almost miss it: a still shot from a grainy video, blown up so large that if I stare at it too long without looking away, Donovan appears to be made of brown and black squares and rectangles.

The news anchor says they've made contact with a woman who used to live in the same apartment complex as Chris and Donovan. Some crap town in Nevada.

The woman's name is Candy DeGregorio. She's wearing a postal worker's uniform and the lines around her mouth are deep, like she's been pulling on cigarettes for the better part of her forty-five years.

"He was a real sweet kid," she says, licking her thin, dry lips. "Around the same age as my boys, so they ran around together all the time, walked to school, stuff like that."

The apartment building behind her is in bad need of a paint job and all the windows have lopsided or missing shutters. The earth around the building looks dry and dead, but not in the way that means winter is on the horizon. The camera zooms in on the part of the complex where Donovan lived with Chris. The curtains are drawn and police tape is stretched over the scarred front door.

Then, without warning, the camera switches to the video Candy provided. It's shaky and a little fuzzy, filmed on a cheap camera. Maybe a cell phone. But there's Donovan, at a skating party. I watch him race from one end of the rink to the other, neck and neck with a blond kid who must be one of Candy's sons. They do it again, flying back to the other side, where they skid to a stop at the end and high-five each other.

There's another clip after that, but it's just a few seconds long. This one is of Donovan at the snack bar, cramming cake into his mouth with the same blond kid and generally looking like he's having the fucking time of his life.

I am certain none of us breathe while the videos play. They were taken two years ago, but he was already tall. Long legs with arms to match. Hair separated into small twists, the start

104

of dreadlocks. Who did his hair? Did Donovan say he wanted dreads? Did Chris pay someone to do it?

"We thought his name was Jamie," says Candy DeGregorio's voice in the background. "Look, we live in a small town but we don't get a lot of bad folks around here and I thought that man was doing a good thing, being a good person and taking in someone who needed help."

I hate Candy DeGregorio.

I dig my fingernails into my palm as hard as I can because they just keep playing the first video and the more I watch it, the more I wonder if I have any reason to think he didn't leave on his own. *Skating parties?* As those few seconds play over and over, I start to reimagine the life he lived. As Jamie Fenner.

Jamie, trekking to school with Candy's sons, when he could have snuck off to call home and tell us where he was. Jamie, *in* school, sitting in a classroom with a kind-faced teacher who would have listened to him say his name was really Donovan Pratt. And Jamie with Chris. At home. Eating dinner together and watching TV together and—what? Sleeping in the same bed? Doing the same things Chris and I used to do? Together.

The news plays the video from the skating rink over and over, those few seconds that show us the life he led, that his existence wasn't only behind closed doors.

Mom's hand is on my arm. I feel her looking at Dad over the top of my head. I wonder what their eyes are saying, what private conversation they've started that will be finished when they're safe behind their bedroom door.

I shake off my mother's hand and stand. My copy of *Great Expectations* falls to the floor and I don't bother to pick it up. I step over it—*on* it, cracking the spine for the billionth time—because I have to get out of here right fucking now. I can't look at Donovan, can't think about how many more videos and pictures like this exist in shitty towns between here and Nevada.

"Theodora?"

I'm already walking. Out of the den and down the hall, toward the front room. I need my coat. I need my car. I need to get the fuck out of here before I explode.

"I need to go out for a while." I don't turn around as I say this. My parents are close behind, their footsteps moving as fast as they can without actually stepping on my heels.

"Theo, sweetheart." Mom this time, as we round the corner into the living room. "Why don't you hold on and we can talk about this. I know it was a shock seeing him in that . . . environment, and—"

I shake my head. Tunnel vision. Coat closet. Door. Car. "I don't want to talk. I want to be alone right now."

"Theodora." Dad's voice is still gentle, but stern enough for me to turn and look at him. "This is confusing and that was hard to watch, but things aren't always what they seem. Especially in a situation like this where—"

"Then what was it?" I yank open the door to the closet in the foyer. Snatch my coat down from its wooden hanger. "He wasn't faking. He was—I *know* what he looks like when he's happy. He was *happy* in those videos, so how is it not what it seems?"

"Honey." Mom moves toward me, her eyes wide and her hands clasped helplessly in front of her soft, camel-colored sweater. "This is one piece to the story, and it's only the beginning. They—they have to look at all sides, talk to people who knew him while he was away."

My hand is on the doorknob. I can't listen to them spout off these things that are supposed to make me feel better but actually make me feel like shit because they're trying *so hard* and no matter what they say or do in this moment, it won't change what I saw. "Please let me go. Please. *Please.*"

They look at each other and I know they don't want to say yes, but I'm getting out of this house, with or without their permission. This conversation is just a formality as far as I'm concerned. But I can sound less crazy while we have it. Flies, vinegar, honey, whatever.

"I'll be safe," I say. Calmly, and while I look them in the eyes—both of them—so they'll trust me. "I just need to clear my head. Please don't make me stay here right now. It's . . . I feel claustrophobic."

Dad sighs. "Take your phone. Check in with us in an hour and don't even think about going into the city. Got it?"

"Got it." I use my rational voice.

"And Theo," Mom says as I turn the handle. Her mouth stays open a few moments before she speaks, like an opera singer ready to hit the big note. "We need to talk about you seeing someone. Maybe not tonight, but—soon."

"I don't want to talk to anyone." Wasn't Juniper Hill sufficient? Three full months in that damn hippie house in the middle of nowhere and they don't think I've had enough therapy?

"Sweetheart, he was your best friend."

Her mouth turns down and it makes me want to cry, so I say, "Can we talk about this later?" and they nod and I use that moment to slip out the door.

This is the first time since he's been back that I walk down the driveway without looking at Donovan's house.

I end up at Casablanca's. It's kind of busy for a Tuesday, but our back booth is open, so I don't care. I park myself there and wait. For what, I don't know. I don't even care if Jana comes over to take my order. I just needed to sit down somewhere away from my parents and make sense of what I saw.

I always knew how much Donovan liked Chris. *I* would have run away with Chris if he'd asked me. I didn't know what to call how I felt for him, but it was addictive. I'd never wanted to please someone so much. Even when he didn't deserve it, I wanted to be the one who made him happy.

But he didn't ask *me*. He went with Donovan.

I look around the diner, at the plain white walls, broken up by random pieces of retro art. Generic portraits of bouquets and New England landscapes and a sun setting over a beach somewhere. Framed pieces you'd buy from a flea market, probably castoffs from a doctor's waiting room.

"Your partners in crime ditch you?"

Jana. Usually I can hear her coming from a mile away. Her overdramatic sighs and the fact that she's always yelling at someone over her shoulder give her away. I stare up at her blankly.

"They're . . . they're not here."

She squints at me like I'm up to no good. "Well, what are you having?"

"Tea," I say, as I kick my foot against the bottom of the bench seat across from me. The resulting thump sounds good to my ears, feels good on the toe of my boot. So I do it again.

"What kind?"

"Chamomile." *Thump, thump.*

"That all?"

*Thump, thump.*

I nod and she stares at me until finally I say, "What?"

"First of all, you can stop taking out your problems on my booth. Second, you're going to sit here in this big old booth to drink a cup of tea?" She rests a hand on her bony hip. Her fingernails are painted a bright red and it's a strange contrast against the veins that crisscross the back of her hand. "What's your deal, girl? You come in here every week and stare at that menu, stare at everyone's food, and you never order more than a cup of soup."

I stop the kicking, but give her the dirtiest look I can muster. "How is that your business? I'm still a paying customer."

She lets out her signature sigh before turning around.

"I'm a regular, too," I call after her.

She pretends not to hear me.

I'm sitting with my back to the rest of the diner, with just the dingy wall ahead of me, but I wish I'd brought something to do. Even my English essay would be better than nothing, because when I'm doing nothing, all I think about is Donovan and Chris.

Without Sara-Kate and Phil to distract me, I'm entirely too aware of every sound in the diner, from the dinging of the register to the person who keeps scratching a fork across their plate like nails down a chalkboard. I'm also aware of the heavy footsteps approaching my table. Different from the reluctant trudge of Jana's, these are slow but purposeful. When I look up, Hosea Roth stands next to me, holding a white take-out bag.

"I thought that was you," he says with a hesitant smile. Hesitant because I look as unhinged as I feel? Or because he's here alone and I'm here alone, and we keep ending up in the same places? Alone.

He's wearing a jacket this time. A black one over the same gray hooded sweatshirt. I find myself wondering again about the black T-shirt. Maybe it's not part of his uniform in the cooler months. I don't say anything. I just stare at his jacket and think how strange it is that he's suddenly around all the time. There's always been some overlap in our circle of friends since I got to high school, but he was just Phil's dealer. Until now. I never really thought about him before he showed up at my dance studio, because I didn't know how much there is to like about him.

"Theo? Everything okay?"

"Where are you going?" I ask, turning the pepper shaker around the table in wide, slow circles.

Because I want to know, but asking also means I don't have to answer his question.

Hosea is taken aback and I guess I shouldn't have asked but I don't care. If nothing else makes sense today I don't have to, either.

"Home, I guess. Had to make a drop-off at this party a couple of blocks away." His cheeks are two pink circles again, flushed from the cold. I want to press my hands over them.

"Oh." I look down at the table again. Squeeze my fingers around the pepper shaker. Wish the news that he's not staying wasn't so disappointing.

He opens his mouth. Pauses, then: "You look pretty bummed. You sure everything's okay?"

I abandon the pepper, poke my finger at the yellow stuffing that bursts through the cracked red vinyl of the booth. "I saw Donovan on the news tonight. There was video. From when he was gone. He was laughing, like those people were his *friends.*"

Hosea looks at me for a while before he speaks, his gray eyes searching my face like he doesn't quite know what he's looking for. "I don't have to be home right away. Want to go for a drive? It helps clear my head sometimes."

"Okay." It's automatic, though I still have an English essay to finish, I barely know him, and he has a girlfriend. But it's just a drive, and maybe it will clear my head.

"Then let's go." He cocks his head toward the door, but not impatiently.

Still, I shrug into my jacket right away, afraid he'll revoke the invitation if I don't move. On the way out, I stop in front of the counter and stare at Jana until she looks over, annoyed. She's flirting with a trucker young enough to be her son.

"What?" she spits out.

"Never mind on that tea. I have to go."

"You kids keep coming in here and ordering things then disappearing and wasting my time, I'm gonna make sure you don't come back."

"You love us too much to do that," I say, and I even manage a smile in response to her scowl because I know how much it bothers her. "See you Thursday!"

She grumbles and waves me away and it's just as well, because Hosea is waiting.

## CHAPTER ELEVEN

HOSEA STEERS THE CAR WITH ONE HAND AND HOLDS A
sandwich in the other. A BLT. An unlikely choice for eating
and driving, but he's surprisingly graceful.

His car is a carrot-colored hatchback with a faded black racing stripe down the center. It only starts after a couple of tries.
It's cramped inside, so small that his seat is pushed back almost
twice as far as mine to accommodate his long legs. My eyes
sweep over the pack of cloves in the console and I think about
Ellie, how she'd be furious if she could see me sitting here right
now. But she won't find out. Somehow, I know Hosea won't
say anything to her any sooner than I will. And knowing I have
a secret with him is even more satisfying than Ellie learning we
hung out alone.

There's hardly any traffic. Everything in Ashland Hills
shuts down by nine and it's a quarter till. I stood outside
the cloudy windows of Casablanca's as I called my parents. I
looked in at Jana and the trucker as I told my father I stopped
by Sara-Kate's house, that I'd be home soon. It's safer than

Phil's; he lives so close that they could easily bump into him or his mother.

Hosea doesn't talk much. He's eating and the radio doesn't work but the silence makes me nervous. I don't know him well enough to be comfortable, to guess what he's thinking. To wonder if he regrets inviting me to go on this drive. I watch him take another huge bite of his sandwich, watch his jaw move sternly as he chews. I watch all of this from the corner of my eye and then, just before he takes another bite, I say, "Are you going to study music next year?"

He lowers the sandwich a bit and looks over at me like I'm crazy. "What, like major in piano?"

I shrug. "Lots of people do."

We're driving through downtown Ashland Hills, which is just three short blocks with the usual suspects lined up on each side: the supermarket, bank, library, coffee shops, boutiques, and restaurants. We don't have a local dance studio, which is why I ended up at Marisa's. My parents like living in a small community—they say it's easier to get things done. Chicago is loud and busy, but sometimes I think I'd rather deal with the hassle than live in a town where everybody knows your business.

Hosea eases his foot down on the brake as we approach a stop sign. "I've never thought about studying music," he finally says. "Not seriously."

"Why not?" I inhale and decide I like the smell of his hatchback. There's an old-car mustiness to it, but it's mostly cloves and that familiar boy smell, like deodorant and soap and a hint of sweat.

Hosea finishes the last bite of his sandwich and brushes his hands against his jeans before we start moving again. "You know you have to be good enough to even audition for one of those places, right?"

"But you *are* good enough." I look at him, think about the way he turns into a different person when he sits behind the piano. How he makes such familiar pieces sound brand-new, how beautiful and evocative the notes become under his fingers. He doesn't say anything and that's when it hits me. "Is that why you asked me not to tell anyone about your job at the studio? You don't think you're good enough?"

"I know I'm not. I should be competing or performing by now." He pauses. "I haven't even taken lessons since I lived in Omaha. I'm not exactly on the fast track to a conservatory."

"Some people don't need lessons." I fold my hands in my lap. "It's called raw talent."

"You're not so bad yourself." His grin makes my face warm and I look out the window because I don't know what to say.

We wind through the quiet streets in silence for a while. Pass the Ashland Hills train station, then loop over to Klein's neighborhood. The hatchback's engine thrums as we drive by the sprawling houses, some of them dark save for the glowing porch lights.

"Whose party were you at earlier?" I ask when the silence is too much. It's not uncomfortable, but with the radio broken, it's easy to let my thoughts wander back to Donovan.

"No one from school. Just this guy I used to be friends with." He shakes his head. "That's the last time I'm going over there, though. He's in over his head."

"How do you mean?" I look out the window at an older woman walking her terrier. She's bundled up in a parka, scarf, mittens, and a knitted hat, like it's February. The dog is utterly unconcerned, taking his time as he finds the perfect place to relieve himself.

Hosea pauses, then: "He's into some hard shit now. Shit I don't touch."

I look back at him because his voice changed. It's more serious. Somber, almost. "Like what?"

"Like everything. Tonight it was crystal."

Oh. Nobody at school messes with meth. "How do you know him?"

"He was the first person I met when I moved here. He's a couple years older, but he grew up around the corner from my Grams and he was always cool to me, you know?" Hosea sighs. "He's the closest thing I ever had to a brother and now it's like I don't know him."

"That's how I feel about Donovan." I absently run my index finger along the cracked dash, come away with a fingertip of dust. "I mean, sort of."

We're at the edge of town now, where the houses thin out

and give way to more land. He pulls off to the side of the road near a paved driveway with a closed gate and a large house set back from the street, shadowed by trees. Hosea leaves the car running for the heat.

He fiddles with the pack of cloves in the console but never attempts to take one out of the box. "Klein said you were with Donovan before he disappeared."

"Yeah." I shift in my seat as I think about that morning.

I'd walked in the unlocked front door of Donovan's house like I always did, because the rest of his family was gone. His mother was on her way into the city to open the museum gift shop while his father dropped off Julia at kindergarten on his way to the office.

The Pratt house was messier than ours, but I didn't mind. It was clean but lived-in and you never felt weird about flopping on a couch or putting your feet up on the coffee table. I stepped over a pair of mud-caked cleats in the foyer as I searched for their owner. He wasn't in the kitchen where I'd assumed he'd be scarfing down a bowl of cornflakes next to the breakfast dishes soaking in the sink. And he wasn't sitting at the bottom of the staircase, tying his shoes before he ran out the door.

He was up in his room but when he heard me on the stairs he immediately stepped out into the hallway. And he wasn't in his pajamas like I thought, but dressed for the day in jeans and a long-sleeved T-shirt with a short-sleeved one layered over it.

I had to describe that outfit to what seemed like everyone

in town, because they wanted to know the last thing he'd been seen in. White sleeves with a short black T-shirt over it. Or was it the other way around? Were the jeans dark or light? Was I positive they were jeans and not shorts? Was he wearing a belt? What brand were his sneakers?

But I never got to see his shoes because he pushed me out shortly after he greeted me.

"Hey, I'll just catch up to you at school," he said. Quickly, like he had things to do.

"What are you doing?" I asked, my hand firm on the banister as I waited for an answer.

He ran a hand over his head. He was in need of a haircut, which wasn't like him. Usually his dad buzzed his head every couple of weeks, and Donovan stayed on top of this because he didn't like longer hair, said it made his head itchy and hot.

"I need to take care of something before school." His deep brown eyes moved from my face to the stair rail and slid across the carpet. "You should go on without me."

Take care of something? We were thirteen. It's not like we had errands to run.

I looked at him for a long time. Until he looked at me, too, and then looked away and back again.

"What, Theo?" he said, turning his hands up like I'd seen my parents do. The universal symbol for *What do you want me to do?*

"You're being weird." I tugged on the straps of my backpack.

"We don't have to do everything together." His eyes were

elsewhere again. On the picture that hung next to the stairs—a portrait of him with Julia when she was just a baby, taken in the hospital before his mother was discharged. "I'll meet you at school later and we can ride home together, okay?"

"Do you have a note?" I pressed on, not wanting to let him get out of this so easily.

Was this my punishment for not telling him about everything I'd done with Chris? Making up secrets of his own and throwing them in my face? It wasn't fair. Hadn't I been punished enough when Chris disappeared without saying goodbye?

"Theo." He sighed and leaned against the doorframe, dug his toe into the carpet. "You're gonna be late."

"Fine." I turned but I didn't walk down the stairs. Not before I looked over my shoulder to say, "But I'm not covering for you."

"I didn't ask you to, did I?"

Those were his last words to me.

Hosea clears his throat from across the car. "That must've been tough, him being gone all this time."

"Yeah," I say, with a small nod for emphasis. "It was."

I look at Hosea and wonder what it would feel like to kiss him. To touch him. To really be with someone like him. He pays attention when I talk. That was one of the things I hated about Chris. He never seemed to take anything I said all that seriously, but Hosea listens. If Ellie weren't in the way, we could be together—really together. No abandoned parks, no quickies against the sink of a gas-station bathroom when I wasn't even sure how to do it in the back of a car. We could hold hands between classes and go on dates and he would be my actual boyfriend.

I steal a look at his hands, strong but almost elegant, and I can't imagine he would ever be anything but gentle.

"Did the drive help?" Hosea dips his head a bit as he looks at me. "Even a little?"

"Yeah." I thread and unthread my fingers in my lap. Smile at him for being so nice to me. "It did. Thanks."

"Good." His hand rests on top of the gearshift, inches from my knee. "You know, Marisa would be pretty pissed if I'd just left you in that diner."

I hold my leg still as can be. Waiting. Wanting. "Why would she care?"

"You're her star dancer. I couldn't leave you all bummed out like that." He smiles a little, then says, "You're special."

"I'm not that special," I say, and it doesn't come out as carefree as I wanted, but that's okay because it's true. Special girls are worthy of a proper breakup, don't have to wonder if their boyfriend was using them to get to their best friend.

"Right," Hosea says softly. "I know shit about ballet but when you're out there, you look pretty damn special to me."

I'm afraid to look at him, for fear of what I'll see. His voice was serious but maybe he's kidding. Maybe this is the kind of thing he says to girls all the time; maybe it's no big deal that he said it to me. But I force myself to turn my head, to meet his gaze, and whatever this is, it's not just in my head. He feels it, too. It's real, reflected in his gentle eyes. They search my face again, just like earlier at the diner. But there's an understanding this time. A look that will quicken my pulse every time I replay it in my head.

I don't know who leans in first, but moments later we are close enough for our foreheads to touch, close enough for me to breathe him in. I slide my hand up the nape of his neck at the same time he slips his arm around my waist and pulls me closer. We're so in sync, it's like our own private pas de deux, like we learned the choreography years ago, are only now putting it to practice.

Hosea's kisses are whispers, just the slightest touch that keeps me wanting more. He pulls back, looks at me, smiles. My palm is still cupped around the back of his neck as he leans in to kiss me again. Deeply this time so there is no doubt as his lips meet mine; this is real.

I run my hands through his soft, soft hair and he keeps his around my waist, tickles a trail up the small of my back with his fingers. For a while, we are the only two people in the world. A burst of light in this small, dark car, on this deserted road. A tangle of heat and breath and touch and taste and I want to stay like this forever. Being with him is safe and wonderful and—

"Theo."

It's not fair the way he says it as he pulls away from me, like he's the only person who is allowed to say my name. It makes me want to keep kissing him for hours, ignore the fact that we have school tomorrow and my parents expect me home any minute now. It makes me forget about Donovan and whether anyone will find out that Chris Fenner and I used to kiss like this.

Only . . . this feels real in a way that things never did with Chris.

"Sorry." Hosea brings his hand up to my face, where he runs his thumb along the curve of my bottom lip. "We should probably—"

"I know." Of course I should have expected him to pull away. Of *course* we can't keep going. I kissed him and he doesn't belong to me and I liked it. I'm not special, but I *am* That Girl.

He looks at my mouth, brushes his fingers against my lips one last time before he pulls away completely. He reaches into the console for his pack of cloves. I sit back in my seat, buckle my seat belt, and pull my phone from my bag so I'll have something to do.

Hosea pinches a clove between his lips and pulls out onto the street again, en route to Casablanca's. Neither of us says another word and we don't look at each other for the rest of the ride, but longing melts through me in a thousand waves.

Hot and slow and bittersweet to the core.

## CHAPTER TWELVE

ONCE, SARA-KATE AND I PLAYED FUCK/MARRY/KILL:
Teachers Edition and I ended up marrying Mr. Jacobsen.

Kill was easy enough—Mr. Gellar is the biggest waste of
space in the school and not just because he teaches chemistry. The Fuck part was a no-brainer because we had a really
hot student teacher in English that year. His name was—no
joke—Grant Fineman. But Jacobsen was the only real option
for Marry, so it flew out of my mouth too easily and Sara-Kate
teased me for weeks.

So maybe his hair *is* thinning. And his belly isn't getting
any smaller, but I can tell Jacobsen used to be cute back in the
day. Or "kind of a fox, in a retro way," according to Sara-Kate.
Whatever. He has a nice smile. And he's a good teacher. He
doesn't have to think up gimmicks or games to interest us in
the justice system. He simply talks like he's telling us a really
good story.

He finds me in the atrium the Thursday before Halloween.
I'm standing with Sara-Kate and Phil before homeroom and

nobody blinks an eye when Jacobsen pops his head into our circle and asks if he can talk to me for a minute. It's never anything bad with him. I don't think I've ever heard him raise his voice, not even last week when he kicked Leo Watson out of class for texting.

We walk over to an empty part of the hallway, a little sliver of space between the custodian's closet and a water fountain I've never seen anyone use. They paint the walls every summer, but someone has already scuffed the latest coat of beige with the heel of their shoe.

"I've been meaning to ask how you're doing, Theo. Everything all right?" Jacobsen looks relaxed in a polo and khakis with a brown belt that matches his shoes. His tone is easy, like he makes a special point to check in with me every couple of weeks or so.

"Everything's great, Mr. Jacobsen." I push my shoulders back and stand tall, make direct eye contact to assure him this is true.

Because what would he say if I told him how everything is *really* going? What would he do if I said my ex-boyfriend is sitting in a jail cell, awaiting arraignment? Or about the fact that I'm the type of person who kisses other people's boyfriends and likes it?

"Theo, Principal Detz is asking the faculty to help out as much as we can in . . . the wake of Donovan Pratt's return," he says, nudging the base of the water fountain with his toe.

And?

"And," he says, reading my mind, "I wanted to give you a heads-up that I've planned my lesson today around Stockholm syndrome."

"Stockholm syndrome."

"Yes, it's—"

"I know what it is."

When the victim sympathizes with their captor. Like people who have been abducted and don't hate their kidnapper. Maybe they even like them a little bit, start to feel like their abductor cares for them. Everyone talks about Patty Hearst, but that was a million years ago and she can't be the only one.

"I think it could be helpful." Jacobsen is talking again. "An open discussion. But it's your call whether or not you want to be there. I can write you a pass to the library. Or maybe you could talk to Mrs. Crumbaugh. I'm sure she'd be happy to make time for—"

"I'll be there."

Why not? It's all hypothetical at this point. Chris is just a suspect, and maybe everyone else thinks they know what he did, but I won't know for sure until I talk to Donovan.

What would Jacobsen do if I raised my hand today and asked, *How do you know if your best friend and boyfriend ran away together?* Or, *Could you find a way to be happy, even if you'd been kidnapped?* Because I know he saw the video. Everyone saw the video.

Jacobsen pauses long enough to look surprised by my answer, then says, "I'm sorry we're able to tie the lesson to something that hits so close to home, but I'm glad your friend is back, Theo."

"Yeah. Thanks. Me too."

And then he pats me on the shoulder and I smile as I walk back to Sara-Kate and Phil because otherwise he'll know something is off and I can't risk that. Besides, world gov only lasts an hour. I can put up with anything for an hour.

Until that hour arrives and suddenly it's like everyone in class has everything in the world to say about Stockholm syndrome.

"Okay, but here's the thing." Klein Anderson is talking. He sits two rows ahead of me. I watch him chew on the eraser of his pencil, which is about the most action that thing has gotten all semester. "We're not talking about a few months with some militant kook. He was gone *four years.*"

"Yeah, and imagine what he went through for that long," says Phil. He's sitting in the row between Klein and me, sliding his pen lazily across a blank sheet of notebook paper.

This is the only class I have with both him and Sara-Kate, and I've always loved that until today. Today—right now—I want everyone to shut the fuck up. Including him. They don't know everything about this case. They don't know *anything.*

"What about the video?" Klein counters. I think he would have stopped if he wasn't arguing with Phil, but their friendship is so tenuous. The line between hatred and respect is thin enough for them to enjoy testing it. They push and pull and poke at each other until one of them is seconds away from snapping.

"What about it?" Phil's voice is calm but when I look over,

his mouth is holding so much tension, I think his lips might crack from the pressure.

"It's not like he was some little kid who couldn't figure out how to get away," Klein says, his head darting around the room for support like a pastor looking for an *Amen*. "He was thirteen. You know what I was doing at thirteen? Not running off with strangers."

Thirteen. I learned how to put a condom on a guy when I was that age. Not every time. Only when Chris felt like it. Which wasn't often.

"Don't you think that's a little disingenuous?" Phil shoots back at Klein. "The guy didn't see him on the street and randomly pick him up. People are saying he worked at the convenience store. He was probably talking to him for weeks before the whole thing went down. The guy was setting him up— grooming him."

Grooming. It sounds so textbook, like Chris opened up a manual on how to abduct a child and followed the steps one by one. It's hard for me to think of him as a predator, when all I can see is Donovan laughing in the video.

"Good point, Mr. Muñoz." Jacobsen brings the attention to the front of the room again. He stands in front of the whiteboard, to the side of his desk. "The fact that the victim knew the defendant puts a different spin on the case. Is the extent of the victim's danger diminished when we learn that he had a seemingly normal relationship with the defendant prior to the abduction?"

Bingo. Is it? I will give one million dollars to whoever can answer that question right now. I'd also come up with one million dollars if it meant Donovan would answer his phone.

"Absolutely not. He was brainwashed," says a voice from behind me.

Sara-Kate.

"We don't know what it's like to be kidnapped," she says, her soft voice growing stronger as she continues. "Or how hard it would be to get away. None of us do. Lots of times . . ." She pauses and I feel her eyes on me before she goes on. "Lots of times they're threatened. Maybe he thought he would be killed if he ran away. Or that someone in his family would be killed. He has a little sister . . ."

Killed? That's extreme. Chris may not be the person I thought he was, but he'd never kill someone.

But who *was* the real Chris? Was it the one who offered sweet words and sweet sex, the guy who traced figure eights on my back, told me he loved me? Did he say and do those things with Donovan, tell him they belonged together? Or is the real Chris just a sociopath?

I wish I could tell Sara-Kate the *good* things about Chris. Like the way he told a story. He had hundreds of them. About growing up in Michigan playing Little League, and learning how to fish with his older brother, and cutting class to sneak into Detroit for the day, looking for trouble. It didn't matter who or what he was talking about. The way he gestured and looked at you when he talked, the way his amber-colored eyes danced, made you feel as if you'd been right there with him. I could have listened to those stories forever. Now I don't know if any part of them was true.

"Yeah, and the fact that he may have known him doesn't mean he wanted to run away with him," says Phil. He's really doodling now, the pen crosshatching furiously across the page as he talks. He looks at Klein as he says this next part. "How do you know he wasn't just trying to stay alive?"

"Okay, fine." Klein again. "Maybe I don't know what it's like to be kidnapped, but I *think* if some dude was trying to fuck me every night, I'd find a way to get out of that situation a little faster than he did."

The room falls completely silent.

It's not because of Klein's language. Jacobsen doesn't care how we talk, so long as we pay attention to the lesson. I've only seen him flinch once, and it involved the c-word. It's not for everyone.

But what the *fuck,* Klein? His revelation is hardly new and yet the way he said it—so loudly, so matter-of-factly—makes me feel like someone drove their knuckles square into my stomach.

"Let's reel it in a little, Mr. Anderson," Jacobsen says evenly.

He's looked about five seconds away from shitting his pants the entire time we've been talking about this, and now he's afraid Klein has said the thing that will break me. I don't move.

I keep my eyes on the whiteboard behind Jacobsen, on the part where he's scrawled STOCKHOLM SYNDROME in red and underlined it twice.

Klein shrugs and leans back in his seat, slings his arm over the back of his chair. "I'm just saying what everyone's thinking."

The room rustles uncomfortably. In the front corner of the room, Lark Pearson does one of those awkwardly obvious cough-laughs. Directly in front of me, the back of Leo Watson's neck turns red from the collar up, and next to me, Joey Thompson drops his pencil, which is quickly followed by his notebook. My eyes travel up to Jacobsen, who's gripping the edge of his desk so tightly, his knuckles have turned white.

"And I'm just reminding you that this is a sensitive subject," he says. "Honesty isn't an excuse for you to shoot off at the mouth."

His gaze flickers over me briefly, but it's long enough for Klein to make the association.

For *everyone* to make the association.

Klein whips around in his seat to catch my eye, to silently mouth, *Sorry, Legs,* even though the whole class can see him and knows what he's saying.

I look away instantly. He doesn't know as much as he thinks he does.

No one is all bad or all good.

## CHAPTER THIRTEEN

IT'S IMPOSSIBLE TO PRETEND HOSEA ISN'T IN THE ROOM as I dance.

Hard to forget that he's behind the piano in the corner, that with a few piqué turns, I could be standing beside him. That a few seconds after that I could sink down into his lap, tuck that stray piece of hair behind his ear and feel his hands travel across the small of my back.

But it's as if we have some kind of unspoken agreement. Our eyes can meet in the mirror but not across the room. A nod is okay, but never a smile.

We've been texting since the night we kissed. We exchanged numbers when he dropped me off at my car; he asked for mine first, said I should have his, too, in case I ever needed to talk. We only text every few days and never about anything important—usually it's just about school or something funny that happened at ballet or to simply say hello—but I smile when my phone dings with a new message and a little thrill goes through me every time I see it's from him.

Last night I locked myself in my bedroom and stood naked in front of my full-length mirror and pictured his arms wrapped around me from behind. Keeping me warm. Safe. I twisted and turned and stretched in slow motion as I wondered how he would see me. If my breasts are too small for him or if he likes my nearly nonexistent hips the way Chris did.

Ellie probably takes everything about him for granted. Like how it feels to run her fingers through his hair, or how his kisses are the perfect combination of soft and warm and wanting. I wouldn't take him for granted if he were truly mine. Not a single part of him.

I think about Hosea much more than I should, but when I'm dancing, all I think about is Chris.

I stand in first position next to Ruthie as Marisa guides us through plié, demi, and grand. We bend at the knee, halfway and then deeper, lifting our heels and pushing down on the balls of our feet. Perfectly synchronized because these movements are ingrained in our memory. Plié is so soothing, so methodical; it's easy to let my mind wander. To think about him.

I'll never forget Donovan's face the first time he caught us behind the store. There was an old picnic bench in back, to the right and down a few feet when you walked out the door. Chris and I would sit out there on his breaks, him puffing on a cigarette and me leaning in for the occasional drag. He would straddle the bench and sit close enough for his knees to touch the side of my leg. Sometimes he would rest his big hand on my thigh; squeeze my knee and tickle me until I begged him to stop, sprinkled tiny little kisses on his stubble-covered chin.

The day Donovan caught us, Chris was practically all over me as soon as we stepped outside. We didn't even make it to the picnic table.

He pushed me up against the wall and shoved his tongue in my mouth and I thought it was sexy. It was the way high school girls kissed their boyfriends. It was passionate and it meant he really wanted me because he was brave enough to do it where someone could walk down the alley and see us.

He had just slipped his hand under my shirt when the back door to the store creaked open. I knew without looking that it was Donovan. Chris didn't stop right away. He kept going, kept moving his hand beneath my shirt, kept pushing his tongue around in my mouth until I pulled away. I'd turned my head to look at Donovan and immediately wished I hadn't. His face was a blend of confusion and horror and something else I couldn't quite place at the time, but what I later recognized as unease.

"Oh, hey, man," Chris said, looking over at the same time he disengaged his hand from under my shirt. "What's up?"

"Someone needs to pay for gas." Donovan's voice cracked as he said this, and I couldn't tell if he was more humiliated by the fact that it happened in front of Chris or that it happened right after he'd caught us in the middle of second base.

Chris made a little clicking sound from the side of his mouth and said, "Nice work. Thanks for keeping an eye out, man."

He gave my waist a hard squeeze, patted Donovan on the

shoulder before he walked back inside. Donovan stared at me for a long, heavy moment before he followed.

Maybe I should have apologized but it's hard to say you're sorry when you're not sure why you're saying it. Donovan looked so concerned, like I was in over my head or something. But Chris was my *boyfriend*. And they were friends. Donovan didn't need to worry about me. Or maybe he was just worried that having Chris around was changing our friendship.

I readjusted my shirt and smoothed down my hair and when I went inside, the store was empty again. Chris was helping Donovan choose a comic book. Any comic he wanted, on the house.

We were silent the whole way home that day. Once, I glanced over and caught him smiling and I pretended it was because he was happy for Chris and me and not because of the X-Men comic tucked under his arm. We never spoke of the incident again, never even hinted at it, but it was clear something had changed between us.

After ballet I walk back to the dressing room alongside Ruthie. She dabs at her neck and chest with the sleeve of her shrug.

"What are you doing this weekend?" I ask.

Ruthie kind of laughs and when I look over, she's rolling her eyes. "I'm on lockdown."

Again? Ruthie is probably grounded more than anyone I know. It's the status quo around Chez Pathman.

"What happened this time?" I stretch my arms above my head, roll my shoulders back as we walk down the corridor of exposed-brick walls. The windows to our left look out over the bustling city sidewalks below.

"A week of in-school suspension." Ruthie folds her shrug into a tiny square as we're walking, so it fits neatly into her palm. "Which is so not a big deal. I mean, I sit in a room alone and finish all my work before lunch and they act like it's punishment."

Lainie McBride has been walking behind us this whole time. You can always tell when she's near; she's basically allergic to the world, so she's constantly sneezing or wheezing or popping an allergy pill. It's disgusting.

She catches up to us, hovering over our shoulders, and sniffs right in my ear. "In trouble again, Pathman? Don't they take that kind of thing into consideration for summer intensives?"

"Fuck off, McBride." Ruthie's eyes are the iciest shade of blue, probably similar to what they look like before her fists start talking. "It's about the dancing. Which I guess you wouldn't know, since you weren't supposed to be here in the first place."

It's true. Lainie tries hard, but she's the weakest in our class, and only joined the senior company when Meridith Bryant moved to New Jersey and Marisa had to fill a spot quickly.

Lainie pushes ahead of us and through the dressing room door just in time to let it slam in Ruthie's face. Not the smartest move, but she knows Ruthie wouldn't do anything to jeopardize her place here at the studio—and especially not her possible spot in a summer program.

"*Such* a fucking bitch," she mutters as we pass Lainie's locker.

Lainie pretends not to hear her, but she scoots a little farther back on the bench.

"Forget her," I say as we sit down on the opposite side of the room. I lower my voice. "Why'd you get suspended?"

She turns away from me as she tugs down the straps of her leotard. "Same reason as always. People are assholes, and I'm not going to sit there and take it while someone talks shit about me."

Ruthie's parents send her to a really good, expensive private school. They support her dream. They're kind and patient and they put up with her mean streak. I guess that's what you do when you love someone—take all of the bad even when it outweighs the good.

Sort of like being with Chris. I loved the gentle version of him, but to be with him, I also had to put up with the Chris who wasn't gentle—who made me feel ashamed as I slipped on my underwear when we were finished.

"Well, your parents can't ground you forever, right?" I say as I toss my tights into my bag.

She pulls a sweater down hard over her curls. "It's going to take them a while to forgive me for this one. The girl I got into it with is sort of a family friend. Her parents gave my school a letter of recommendation . . . I'm pretty sure they're the only reason I got in."

"Shit, Ruthie." I stand up from the bench to slide on my yoga pants as I think about what it's like to be her.

"Yeah, well." Ruthie looks away from me before I can make eye contact. Bends over to knot the laces on her black Converse. "It's kind of a big deal and everyone blames me because I'm the one with the record or whatever."

She doesn't sound angry. She doesn't look it, either.

Even with her head down—even when I can't see her face—she just looks tired. And maybe a little bit sad.

# CHAPTER FOURTEEN

I FEEL BAD ABOUT KISSING SOMEONE ELSE'S BOYFRIEND.

But not bad enough to stop.

I thought what happened with Hosea might be a one-time thing. We've been texting, but we haven't seen each other outside of ballet or random hallway sightings at school. And it would be the right thing to do—to stop seeing him before I fall too far. Yet a big part of me hopes that kissing him, that being with him, *wasn't* a one-time thing. We would be good together—I know it—so I wish guilt didn't rush through my veins every time I think about being That Girl. Because I don't know if it's a title I'd ever be comfortable owning.

Then, the Monday after Halloween, he texts me.

It comes through a few seconds after the lunch bell, so I read it as everyone is rushing out of English, toward the cafeteria. I stand at my desk and pull up his message with shaking fingers.

*Meet me in the old science lab? I want to see you.*

The old lab. Of course. No one ever uses it. I cover my smile with my hand, but I can't do anything about the goose bumps that prickle along my arms as I text him back:

*See you there.*

It was too fast. Maybe I should have waited a little bit, left him wondering. But I couldn't have stopped myself, even if I'd wanted to.

I shoot Sara-Kate a quick text that says I have to study during lunch, then duck into the nearest bathroom for a quick mirror check. I put on a fresh coat of lip gloss. Stop. Really look at myself. And it's strange. The same old me looking back as always—dark eyes, thick hair, skin a warm brown with reddish undertones. But for the first time in a long time, I look . . . happy.

I peek out into the hall to make sure it's empty, then book it to the science lab. It's more of a supply room, really. No one has class here anymore after some super-brainy kid's parents donated a ton of money to build a new lab a few years ago.

I take a deep breath when I'm standing outside the door. Smooth my hands over my fitted white button-down with the tiny yellow flowers, look down at my dark jeans to make sure they're still tucked snugly into my boots.

The knob turns easily. I step in, close the door behind me, lean my back against it as I search the room for him. Or maybe I'm here first? But I follow the rustling sound to the far left corner and there he is.

We look at each other for a long second. He smiles and I smile and we walk toward each other until we meet in the middle.

"Hi," I say when we're so close the toes of our boots are touching.

"Hi." He removes his hands from the front pocket of his hoodie. Traces my collarbone and lingers there only slightly before his hand slides up my neck and along the line of my jaw. His thumb strokes my earlobe and I lean into his palm, move closer, shut my eyes as I give myself to the moment.

Our first kiss is soft. Sweet. Short.

"I'm glad you came," he murmurs, our lips inches apart.

"Me too," I breathe back, wondering how such a small kiss can leave me so flustered. "But how'd you think of the lab? Shouldn't this room be locked up?" I look at the microscopes and Bunsen burners and boxes of rock samples perched on the tables around us. The light that manages to shine through the hazy windows reveals that everything is covered in a thick layer of dust.

His body heat melds into mine. Does he know my heart is pounding double time? Can he feel how I feel about him?

"Should be. Never is." He shrugs. "Gas is turned off on the tables and they took out all the chemicals. Klein told me about it a while ago."

"Does he still come here?" I look toward the door, wondering if this is too good to be true. I never would have thought to meet up here, but I've only recently become a person with so many things to hide.

"We're fine." He takes my hand in his. Squeezes. "I promise."

We move farther into the room and off to the side. My back against the edge of a lab table, his arms braced on either side of mine as he presses against me. My hands are cold. I look at him as I slip them between his hoodie and T-shirt so they're sitting at his waist. His mouth turns up in a slow grin as he leans in to kiss my neck.

"Hosea." I say his name quietly, but he stops. Looks at me as I wait for the right words to come. "Do . . . do you bring her here?"

His eyebrows lift in surprise. "Ellie? No." He pauses. "Never."

Of course not. He doesn't have to bring her here, because she's his girlfriend. They can be together anytime they want; they don't have to sneak around.

"Hey." He tilts his head to the side a little, his gray eyes soft. "What's wrong?"

I look down at my hands still resting on his waist. "Nothing, I . . ."

*I'm being stupid.*

*I should just enjoy this.*

*I shouldn't be upset that you're with her.*

"This can be our place . . . if you want," he says, his gaze locked firmly on me. "Just you and me, okay?"

I nod. And I know it means I'm saying that what we're doing could happen again, that I'm not strong enough to resist him. But these feelings aren't going to disappear. I *like* these feelings. I was afraid I'd never have them again, after Chris. And besides, right now, all I want is to say yes to Hosea.

"Okay?" he says again. He's still looking at me and we share a private smile that sends ribbons of warmth dancing through me.

"Okay." Maybe it's not so bad being That Girl.

I tip my head back and close my eyes and his mouth comes down on mine, soft and warm and familiar.

At least That Girl gets what she wants.

My lips are swollen when I leave the science lab.

We kept all our clothes on, but our hands were busy. My shirt is rumpled. Bunched in weird places. I tug it down at the bottom and decide to stop off in the bathroom for another mirror check. I left first and Hosea will follow in a little bit, just to be safe.

There are still a few minutes before lunch ends, so I figure the bathroom will be empty—but I figure wrong. Lark Pearson is standing at the far end of the room in front of the sinks, reapplying her eyeliner. She leans forward in a way that makes her ass stick out, emphasizing the fit of her painted-on jeans.

She gives me a long look in the mirror as the door closes behind me. I wait for her to speak, but she never turns around, and then finally, she looks away. I keep an eye on her as I move toward the farthest stall, and still she doesn't say a word. Just stares straight ahead at her reflection as she rims the lids of her blue eyes with layers and layers of black liner.

I step into the stall with every intention of staying in here until she leaves. Even if it makes me late to my next class. I've closed the door, am just getting ready to slide the lock into place when her voice echoes out across the room.

"Got any more smokes?"

I freeze. There's no pretending I didn't hear her. We're the only ones in here. I crack the stall door to look at her. "What?"

Lark drops the tube of eyeliner in her purse, then turns around and flutters a hand in the general direction of my chest. "Cloves. Got any more?"

Shit.

How could I forget? Hosea gave me one before we left the lab. "To remember me by," he'd said, pecking my lips as he tucked it into the triangular pocket of my button-down.

And now it's just sitting there, poking out of my shirt like I'm marking my territory.

I ignore the bad feeling that blooms in my chest as I shrug. "Sorry, it's my last one."

I start to close myself into the stall again as Lark makes her way to the door, but she pauses in front of me. Puts her hand on the edge of the stall door before I can fully shut it. *Shit.*

"Since when do you smoke cloves?" Her raccoon eyes are scary up close as they assess me.

"I've always smoked cloves," I say, forcing myself to not look away from her. "When they're around."

"Well, the only person I know who smokes cloves around *here* is Hosea." Lark squints at me and her breath smells faintly of old coffee and I wish more than anything that someone would walk in and save me.

"Maybe you should know more people," I respond with another shrug. Calm and cool. Totally relaxed, like my palms aren't sweating.

Her mouth falls open, but she recovers quickly. "Bitch," she says in a loud, clear voice before she slinks out of the bathroom.

I snap the clove in half, watch the two ends swirl down the toilet bowl as I flush away the evidence.

## CHAPTER FIFTEEN

THE RAINBOW DIET IS WHAT DID ME IN.

I'd been gradually cutting back on everything. It started with processed foods, then baked goods, then pasta and rice and bread. I never went to the trouble of pretending to be a vegetarian—even my parents couldn't argue that cutting out red meat and pork was a bad thing.

But the rainbow diet was another beast. I found it on a pro-ana site. It was easy enough to follow, in theory. Mom already bought most of the fruits and vegetables on the list, and neither she nor Dad would be suspicious if they saw me eating more produce.

It was hard when I had to eat dinner with them every night, so I started staying at the studio late, or saying I'd eaten at Phil's or Sara-Kate's, or that I didn't feel well and it would be better if I went to bed without supper.

I managed to keep it up for almost two straight weeks. The days were separated into colors: red produce on one day, white on another, and green and orange and yellow and purple. No more than 300 calories a day if I planned it just right. Wednesdays were the hardest. That's when I fasted completely, when I could have nothing more than water. I danced on those nights, too, and I was so proud of myself when I finished, when no one had figured out that I hadn't eaten since the evening before.

The second Wednesday was the one that gave me away. It was late June but already the days were so hot and humid that you wanted to take a shower as soon as you stepped out the front door. Phil and I had begged his mother to drop us off at the mall instead of the pool with her and his younger brother, Glenn. She protested at first; all of us were getting used to Donovan's absence and parents were still nervous about leaving their kids unsupervised. He'd only been gone for a couple of months. Almost as long as it had been since I'd last seen Chris.

But we begged until Mrs. Muñoz called Mom to make sure it was okay with her. It was. She was just as nervous as Phil's mother but I'd heard her and Dad talking once when they thought I was upstairs. She'd said they couldn't let the fear control us, that we had to keep living our lives and not give anyone that power. So as much as it pained her, she let me go to the mall that day with Phil.

Mrs. Muñoz stared both of us down as she dropped us off in front of the movie theater/food court wing. "You keep your cell phones *on* and pick up if you see me calling, no exceptions. And do *not* talk to anyone you don't know. Also no exceptions."

"Ma, we'll be right here at four o'clock," Phil said before he kissed her on the cheek. "Three fifty-nine, even."

I was pretty sure she had tears in her eyes as she drove away.

I knew for a fact that Phil had only gotten out of bed at eleven, a half hour before they picked me up, but his first stop was still the food court. I had mixed feelings about the food court. One part of me wanted to stand in the middle and revel in the decadent smells—fried chicken strips and enormous slices of greasy pepperoni pizza and creamy frozen yogurt and thick-cut waffle fries. It wasn't what I needed to smell on a Wednesday, my fasting day.

But the other part of me was frozen with fear, because everything about the food court reminded me of Chris: the fast-food wrappers balled up in the corners of his car, the fountain sodas that took up residence in the sticky cup holders of the console. Even the stacks of thin paper napkins on the tables made me think of him. He always kept a bunch in his glove compartment; he used them to wipe himself off after we'd finished having sex.

"I'm getting a gyro to start out." Phil took a step toward the Greek place, but his eyes were all over the food court. "Maybe a corn dog before my mom picks us up. Or tacos. And fries. A shitload of fries. What are you having?"

I didn't answer. My stomach was growling so loudly, I could barely hear myself think. I pinched. Directly under my ribs on my right side. For one, two, three, then four beats. It was a little after noon, so I only had a few more hours until I could eat again. Seventeen more hours, to be precise. But I'd be sleeping for seven of those, so really just ten more hours.

"Theo?"

Phil's voice sounded tinny. I wasn't looking at him, anyway. I was staring at the meat behind the counter of the gyro restaurant. A vertical cylinder of meat turning on a spit. How could anything that looked and sounded so questionable smell so wonderful? I couldn't remember the last time I'd touched beef or even chicken. Or lamb. Was it lamb? I'd always thought lamb was disgusting but if that's what they were shaving off and stuffing into the grilled pita bread, it wasn't disgusting that day.

I couldn't even remember the last time I'd had anything besides fruits and vegetables. Maybe I could switch out that day for the next one on the diet. Thursday could be my fasting day and maybe a gyro wouldn't count because Chris and I never ate at a food court. Only in his car or on the swings of the abandoned park or at the picnic table behind the convenience store.

"Theo?"

I pinched myself again when Phil said my name. Harder, to make sure I wasn't cheating myself. But everything started to get fuzzy. The sounds from the food court grew louder, like they were living inside me, and Phil's voice got smaller. I was dizzy and warm. My whole body, then the warmth rushed to the tips of my ears. My ears were on *fire*. I think Phil touched my arm then, kind of shook me to make sure I was okay, but I was too far gone.

I kept staring at the rotating meat and I had to think of something to keep my mind off of how delicious it would taste, so I pictured a lamb impaled on the spit instead. White and fluffy and adorable with big, long-lashed eyes, but still my stomach moaned, so I imagined the man behind the counter slaughtering the lamb with a sharp, shiny butcher knife and I hit the floor when I saw blood.

Phil ratted me out.

Not that night. Not right away. After I'd finished convincing the mall employees that I was simply exhausted from the heat, that all I'd needed was water and a few minutes to sit down, I had to work on Phil. I pleaded with him to not tell his mother. I talked him into a matinee of the new Wes Anderson, told him that the air-conditioning would make me feel better.

I don't think either of us knew anything about the movie by the time it ended. Phil spent as much time looking at me as he did the screen, and I was sucking hard on ice chips, pretending I hadn't just scared the shit out of everyone—myself, most of all. I'd been really weak on the new diet, but it was working. I'd already lost two pounds, so I'd powered through it. But fainting? I'd never fainted in my life.

Luckily no one I knew had been around. A miracle in itself, possible only because Ashland Hills doesn't have a proper mall and we had to go to the next town over. But what if it happened again? That's not something I could explain away. If anyone else found out I'd fainted, they'd surely connect the two and take me to a doctor and everything I'd worked so hard for would be ruined.

As soon as the credits began rolling and the lights came on, I'd turned to Phil and clutched his arm in a death grip.

"You can't tell."

"Jesus, Theo. That hurts." He'd yanked his arm out of my hand. Then, "What are you talking about?"

"You know . . . What happened today." I dug my fingers into the plush armrest instead.

"Theo—"

"You can't tell, Phil. It was an honest mistake. I forgot to eat breakfast and it's a thousand degrees outside and it was a mistake, okay?"

"You already said that." His eyes narrowed as he looked at me and toyed with the sleeve of his vintage Jethro Tull T-shirt. His love for old British rock bands was unrivaled at the time.

"Because you have to believe me."

"How do you forget to eat?" Phil frowned so deeply at me then that if his mother had been there she would have warned him that his face might stay that way.

"Phil, please. If you tell my parents they'll get pissed and we'll have to have another meeting with Marisa." I squeezed the armrest to hide how badly my fingers were shaking.

"*Another* meeting?"

Shit shit shit.

If I'd been paying better attention the next evening, I would have realized Phil had every intention of telling. He came over for dinner and he was overly polite, even with me. Like always, he helped my father with the dishes while Mom and I wiped down the dining room table. And I was stupid not to suspect anything while they were alone together. Or when Phil looked into my eyes a bit too long before he stepped out the front door. He was trying to tell me right then and there that he was sorry for what he had done.

I was too tired to notice. I was too fucking tired of everything. Of pretending to eat, and pretending to be okay with the fact that my friend was still missing and my boyfriend had left me. Of pinching myself till I left plum-colored bruises. I was tired of pretending that I was as strong as the girls on the pro-ana boards: StikPrincess and Dyin2BThinnn and Paper-Gurl. None of them ever talked about fainting. None of them were sitting there in the second week of their rainbow diet nibbling on a chicken kebab because they were too tired and too dumb to figure a way out of the meal. Thursday was my red day. My dinner was supposed to be half a red pepper, not half a red pepper with fattening meat attached to either side. Or was Thursday orange? I was too tired to get up and check my computer.

It didn't matter. The damage was already done.

My parents didn't know what else to do with me. I hadn't ever been in any real trouble up until then. I was a solid B student, fully dedicated to ballet, and more than capable of taking care of myself in the hours they couldn't be with me. When they realized how little they'd actually seen me eat in the past couple of months and how worried Marisa and Phil were, they freaked out and sent me away while they tried to figure out where they went wrong.

Because they'd talked to me about Donovan. A lot. They made sure I knew that the case wasn't closed just because he hadn't turned up yet. They asked how I was feeling. Constantly. And if they thought I was spending too much time alone, Phil would magically show up at the door, asking if I wanted to go to the pool or see a movie or come over for lunch.

Maybe if I were a better person I would have told them about Chris. But every time I wanted to pick up a pen to confess it all in a letter or tell them in one of the two phone calls I was allowed each week at Juniper Hill, I stopped. I backtracked. I remembered what Chris said, that no one would understand what we had. That we hadn't known each other very long but our love was irreplaceable and true. He said what we had was special and if anyone else found out they'd try to ruin it for us.

I had seen the look on Donovan's face when he found us behind the store. I believed Chris. Even after he left me without saying goodbye, I believed him.

Phil wrote me letters. One for each week I was in Wisconsin. The old-fashioned kind, with paper and an envelope. I never wrote him back.

But I read every single note. They didn't say anything important. He spent the first three apologizing and explaining how worried he'd been, how he didn't think he had any other choice. The next few were about his summer and those letters are evidence that Phil is a hell of a lot more boring when I'm not around.

I kept them all. In a box at the back of my closet with the articles about Donovan. My parents were especially sneaky back then, and the newspapers would go missing in our house almost as soon as they landed on the front doorstep. But I could still use a computer, so I printed them out and paper-clipped them together under the only thing I have from Chris: a dried daisy.

He'd get them from the store. They were two-day-old flowers, discounted to almost nothing. I didn't care. We'd be driving out to the park, and when I turned my head to look out the window, a single daisy would appear on my lap. I looked past the curling petals and drying stems because two-day-old flowers were still beautiful in their own way. They were extra-beautiful to me, because no one had ever given me flowers besides my father.

Sometimes I wonder what Phil would do if he knew his letters were sitting next to something Chris gave me. I think about what his face would look like as I told him about my ex-boyfriend, how quickly he would relay the story to my parents.

I don't know what I would tell him anyway. Phil's never been in love, so I don't think he'd understand a boyfriend I had to keep secret. Especially not then. He knew love— just not the kind I did. He would have done anything for his mother, for Glenn. But he didn't know that the love of someone who isn't related to you is even better, even more special, because they don't *have* to love you. They love you because they want to be with you, because they chose you.

Or at least that's what I used to believe about Chris.

# CHAPTER SIXTEEN

STUDY HALL IS A PARTICULAR KIND OF HELL.

It wouldn't be so bad if the rules were actually enforced. But I'm in a classroom notorious for juniors and seniors who could not give less of a fuck. And it's not just the students. Gellar oversees this period and he's useless when he's not rattling off facts about inorganic and organic substances or slashing a fat, red C-minus on my chemistry midterm.

I usually sit in the middle of the room, in the row closest to the door. Far enough from the slackers to avoid being associated with whatever they're getting into, but not too close to the front. You miss everything up there and I like to know what's happening, even if I'm not involved.

Two days after I meet up with Hosea in the science lab, Klein slips into the room shortly after the bell rings. He never carries a notebook or pencil to this period, doesn't even pretend he's here to do anything other than act like a total asshole. Gellar's eyes don't leave his crossword puzzle. He stopped calling roll and marking tardies the third week of school. It's a wonder anyone shows up at all.

Klein usually sits at the back with his druggie friends, but today he slides into the seat behind mine. He scoots his desk up until he's nearly sitting on top of me, then moves his mouth so close to my ear I feel violated.

His breath is on my skin. "You didn't hear this from me, but Ellie Harris is pissed at you."

My stomach clenches into a hard knot. I turn my head to show I heard him, but just slightly. I won't look at him dead-on or he'll be able to read my eyes. "What did I do to Ellie Harris?"

Besides kiss Hosea and want Hosea and wish that he were *my* boyfriend? But this isn't just about hooking up. We have a connection. We have a *place.*

"She thinks he's fucking around on her," he says, his voice low.

"So?" My heart thumps three times in rapid succession.

Klein cranes his neck so uncomfortably close that I have to look at him. Dark circles are lodged under his eyes, and his lips are dry. He looks as if he hasn't been to bed in days.

"She thinks he's fucking around with *you,* Legs." The desk groans as he leans forward, as he claps a hand down on my shoulder so hard that I wince. "Said she's seen you guys talking a lot lately."

A lot? The gazebo at Klein's party and—

"Where?" I twist halfway around in my seat to get a better look at him. He startles, then his green eyes narrow to slits.

"Well, shouldn't you know the answer to that, Legs?" I want to slap the smirk off his face.

But shit. Maybe someone *did* see us around the science lab? But we were so careful. We waited until no one else was around, and left at different times, just like we arrived. Lark. Did she tell Ellie she saw me with the clove? Maybe, but she can't prove that I got it from Hosea. Or maybe someone saw us driving around that night I saw the video of Donovan? But no. That would be enough evidence for her to confront Hosea, not simply speculate to Klein. If he's even telling the truth.

"Gossip is gross," I say, throwing him my hardest death stare. "You should mind your own business."

He holds up his hands in fake surrender. "Hey, I'm just giving you a heads-up. No judgment here. But Hosea's my buddy and you're . . . well, anyway. I thought you should know."

I turn back around. "And I think you should leave me alone."

His hand squeezes down on my shoulder again—too hard, again—before he pushes his desk back, stands up, and retreats to the rear of the room with the other burnouts. "Good to see you, too, Legs."

The classroom door opens and Gellar's head of wispy gray hair finally shoots up. An office attendant shuffles in with a blue hall pass. Everyone who's noticed is cringing, praying that pass isn't meant for them. Blue means Crumbaugh, and in a room like this there's a good chance anyone could be called up to her office. Gellar glances down at the name before he mumbles, "Theo Cartwright."

This day is getting worse by the minute.

I have no idea what Crumbaugh wants, but I sigh and tuck everything into my bag and follow the hall monitor out of the room. The only consolation is that I don't have to feel Klein's eyes piercing through me for the next sixty minutes. I look back at Gellar. Eyes down, he licks his thumb before turning the page in his book to a new puzzle.

I don't know what to expect when I get to Crumbaugh's office, but it is not my parents.

Yet there they are when I walk in. And there's an extra chair pulled up for me between them. I sit but I don't have the patience for pleasantries, so when Crumbaugh says hello to me with a weak smile, I look at my parents instead.

"What are you guys doing here?" I push the steel legs of my padded chair back a few feet. Not so close to Crumbaugh's desk.

"Sorry to take you out of class," Dad says, and he already sounds unsure, so that's not a good sign.

"We came right over as soon as . . ." Mom trails off like she doesn't know how to finish that sentence. Like she's not even going to try. She's wearing makeup—a touch of mascara on her almond-shaped eyes, her thin lips a muted burgundy. "And

Mrs. Crumbaugh was kind enough to let us use her office to talk to you."

Yeah, kind enough to let us use her office while she sits two feet away listening to our conversation. That totally makes her the best.

My palms sweat because they must have found out about Chris Fenner. And instead of going straight to the police, they're going to make me talk about him, here in this room with the guidance counselor.

"Babygirl—" Dad clears his throat, looks swiftly at Crumbaugh and back at me. "Theodora, there's been a new development. With Donovan."

"He's talking?" My voice is so shaky it takes even me by surprise.

"Well, no," Dad says. He leans forward a little, his hands on his knees. "But the arraignment for Donovan's abductor was this morning."

Right. How I managed to forget that for even a second is beyond me. Maybe my conversation with Klein wasn't the worst thing that could have happened.

"He pled not guilty." Dad sounds as if it physically pains him to say so.

Not guilty.

I will have to testify.

A headache throbs immediately behind my eyes. It pulses steady and hard in the same spot as I think about what this means. Chris Fenner was many things—charming, focused, pouty when he didn't get his way—but he wasn't stupid. Whether Donovan went voluntarily or not, Chris must think that he won't say anything to get him in serious trouble.

"It's a complicated case." Dad pushes up his glasses. "Donovan isn't talking, and he also wouldn't let anyone touch him when they got him back here. Of course some of that—that *man's* DNA was found on his clothing—"

"DNA?" I practically whisper as I stare at the perfectly pressed sleeve of his white dress shirt. He's wearing small, oval cuff links. Silver.

"Not—no. Hair. Skin cells." Dad scratches at his clean-shaven chin. "Anything you'd find on someone who'd been living in the same house, but not enough to prove anything that happened was . . ."

"Of a sexual nature," Mom finally pipes in, her eyes cast down on her lap. She crosses and uncrosses her thin legs a couple of times. Runs a hand over her short, curly hair before she brings it down to her lap. "They couldn't prove anything like that happened."

I think the room would collectively blush—my mother more than anyone else—if we weren't so disgusted by the topic at hand. My eyes rest on the finger-painted picture hanging on the wall behind Crumbaugh. It's framed.

"They couldn't do a . . . thorough test," Dad says. "It was Donovan's choice and he refused . . ."

Shit.

"Maybe this Chris guy was an idiot who didn't understand you can't go running around with kids half your age," Dad says. "Maybe he didn't do anything to him." He shakes his head. "But it's just so rare."

He clears his throat. "The prosecution's testimony will be crucial to the case. Donovan's old neighbors and classmates— *anyone* who can speak about him or the situation so we can make sure this guy gets the maximum sentence."

I can't focus. My eyes flicker back and forth so rapidly, I get just snatches of reality—my mother's knee and my father's teeth and that stupid fucking mug of Crumbaugh's with the hot-pink lipstick pressed into the rim.

Dad: "And the people who saw him the day he went missing." His voice softens. "They will have to speak, too."

"When is it?" My voice is strangled. Mangled by fear.

"It's set for the third week in January. A little less than three months."

I am numb.

If I don't say anything, Chris will probably do a few years of time, followed by parole and community service. Then he could move wherever he wanted and start a new life. If I don't say anything, they won't have much to go on at all. Not unless someone else has the kind of story I do.

# Part Two

# CHAPTER SEVENTEEN

I SPIN AROUND ON ONE FOOT, THE ROOM SWIRLING BY me in blurs of color and light. My leg extends from my hip in a straight line before it whips around to meet my body, over and over again. Spotting saves me from a serious case of dizziness; I train my eyes on a specific point across the room and never look away, not until that last possible second when I have to turn my head to keep up with my body. Air speeds by me so fast that it clicks in my ears, strong and steady like a metronome.

Fouettés.

Ruthie swears Margot Fonteyn was the greatest Odette/Odile. We've both watched endless productions of *Swan Lake,* from those put on by the senior companies before us to videos of famous performances to a night at the Joffrey that has been my best birthday present yet. Fonteyn was marvelous, the textbook example of the role, no doubt about it.

Natalia Makarova's version is everything to me, though. I cried when I first saw her perform. Her control and precision appeared so effortless, her acting so natural that I truly believed she had turned into Odile, the seductive black swan that danced through the night.

Odile is known for her thirty-two fouettés in a row. No break, just balanced on that one pointe shoe, the movement signifying the beautiful strength of ballet. I can execute twelve nearly flawless ones without stopping and sixteen if I really push myself. You get in a zone, like a human spinning top. Ready for the next one—always ready for the next one—because if you aren't you'll lose the momentum. Interrupt the machine. Break up the story.

I won't make it all the way there, but I want to get as close to thirty-two as I can. I have to dance better than ever to catch the eye of the audition tour judges for summer intensives, but I don't just want them to notice me—I want to *astound* them.

My feet are cramping, the bones aching for relief. I turn once more, then stop. The finish is sloppy, but I have the room to myself, so no one else saw. And I've been going for a while. My leotard is soaked.

I stare at myself in the mirror. I used to do this, just stand here and stare, until my body appeared so contorted, I could have been looking at it through a fun-house mirror. Until I was just a misshapen blob of a person with a neck made of putty and noodles for legs. I used to stare until I was satisfied, until I looked nothing like the actual girl who stared back at me. I hated the distorted twist of my limbs and torso, but I hated my real reflection even more. It was never thin enough.

I turn to the side now and assess my profile. Run my hands down the length of my body and wonder what Chris would think about me. Back when we were together, some of the girls at school had already transitioned to real bras, but I barely needed the training kind. I liked that I was thinner, more disciplined than my peers, but I hated that you could mistake me for a child if I turned the wrong way.

Chris didn't mind. He told me I was perfect the way I was, that he wished all the girls he'd dated had looked like me. I had no reason to doubt him. My chest may have been the flattest in the seventh grade, but that didn't stop him from treating me like someone older, like one of the girls he'd known whose body didn't look like mine.

One day, he got mad at me. We were at the abandoned park, already in the backseat of his car. His shirt was off. I'd gotten into the habit of removing it as soon as I could because Chris's shirts always smelled like mildew, as if they'd been left in the washer too long.

I usually wore a cotton triangle bra. Simple and unlined and enough to save me from complete embarrassment in the locker room during gym class. But that day I wore my new bra. The one I bought with my own money and on my own time, so my mother wouldn't ask any questions. The one I hid in the back of my closet so she couldn't find it when searching for stray laundry.

I wanted to show Chris how grown up I was. He looked especially cute that day; he'd just gotten a haircut and it showed off more of his chiseled face, of his smooth cheekbones and strong brow. And I liked the way he looked with his shirt off. He worked out—a lot, from what I could tell. His chest was smooth and broad, his arms ropy and strong with lean muscle.

But he didn't seem happy about my bra. His face darkened as his fingers tangled around the clasps in back and after a few moments he gave up, threw his hands in the air, and said, "What the fuck is this?"

"It's new." I squished down into myself. My back suctioned to the sticky vinyl seat, my arms folded over the black lace cups of the bra that was causing all the trouble. "I thought you'd like it." I paused, and after several seconds had passed and he still hadn't said anything, I added, "I guess not."

"Don't start pouting on me now, Pretty Theo," he'd said, in a gentler voice. He lightly ran a finger along the bridge of my nose. "I just like the other ones better."

"They aren't . . . babyish?"

They had to be. They were made for girls who don't have real breasts yet. For little girls. He must have thought of me as a little girl when I wore those, not the thirteen-year-old mature enough to date someone five years older.

"Hey, hey. You're not a baby," Chris said, his voice steady and firm as he blinked at me with those eyes that I loved. "You're not like other girls your age."

He gave me a long, wet kiss on the mouth as if that signaled the end of the conversation, then glanced at the dashboard clock before his hand moved down to his belt buckle. I knew what that meant. As if I'd needed confirmation, he said, "Come on. I have to be back at the store in twenty."

Still, if Chris liked me as I was, small chest and little-girl body, how could I complain? I would have done anything to continue being the object of his desire. I never put on the black lace bra again after that day. It's at the bottom of the box with Phil's letters and Chris's daisy because I don't know where else to put it. And I couldn't bring myself to get rid of it because good memory or bad, sometimes I'd needed proof that our relationship had existed.

I look at the mirrored wall of the studio and wonder what Chris would think of me now. What will he think when he looks at me across the courtroom with those amber eyes that used to be able to persuade me to do *anything*? And what will I say when they ask me if I knew him? It's been four years.

Four years that remain almost a complete mystery.

I *have* to talk to Donovan. I have to keep calling until he answers the phone. I'll go over to his house if it comes to that, but I have to know:

*Did you want to go?*

If he can answer that one question, I'll know what I have to do. Keep quiet about my relationship with Chris and go on with my life, or confess everything to send him to prison.

Everyone thinks he abused Donovan, but I have to hear it with my own ears.

My eyes focus on the mirror again. My hips are more rounded now—too round for my liking. My thighs are a bit larger than when I was with Chris, but most of it is muscle. They were the first place I gained weight after Juniper Hill, and sometimes I'd sit on the edge of the tub before my shower and squeeze my hands around them. Evaluating every millimeter of my skin, looking for signs of cellulite.

I don't do that now. Not every day. But I've gotten lazy over the last year or so. Forgetting that a slice of pizza here or a cup of frozen yogurt there adds up. Everyone tells you "a spoonful of this" or "a little bite of that" won't hurt, but those spoonfuls and bites could be the difference between sixteen fouettés and thirty-two. Between dancing at Marisa's studio for another year before I graduate or going to year-round ballet school.

Or it could all mean nothing. The trial is a little over two months away, and auditions start a week after that. If I find out Chris abducted Donovan, if I have to tell my story to a courtroom, I'll be judged for much more than my dancing. Or worse, they might not give me a chance. They might recognize my name, my face, and politely but firmly suggest it'd be better if I focused my energy elsewhere. Ruthie said it was about the dancing, but I can't imagine anyone would want me affiliated with their program if my ex-boyfriend turns out to be the worst kind of criminal.

I run into Hosea in the lobby of the studio. He's coming from the direction of Marisa's office and looks surprised to see me. This is the first time we've been alone since the science lab.

"Hey," he says, rearranging his backpack on his shoulder as he smiles at me.

They're becoming easy now, his smiles. It shouldn't be so hard for me to ignore someone who has a girlfriend. Especially after what Klein said. What Ellie suspects. And how bad I feel when I think about what we've been doing.

We still text. I'm happy to know he's thinking about me, that he wants to be with me, but sometimes I think it's better that we can't be alone very often. Because he may never break up with Ellie. Or worse, what if he broke up with her for me, only to end things if I tell people the truth about Chris and me at the trial?

"Hi." I smile back at him. Cautious, but grateful that for the most part, the studio is a safe place.

"How often do you stay late?" he says before I get a chance to ask what he was doing in Marisa's office. He holds the door open for me and I look at him before I cross through, simultaneously appreciating and hating the gentlemanly gesture. It makes it that much harder to stop liking him.

"A few times a week now. Just getting in some extra practice."

"Like you need it." He closes the door firmly behind him, then digs around for his keys in the front pocket of his backpack. "You want a ride?"

"I can take the train." It's automatic, something I've become accustomed to saying when people offer. And I'm glad, because otherwise I would have hesitated. Possibly said yes as soon as he asked, because sometimes it takes a while for my heart to catch up to my brain. And of course I would rather ride in his car.

"Do your parents pick you up at the station?" He looks at me curiously, and I wonder if he knows how hard I've been trying to avoid him.

"No, they trust me enough to drive there." I slip on my wool gloves before sticking my hands into the pockets of my peacoat. "Just not into the city."

"Well, it's on my way, so I'll give you a ride," he says, already starting to walk.

I stand in place on the concrete. "I shouldn't. I . . . *We* shouldn't."

He stops, turns to look at me. Eyebrows wrinkled, gray eyes blinking in confusion. "I know we haven't met up lately, but . . . did I do something to piss you off?"

I stare at the brick on the building's exterior. Red. Weathered. It matches the corridors inside. "No, I just . . . Things *happen* when we're alone and maybe we should try to be good."

"Oh." He shifts his weight, shifts his backpack. Doesn't quite meet my eye. He looks out at the street, packed with honking cabs and hissing buses and commuters road-raging their way back to the suburbs. Then he nods. "We'll both be good, okay? It's not just about that. I like talking to you, Theo."

Oh. Maybe I'm weak, but knowing it's not just physical, that he doesn't *expect* anything . . . it makes me feel better about accepting his offer. So I do.

He's parked a couple of blocks over from the studio, and as soon as we're out of sight I feel him move closer. A moment later, his arm is around me. I'm stunned at first. No one has ever been affectionate with me in public. Well, Klein, I guess, but he doesn't count.

"Is this okay?" Hosea asks when I remain silent. "I swear, I'm not trying anything. You looked cold."

I take in a breath. Let it out. This isn't being good, but I say, "It's fine."

And a few seconds later, I relax into him. Because being under Hosea's arm *feels* good and I need to feel good right now. Friends can put their arms around each other. I do it all the time with Sara-Kate and Phil.

We fall into step together as we make our way across the cold pavement. It's supposed to snow this weekend; if we get as much as the weathermen are saying, we might have a white Thanksgiving in a couple of weeks. I don't mind the snow, but it makes my parents flip out even more about my driving. They start dumping sandbags in the trunk of my car and yelling out safety instructions every time I leave the house and I think they'd put snow chains on my tires if I let them.

I hate when we reach Hosea's car because it means he has to move his arm. I felt so cozy under there. Comfortable, like I belonged.

And then I squash that. We're friends.

He opens the door for me again and I say thank you as I slide into the passenger seat of his little orange hatchback.

Fasten my seat belt and sit with my gloved hands in my lap as I wait for him to get in.

The engine starts up after a few tries and he twists the knob on the heater but the car has been sitting too long. The vents send out a rush of cold air, so he turns it off again. "I hate this thing. Nothing works."

"It's not so bad," I say, squeezing my fingers together so he won't see them shake from the cold. "At least it still runs, right?"

"I guess." He kind of laughs as he rubs his hands together and blows on them. "Klein won't ride in here. He thinks any car without seat warmers should be taken off the road."

"Classic Klein." I shake my head, then: "I'm not exactly his biggest fan right now."

I look at the people sitting in the tiny café across the street from our metered parking spot. Two girls in dark sweaters, laughing over giant mugs of coffee. It reminds me of Sara-Kate, how it's so strange for me to be keeping *another* secret from her. But there's no need to tell her, because nothing's going to happen between Hosea and me. We're both being good. And there's nothing to tell if we're just friends, right?

"What did Klein do?" Hosea looks at me. Waiting. Ready. Maybe a little nervous.

"He said Ellie is pissed." I turn back to him, move my eyes down to the elbow of his black coat. "At me."

He casually reaches for the pack of cloves by the gearshift. Turns it over in his hands a few times before offering me one. I decline and he lights one for himself, takes a long drag before he puts the car in drive and starts down the side street toward the expressway.

"Well, nobody's said anything to me," he says, exhaling his smoke toward the sliver of open air at the top of the window. "Klein knows I don't put up with that gossipy bullshit."

I don't want to care, but that statement lets me know I do. A part of me deflates as he says that. I know it shouldn't matter because he's *not* my boyfriend. But it makes me feel as if he's downplaying our connection. As if I'm in this alone and imagined everything that's happened between us.

"But it's not bullshit. This. Us." I spread my hands around the interior of his tiny car.

"I didn't mean it like that," he says impatiently. "Of course it's not bullshit. It's just . . . I'm not exactly in the habit of cheating on my girlfriend. And then you . . ."

I'm dying to know what's on the end of that sentence, but when I look over, his eyes are flashing and I know better than to ask before he's ready to tell me. I don't want to push him away.

So I stare out the window as the lights of downtown Chicago twinkle around us. I remember when I'd come into the city as a kid, how I thought it was magical. The buildings seemed positively gargantuan back then, and I loved the overhead chugging of the El as we walked the crowded sidewalks, navigating our way between the patches of stores.

The car is too still. The busted radio means we're dependent on the sounds outside to break up the silence: the uneven rumble of the engine, the hum of cars in the lanes parallel to us, the long, high wail of sirens in the distance.

Hosea exits smoothly off the expressway, makes a couple of right turns, and pulls onto a quiet residential street near the Ashland Hills train station, then turns to me, ready to finish what he started to say when we were back in the city. He takes a deep breath. "And then you came around and made me feel something . . . new. Something good. It's been a long time since I've felt this way, Theo."

Now the heater is blasting hot, stale air and the car is too warm. I take off my gloves, slowly lay them across my lap, one on top of the other.

"What about Ellie?" I say weakly. I didn't expect him to be so upfront about his feelings. Does this mean he's going to break up with her?

"Ellie is . . . Ellie." He shrugs. "She knows about the music stuff, but she doesn't care. That's why I didn't tell her about my job at the studio. She doesn't make me want to be better, like you do. She doesn't get that it's scary . . . to want something so much and not be sure if you're good enough. I guess sometimes I feel like she doesn't know the real me, or something."

"Then she's missing out. Anyone should feel lucky to know the real you," I say. Softly, because I didn't think I would say it out loud.

"That's, like, the nicest thing anyone's ever said to me." His voice is quiet. Then he inhales from his clove one last time and smashes the butt into the crowded ashtray under the dash.

"It's true." I fiddle with my gloves because I don't know what else to do with my hands. Because telling me I just said the nicest thing to him is sort of the nicest thing in itself.

He looks down at the gearshift, where his fingers tap out a quick rhythm. "Did you say something to Marisa?"

I give him a funny look. "About us? Of course not."

"No, I mean . . . what I said about music school. She called me into her office to ask what my plans are after I graduate. She gave me some sheet music she thinks I'll like and said she knows someone in the music program at Columbia College if I wanted to talk about applying. Why would she do something like that if you didn't talk to her?"

"Because it's not exactly a secret that you're good enough to be serious about music, Hosea." I look down at the gearshift, wish his hand was touching me instead. "Marisa likes to help people who work hard."

"She told me to think about what I want to do next fall, and that I could practice on the piano at the studio when there are no classes. For free." His voice is incredulous, his eyes wide. "Do you know how long it's been since I really played a piano? Like, with my own music? I have one at home, but it's hard to compose on that thing. It's an old spinet and it's shitty and . . ."

He trails off as if he's so overwhelmed by Marisa's kindness that he doesn't know what to say.

"You're going to do it, right?" I say encouragingly.

"I think so." He leans against the headrest.

"But?"

"But . . . you don't think she's just being nice?"

My eyes lock on his wrist. I imagine my fingers wrapped around it, his pulse beating warm and quick against my skin. We understand each other. We *like* each other. This isn't my imagination.

"No," I say. "And your piano teacher wasn't saying those things to be nice, either. Neither was I. You're really, *really* good, Hosea."

He looks at me, lets out a long, quiet breath. Then his lips meet mine with urgency. But it's not demanding like Chris, or chaotic like Klein. It's full of intense yearning that makes me pause for a moment to look at him before I return it with an urgency of my own, a kiss so steeped in need and craving, it must be radiating from me. I pull away, look at him as I wonder why I can't seem to control myself with him.

"Hey." He smooths a hand over the top of my head, squeezes the bun at the back. "We can stop. I should stop. I didn't mean to break my promise."

*Too late.*

"No." My chest is rising and falling so quickly. We're both breathing hard. Panting, almost. "Don't stop."

He smiles.

We remove our coats and then he's back with me. He lowers his head to my neck, brushes his lips against the dip in my collarbone. My fingers crawl beneath the layers of his shirts until

I make contact with his skin, slide my hands along the muscles in his back.

His strong piano hands trace the lines of my body and I wonder if it disappoints him. I look nothing like what he's used to, must feel so different from Ellie's curves. But the way he looks at me between kisses and lifts the hem of my shirt, inch by inch, slowly exploring what's underneath—it makes me feel like I'm the only girl he's ever wanted.

He slides his finger below the waistband of my jeans and I flinch. Only a little, but enough for him to notice, to pull back and exhale as he says, "Sorry."

"No, it's not that. It's just . . ."

I feel so light-headed, so happy and confused and wrong and *good.* But I don't trust myself around him and I need to know if there's any hope of a real *us.* An *us* that can be seen in public, that doesn't have to meet up in parked cars on dark streets.

He looks at me expectantly, his face flushed, his eyes filled with the same heat.

"Are you . . ." My voice is garbled. I clear my throat. "Are you going to break up with her?"

His eyebrows shoot up before they sink low in—not exactly a frown, but whatever look that is, it isn't good. He leans back in his seat, away from me, and I think that must be an involuntary sign. A preview of his answer, if I didn't already know by the look on his face.

"It's not that easy, Theo." His eyes are trained on the dashboard, where a ribbon of cellophane curls into a corner. He sweeps it into the console with the pack of cloves it came from. "We've been together almost two years now."

I pretend my throat isn't aching. "But you make me feel something good, too."

"What am I supposed to do?" He throws his hands in the air. "Tell her I met someone else and break things off, just like that? I can't do that totally out of the blue and after two *years.*"

"You're supposed to do what feels right." I look down at my hands. They've gone ice-cold since I stopped touching him. "Doesn't being with me feel right?"

"Do what feels right, huh?" He pushes a loud stream of air from his lips, like he's trying hard to control his irritation. "Easy for you to say when you're not the one who has to make the decision."

I push on the door handle and jump out of the car, yanking out my coat while Hosea stares at the seat. He looks baffled, as if he has no idea why I'm not sitting there. He snaps out of it when I slam the door, steps out of the car immediately.

"What are you doing?"

A full-body chill takes over. It's fucking freezing. I'm standing out here in the stupid cold on a stupid street that isn't mine, arguing with someone else's boyfriend. What *am* I doing?

"I'm walking to the station and getting in my car and going home. Thanks for the ride."

I'm shaking so hard, it's amazing I can get my coat on at all, let alone line up the buttons with the appropriate holes, but I put my fingers to work anyway.

"Theo, come on. Don't be like that," he says in a voice tinged with annoyance.

"Then don't talk to me like that."

"Like *what*?" He's standing next to the car, one hand on top of the doorframe, one resting on the black racing stripe that coasts down the middle of the roof.

"Don't tell me about your dreams and how I make you feel good about yourself and then say you can't decide." My trembling fingers give up on the last few buttons; I pull the sides of my coat tight against me instead. "I don't want to be your secret girlfriend. I don't want you to want me only when no one else is around."

I've done that before and maybe if I'd said something sooner . . . maybe Donovan never would have left and my life wouldn't be such a mess right now.

Hosea shakes his head as he looks at me. "You really think that's how I feel about you? You think I don't want to be with someone as amazing as you?"

I don't know what to believe but it's not my heart. It flips and flutters like he's said something that matters but I know when Chris said things to me with such tenderness, such passion, they were never true. Not in the end.

*You're my girl, Theo, but if you tell anyone about us, they'll take me away. I wouldn't be able to see you, ever again, and you know I can't handle that.*

*I can't stand being without you.*

*You have to promise you'll never tell. Ever. I need you.*

"I can't." I'm quiet but the street is so still that my voice seems to bounce off the thinning treetops, echo from the roofs of the nearly identical houses. "I can't . . . *be* with you in private and watch you hold her hand when everyone else can see."

"Theo . . ." His hands drop their grip on the car, fall slack on either side of him.

But I'm already walking. I can see the lights of the station from here. It's across the street and half a block down. If I peer hard enough I can even see my car, I think. It's nothing more than a black dot illuminated by the soft halos of light in the parking lot, but I see it. And it's not too far to walk to, not even on a frigid night like this. I pull up the collar of my coat, clumsily shove my gloves onto either hand and stuff them in my pockets.

My name floats up from behind me twice more but I keep moving, keep marching along as if I never heard him in the first place. As if walking away from Hosea Roth is hurting him more than it's hurting me.

# CHAPTER EIGHTEEN

IT'S THE WEEK BEFORE THANKSGIVING AND THE GREASY front windows of Casablanca's are decorated with paper turkeys and cardboard leaves, its tables host to plastic gourds that could stand a dusting.

It's the week before Thanksgiving but it feels like Christmas outside. When the heavy scarves and wool hats are out before the end of November you know it's going to be a bad winter. I burrow my nose into my own chunky knit scarf as a blast of cold air tunnels its way through my layers.

The people sitting at the counter turn around and stare at me accusingly, as if I purposely waited for a gust of wind before opening the door. The looks you get for simply existing during winter in Chicago are enough to send you right back out to the cold sometimes. I keep my head down as I make my way back to Sara-Kate and Phil.

Except Phil's not here. I didn't see his car in the lot but I thought maybe he hitched a ride with Sara-Kate. That never would have happened before this year because they never hung out when I wasn't around. I've always been the link between them. Phil was sitting with me in the lunchroom the first day of our freshman year when Sara-Kate approached with a tray of chicken nuggets, her face bright red as she asked if she could sit with us. But she and I were the ones who hit it off that first day. Phil was skeptical, partly because he's wary of anyone new, partly because he thought Donovan would return someday and then there wouldn't be room for someone else.

I don't know what's changed between them, but it's there. It's weird how you can go to school with a person forever and brush shoulders at parties for years and then something shifts. I wish I could pinpoint the moment it happens, but maybe it's not a moment. Maybe it's been there all along and nobody noticed.

I've gotten so used to seeing Phil next to Sara-Kate that she looks incomplete sitting alone at our back booth. Her head is bent over a fat fashion magazine, her asymmetrical bob pumpkin-colored for the holidays.

Sara-Kate looks up as I walk toward the booth and instantly pushes the magazine aside. "Did you know that Casablanca's serves a full Thanksgiving meal every year?" She reaches for one of the menus, which have been stuffed with inserts advertising the dinner. "From open to close you can get a turkey dinner, complete with your choice of white or dark meat, mashed potatoes, a cooked vegetable, a dinner roll, and a slice of pumpkin pie. All for $9.99."

I slip into the booth across from her. "It's kind of sad," I say.

Sara-Kate puts the menu back in its holder. "Considering they can't even identify which vegetable they'll be cooking? A sad Thanksgiving indeed."

"No, having to eat dinner here is the sad part." I place my hat on the bench next to me, but leave my scarf wound around my neck. "Can you imagine Jana on a holiday? She'd probably tell you to fuck off as she set your pumpkin pie on the table."

Sara-Kate laughs as she looks over at the counter, where Jana is screaming at one of the cooks. "It might not be so bad. Better than listening to my great-aunt tell me I dress like a slutty hooligan."

I rest my elbows on the Formica table, gaze at the faded watercolor print of geraniums hanging on the wall beside us. "I wish we could have a friend Thanksgiving. No parents, no smart-ass family."

"We could have all carbs," she says, nodding right away. "Something about that giant bird and those little legs makes me so sad."

Or we could forgo the meal altogether, something I've been doing more of lately. Not full force, like before. I know not to go too far. But with the trial eight weeks away, I need something to keep my mind off the fact that I still haven't talked to Donovan.

I tried to call this afternoon on my way to ballet. Again, the phone rang and rang, and again I waited and waited for an answer that never came. I hung up, counted to ten, and called right back. That time, the phone rang twice before it stopped. There was a quick rush of air and a tiny click before whoever it was hung up. I was so surprised, I didn't get a chance to say hello or ask for Donovan before the line went dead. The police told Mrs. Pratt to keep the landline all these years in case Donovan ever called home or anyone who knew something about him tried to get ahold of her at that number. I wonder why she doesn't shut it off, now that he's back. If they don't start picking up very soon, I'll have to sneak over to their house. Make them let me in. Make him talk to me.

Thinking about food—exactly what I'll eat and when and exactly how much—helps keep my mind off the trial and the fact that I have no idea what to say when I get up on the stand. Marking down what I eat every day deters me from obsessing about how many days I have left until the trial.

(Sixty. I have sixty days left. Exactly two months.)

I look at Sara-Kate. Her lips are moving again. She's speaking and I don't know what she's talking about, but then Phil's name comes up.

"Where is he?"

She gives me a funny look as she nibbles on the end of a fingernail sporting raggedy yellow polish. Her hands are wrapped in fingerless gloves made of soft, pink wool. "I just told you. He's with Hosea."

"Oh." My stomach flip-flops and I try to keep my face neutral, though I can feel her looking at me, trying to gauge my reaction to his name.

I miss everything about him: sharing looks in the mirror across the studio, hearing him say my name. I missed him as soon as I walked away from him and now I don't know how to fix it. I keep replaying that night, thinking about what would have happened if I'd never said anything and we'd kept going. I wonder if I would have had sex with him, if he would have made me feel like Pretty Theo, or if it would have been fast and hard and left me numb inside.

Hosea and I ran into each other so often just a few weeks ago, but now, when I really want to see him in passing, it's like he's disappeared. So I find myself looking for him around corners in the hallway, on my walk from the train station to the studio, in the parking lot on my way into school. Maybe I made a mistake by telling him we couldn't see each other while he was with Ellie. The worst part is there's no one I can talk to because we were never supposed to hook up in the first place.

"Penny for your thoughts?" Sara-Kate smiles at me.

Our freshman year, there was a sign hanging outside Crumbaugh's office with that saying. Whoever made it had taken extra care with the bubble letters and shading, but it only took a week for someone to cross it out with heavy black marker and write $100 FOR YOU TO LEAVE US THE FUCK ALONE.

"I kissed someone." I train my eyes on the magazine to her left. "Someone I wasn't supposed to."

Sara-Kate leans forward, arms splayed on the table, her fingertips inches from mine. Her full lips part in surprise, and she looks so horrified for a second that I wonder if she thinks I mean Phil.

"Hosea," I continue, before her imagination can run too wild. I twist my fingers around the loops of my scarf. "It's happened a few times now."

I exhale a long, full breath. It's a relief to admit it, to let someone else in on this. Maybe it will be easier to stay away from him if I know someone else is aware of my weakness.

"I knew it," she says. But not in that breathy, satisfied way people use when they're getting off on gossip. It's more relief, like she's solved a minor mystery. "Not about him, but . . . I knew something was up. No offense, but you've been acting a little strange lately, Theo. I wasn't sure if it was just about Donovan or if it was something else. Some*one* else."

"He's nice." I put my elbow on the table, cup my chin with my hand as I look at her. "I like talking to him. I like—well, everything."

Sara-Kate sits back in the booth. Scoops her knees up to her chest as she presses herself into the corner of the cherry-red vinyl. "He's a good kisser?"

"The best." I smile in spite of myself. "It feels right. I mean, we didn't sleep together, but just—when I'm with him. He's . . . we understand each other."

"Well," she says, slowly. "That's great and all, but he has a girlfriend."

*Girlfriend.* I can practically see the word land between us.

"Yeah." I look out the window at the parking lot, where a harried father is trying to get two bundled-up toddlers from the pavement to their car seats. They shriek and run around him in circles as he bends down to speak to them. "He's not going to break up with her."

Her forehead wrinkles as she raises her eyebrows. "He told you that?"

Questions like that are usually followed up by statements like, *What an asshole.* She refrains and I am glad. I don't want her thinking Hosea's an asshole.

"He said it was hard for him to make a decision, so I told him not to bother." The dad outside is getting frustrated. He stands up to his full height, points to the backseat with a firm index finger. The kids stop their game and switch gears, squeeze their arms around his legs, stepping on his big shoes with their little feet. "It's over."

Sara-Kate scratches at the knee of her thrifted denim bell-bottoms. "You're sure?"

"Yes," I say, looking straight into her eyes as I wonder if I'm lying. "Completely over. So please . . . don't mention it to Phil."

She gives a solemn nod. We both know he wouldn't take this kind of news so calmly, especially when it involves two of his friends.

So. Now that I've confessed about Hosea, what if I told her about Chris Fenner? Told her everything, from how we met to what we did to how I will have to face him in court soon? Look him in the eye for the first time in four years.

I've always been able to trust Sara-Kate—maybe if I told her, I wouldn't feel sick to my stomach from the moment I wake up until I manage to fall asleep. I've taken so many antacids over the last few weeks, they're no longer effective.

It's just six words: *I have to tell you something.*

Once you say that, you have to tell. You can't leave someone hanging, not once you've gotten their attention.

"Do you think I'm a bad person?" I bring my hand up to touch my cheek. The heat seeps into my fingers.

"I think you're a normal person. With feelings." Her soft, round face looks like a porcelain doll's as she pauses in thought. "But I think it's good that you ended it. Before you fell too hard."

No. I can't tell her about Chris. She disapproves of what happened with Hosea—it's in her tone, in the way she moved away from me. So I change the subject.

"Like you're falling for Phil?" I say with a tentative smile.

She blinks her doe eyes at me, the lashes so curly, I'm surprised they don't tangle. "Nothing's happened."

I give her a look.

"I swear. You know I'd tell you, right?" She fingers the bright green barrette clipped to her dark orange hair. "I'm not saying something *won't* happen, but I couldn't stand to keep something like that from you, Theo."

It's supposed to go both ways but it doesn't.

"Do you ever . . . ," she begins, and stops to press her lips together, to think about what she's going to say before she goes on. "Do you ever feel like time is moving too fast?"

She's just described my entire life, in fact. I look outside. The dad and kids are finally gone.

Sara-Kate fans the edges of her magazine. "Junior year is almost half over and you might be leaving next year and—"

"We don't know that," I say a little too sharply.

Sara-Kate stares at me. "There's a strong possibility. Your ballet teacher said so herself."

I take a sudden interest in the saltshaker. "Well, nothing's guaranteed."

It's not. If I find out Chris abducted Donovan, that "strong possibility" could turn into "no shot in hell" in the span of five minutes. It's like being thrust into a real-life game of What If that I never signed up for.

"Guaranteed or not, I want to hang out as much as possible while we still can. So we have to make sure this year counts. Like, winter formal. We're going to make it the best winter formal ever." She clears her throat. "Not to get all sappy but I don't know what I'll do without you next year if you leave."

It would sound insincere from anyone else, but I know Sara-Kate means every single word.

"Yeah," I say as my stomach jumps, raw and angry. I pinch my side. "Me too, Sara-Kate."

I look away as quickly as I can, feign interest in the menu I've pored over a thousand times, as if I'm going to do anything besides push lentil soup around the cup with a spoon.

I look away from Sara-Kate, but her honest brown eyes haunt me for the rest of the evening.

## CHAPTER NINETEEN

IT'S HARD NOT TO THINK OF DONOVAN'S FAMILY AS Before and After.

Before, Mrs. Pratt managed the gift shop of a busy museum in the city and she was almost as married to that job as she was to Mr. Pratt. But she still made it to every baseball game, every parent-teacher conference. Each time Donovan's father was too busy, his mother was around to pick up the slack.

I remember when the local news interviewed her, shortly after the abduction. She was pleading, staring into the camera with so much hurt and hope that it was hard to look at her. "Whatever you can do to help my son—to help Donovan . . . I would be eternally grateful."

After, Mrs. Pratt was the kind of person who called psychics to her home and only went out to buy more gin.

Mr. Pratt's Before isn't very different from his After, except he's no longer married to Mrs. Pratt. He still works all the time because he's a successful real estate broker for lakefront properties. But now he lives in the city and has full custody of Julia. As soon as I saw the moving van in the driveway that day, I knew it meant he was leaving her—that Mrs. Pratt's things weren't packed into any of the boxes being carried down the driveway.

I know Donovan's Before, too. It was filled with a mother who would do anything for him and a little sister who adored him and plenty of time for comics and baseball and friends. It was filled with the kind of trust that lets you lose track of time and ride bikes home after dark without worrying someone will snatch you up from the side of the road.

Donovan hasn't left the house since he's been back. It's been almost two months. How do they expect him to start talking if he never sees anyone?

I watch. Each time I'm heading out or coming home, I watch their curtains for movement, and if it's dark outside, I look for shapes behind them. Sometimes I take the long way around our street so I can look at the house from a different angle.

A couple of people come to Donovan's house regularly; one is the man who delivers their groceries, but he's only allowed to bring them to the front porch. If you look closely and at just the right minute, you can see the terry cloth sleeve of Mrs. Pratt's bathrobe reaching through the doorway as she picks up the bags of food.

The other person shows up twice a week. A woman. Tall and big-boned with gorgeous red hair that cascades down the back of her sensible suits and trench coats. Mom said it's probably his therapist. I didn't know therapists made house calls but I guess most people would make an exception in this case.

But that's it. No one else in and certainly no one out.

I *have* to talk to Donovan before the trial. If I can see him, talk to him face-to-face, I'll know what I have to do up on the stand. I'll know for sure whether Donovan was a runaway or a victim. I'll know if he and Chris betrayed me together or if Chris Fenner deceived us both.

But every time I think about the witness stand and telling my story to a courtroom of strangers, my skin goes clammy and my mind goes blank. I don't know where I would start, how I would tell them that I didn't know what I was getting myself into when I first kissed the person I thought was named Trent.

I don't know how I would tell them that I never suspected anything between him and Donovan back then—and not for the four years they were gone, either.

# CHAPTER TWENTY

WHEN I'M AROUND HOSEA, I TRY TO PRETEND I'M A block of ice.

In the school corridors, at the dance studio.

Cool, impenetrable, incapable of interaction.

But as soon as he gets me alone—I melt.

I haven't been in the smoking spot behind the athletic field for five minutes before he's heading out the same way I came, taking long, even strides with his black boots leading the way. I'm sitting across from the bleachers, my back against the fence; my breath catches in my throat as I see him.

I'm supposed to be in study hall so it almost doesn't seem like I got away with anything. Gellar didn't even look up when I grabbed the bathroom pass off the edge of his desk. He won't notice if I don't return.

I haven't lit my first cigarette. The veggie sandwich from lunch is sitting in my stomach like an anvil. Even after I discarded the bread (too soggy), the tomato (too mealy), and the cheese (too waxy). I ate mayo-covered sprouts and cucumber slices and even that felt like too much.

It's like my stomach has already decided what to do before my brain can make a choice. I think the worst part is that it's inconsistent, which means I can't plan. One day a small, plain garden salad might be fine but the next day that very same salad could wreck me.

But in this moment, I can't tell if it's the food or Hosea walking toward me that makes my stomach roil like someone's tossing rocks around inside.

I don't know where to look as he approaches. The ice block stays intact only when there are other people near us. My insides are warming, and the closer he gets, the more my fingers tremble around my unlit cigarette. Hardly impenetrable.

He leans against the fence and says, "How's it going?" from above me, and I wish my heart didn't beat a little faster.

I don't say anything because I don't know what to say, and a couple of seconds later, there's the crinkle of plastic and the click of a lighter and he's sitting next to me with a clove between his lips. He offers the pack, but I shake my head, hold up the cigarette in my hand. One of the two I bummed from Sara-Kate this morning. I light the end with the cheap plastic lighter I've been clutching.

He looks down at a small, smooth rock sitting between us, his dark brown eyebrows creased in thought. His angular face is clean-shaven as usual. "I know you hate me right now, but you have to let me say a few things."

His voice is quiet and I knew one of us would have to speak eventually, but he startles me all the same. I don't dare look at him again but I don't get up and walk away, either, so I guess that's enough for him to go on.

"First of all, I want to be with you. I do." He pauses, then continues in the same low, even voice. "But you could be going away soon."

I force myself to look down at the soft caramel leather of my boots as I say, "Who told you that?"

I see him shrug out of the corner of my eye. "Phil."

Matter-of-fact, like I should have known. And I should have. But he asked me to keep his secret from Phil; why is it okay that they get to talk about me?

"Why didn't you tell me?" He blinks up at the colorless winter sky, the clouds that cover Ashland Hills like the world's most depressing blanket. Then he flicks ash from his clove on the other side of him, away from me. "Phil made it sound like a pretty big deal."

"I guess I didn't think you were interested." And I'm not sure summer programs will even *be* an option for me. I'm not halfway done with my cigarette, but I blow out one last puff, stub it out, and toss it into the Coffee & Jam paper cup a few feet away. It's a fresh ashtray. Half full of someone's coffee from this morning and a couple of butts from people who sat here before us.

"You listen to me talk about music." He pulls on the end of his hair.

"That's different. Music helps us keep rhythm . . . It gives us structure and helps tell the story. You don't need ballet to perform."

"So? I still like seeing you dance to what I'm playing. You make my music better."

Neither of us utters a word after that, not until he says, "Theo." He sighs out my name with his sweet-smelling smoke and all I want to do is put my head on his shoulder. Listen to him say my name for the rest of the afternoon. "And second—"

"Second?" I manage to croak out, even though his hand is on my arm now and I don't even know what we were talking about in the first place.

"Yes." He leans his head close to mine and his breath is warm on my ear. "The second thing is that I think about you all the time."

I shiver from the way his words tickle my skin, from the familiar scent of him, but I don't respond.

He clears his throat, leans back so we're no longer close enough to kiss, so his back is flat against the fence. "Phil also told me about the trial . . . that you have to testify. And I wanted to make sure you were okay."

"I'll be fine," I say, so nonchalant I doubt it would be convincing to anyone, let alone Hosea. I wish I hadn't been so quick to toss out my cigarette. I need something to do with my hands so they won't look so nervous, so Hosea won't know that I'm not fine at all.

He stretches his legs in front of him, lazily crossing them at the ankles. "I had to testify once."

I'm not sure I heard him correctly, and when I try to read his face it's completely devoid of expression. He passes his clove to me and I look at it for a long moment before I put my lips where his lips have been, like a secondhand kiss. Our fingers touch as I hand it back to him, linger for several seconds too long.

"My grandma . . . she took my mom to court because they said she wasn't competent enough to take care of me."

"Why?" I make a point to sound gentle.

"She has an anxiety disorder." He pauses to drag one last time, the end of the clove burning red but muted under the ash. "Agoraphobia . . . She can't leave the house or deal with crowds. Not without having an attack."

I stare at his boots for a while. "When did you figure it out?"

He puts out the clove and bends his fingers back and forth. Looks down at the ground as he says, "A long time before I told anyone. I thought . . . that I could handle things for us. But I was a kid. I couldn't drive or make money. She had boyfriends sometimes but they never stuck around."

"They made you testify against her." It's a statement, not a question, and it sits between us like a boulder. Hosea moved here in the middle of his freshman year, so he was even younger than me when he had to tell a judge that his mother wasn't capable of taking care of him.

"I did it," he says in this small voice that makes me want to cry. "My Grams made it seem like there was no other choice. And I guess I knew . . . things were getting pretty bad. My mom would spend all day in bed and I'd go to sleep without dinner because I felt like shit begging her to go to the store. Or asking for money we didn't have." He taps his fingers against the cold, hard ground. "But my mom is a good person. Maybe other people couldn't see it, but she did her best. And I knew she really thought she would get better someday . . . that things would be normal."

I study his profile. The slope of his nose from the side, the edges of his turned-down mouth. "Can't you go visit her?"

"She's living with a friend and she's getting better, but the visits make me feel like shit, you know?" He shoves his hands into his pockets as he looks at the school building in the distance. "She cries and *begs* me not to leave her, and I can't—I don't want to make her feel any worse than she already does, so it's better to just stay away. Call every once in a while. I send her recordings of my music sometimes."

"I'm sorry." I crumble a dried leaf in my palm, scatter the bits over the ground like ashes.

"Grams did what she thought was the right thing, but I don't know if I'll ever forgive her." He rubs his nose with the back of his hand. The tip of it is pink from the cool air, and it makes me think of him as a little boy.

"It's not fair, what she made you do," I say.

I hate thinking about him up on the stand, confessing all

the ways his mother had failed him. But even more, I hate to think of him hungry and trapped in a house with someone so helpless. And it's selfish to think this, but I never would have met Hosea if his grandmother hadn't insisted on a better life for him.

I want to comfort him. Hold his hand or put my arm around him or something. But I don't.

He shrugs. "It is what it is. I'm not a kid anymore. I can go back someday if I want to. It's fine."

"But it's not." I brace my fingers against the ground, stop them from touching his arm. "I'm really sorry, Hosea."

He takes in a breath and he lets it out and he doesn't look at me, but he says, "Thanks." Then, "I didn't mean to turn this into a pity party. I just wanted to say that I know what the trial stuff is like and testifying is shitty. And I know you're not cool with me right now, but if you need to talk to someone who's been through it, well—I'm here."

He doesn't know how complicated it really is, so of course he thinks it'll be okay.

"Hosea?" I turn my body toward him.

I want him. Despite the fact that he'll hate me if he finds out who I really am. Despite the fact that everyone I know will hate me.

Maybe that's all the more reason to be with him. Maybe I should seize the moment while I can. Everything could change in two months. I could lose ballet, my friends, everyone's respect. I could be stuck here in this town for another year, with people who only think about one thing when they see me. Being with Hosea is one of the few things that make me happy. I know the risks and I'm still not deterred, so that must be a sign.

He looks at me. Cautious but expectant.

"I don't want to stop seeing you." I hold his gaze.

His slate-colored eyes spark and then darken. "I can't break up with Ellie right now. I'm sorry, but—"

"I want to be with you either way." My voice wobbles but I go on. I have to. "Because I don't know . . . Maybe I *will* go away next year."

*Or maybe you'll never want to see me again if the truth comes out.*

I think about Sara-Kate's words at the diner. "Time is moving so fast and—"

"Life's too short not to be happy," he says simply, with a smile.

"Exactly," I say, so grateful that he understands, that he didn't make me keep talking.

His smile lingers but his eyes are serious again. "You sure you'll be cool with this?"

No, I'm not sure. But I know that the alternative—not being with him at all—would leave me feeling much worse than being his secret.

So I nod. I say, "Totally cool," and I give him a smile so wide he can't question it.

"Good," he says, nodding a little bit himself. "That's really good."

He drops his hand down to the ground. Slides it through the leaves until it's close to mine. I almost jump when I feel it on my own, when I feel his skin against mine for the first time in much too long. I think it's a mistake at first, that he's searching for something he dropped in the leaves when I wasn't paying attention. We're a little bit hidden but we're still in public.

It's not a mistake. He covers my hand with his own and I'm struck by how warm it is, by how very much our hands feel like they belong together. I glance at him out of the corner of my eye to see if he's looking at me, but he's staring straight ahead, his eyes fixed on the bottom of the bleachers in front of us.

So I say nothing as I spread my fingers apart and his dip down into the gaps between them, as we squeeze our hands together and the pads of his fingers brush against my palm.

We sit like that for a long time, for the rest of the period.

I sit in the smoking spot, holding hands with Hosea, and I can't remember the last time I felt so alive.

# CHAPTER TWENTY-ONE

SUMMER INTENSIVE AUDITIONS ARE A TYPICAL BALLET class with barre and center work, combinations across the floor, and a focus on pointe work for the girls, jumps for the guys.

A typical ballet class that also happens to be the most important class of your life.

I stay late to practice at least a couple of times a week, and usually more than that. The thought of my auditions makes my body hot and my head too light, but the extra time in the studio gets my mind off the trial, and that's the most I can hope for at this point. Only two weeks until Christmas, so the trial is just six weeks away.

I'm in an empty studio on a Tuesday night when Marisa walks in. I've just moved to the barre and I look over, hold my breath, wonder if I've done something wrong. She's only ever checked on me a couple of times when I practice solo, and even then, she comes in at the end of my session, not the beginning.

Her hair falls around her shoulders in loose, coffee-colored waves and she's dressed in street clothes. Dark jeans, a long-sleeved white V-neck, and a pair of buttery gray boots I've been eyeing for a while now.

"I just thought I'd sit in with you today," she says as she closes the door behind her. "Lead you through a class, like at your auditions. Is that okay?"

"It's fine," I say, and hope she doesn't spot the apprehension in my tone.

Actually, once I get over my initial nerves, I'm glad she's here. I work best when Marisa is in the room, because she always expects the best from me.

She walks over to the stereo and I adjust my leotard while her back is turned. I feel like I'm shrinking inside this one, which means none of the others will fit me well, either. I can't ask my mom to take me shopping again so soon; we just stocked up on new leotards and tights and two new pairs of pointe shoes at the beginning of autumn. It's too soon to ask for more, and if I tell her how loose this one is, she'll be suspicious.

I wonder if Marisa noticed when she walked in, but all she says when she turns around is, "Full out, no marking."

She leads me through the barre work, assesses my turnout, and studies the movement of my port de bras as I work through the steps. I push myself harder than I have in weeks, maybe even months. I want her to see how much I've grown, that she didn't make a mistake when she said I should audition.

When I move to the center, Marisa tells me not to get too

tripped up on the fouettés, but this is the moment I've been waiting for: to prove that even with everything else going on in my life, I can focus on what matters most. She says not to get too caught up in them, but I know she's dissecting every move, examining how I rise from plié to relevé en pointe, how my working leg extends in fourth position before I pull my foot in to touch the back of my knee. I do this again and again and again. I am in total control, taking charge of these fouettés like the first Odile I ever saw.

I'm gearing up for my tenth fouetté when I see him. When I remember that for the first couple of years after we broke up, the sound of a pants zipper still made my breath hitch in my throat. I stop keeping count of my turns when I recall that the first few times I was too aware of everything: the blood pounding in my ears, the random movement of my arms because I didn't know what to do with my hands.

I got used to it, eventually. The pressure from his palm as it pushed down on the back of my neck. The little moans that escaped when he was close and the blank look in his eyes immediately afterward, like I could be anyone.

It didn't *seem* wrong. Chris was my boyfriend and it made him feel good. All I ever wanted was to make him happy, so I never let on that every single time, it made me want to wash my mouth out with bleach afterward.

My ankle gives out and I lose my balance. Crash down from relevé and nearly tumble to the floor before I catch myself. So damn stupid to let him in my head like that when I have

Marisa's undivided attention, when I'm so close to auditions, I can practically taste the nerves. I take my time righting myself. Look down at the ankles that failed me, at my anxious reflection in the mirror, and finally at Marisa, whose face is a mixture of confusion and sympathy.

"I'm so sorry," I say in a whisper, my eyes dropping to the floor again.

She sighs. "I know you're tired, sweetheart, but you've got to keep pushing."

"I am. I mean, I was trying." I stand in place as I cross one foot over the other and back again. "I'm just a little nervous with this . . . and the trial. It's a week before my first audition."

I still don't understand how two of the biggest moments in my life are barely a dozen days apart. I thought trials like this took months, sometimes years to go anywhere, but that's not the case with Chris Fenner. It's sort of ironic. He was never good at waiting and now the one thing he must be desperate to postpone is moving faster than anyone can grasp.

"I'd be worried if you weren't." Marisa pauses. "Sometimes these things don't run on schedule, so you know if there's any conflict with your auditions and the day you have to be in court, we can work around it. I have no problem explaining the situation to the heads of the programs."

I force myself not to pull at the loose fabric of my leotard, clasp my hands in front of me instead. "You don't have to do that."

"I know I don't have to. I want to." She steps closer, though the studio is so empty, our voices echo off the walls. "And I wanted to tell you that a couple of the schools already have their eye on you."

I dig the heels of my pointe shoes into the floor, lock my knees so I won't fall again.

"I'm guessing this comes as a surprise." Marisa smiles big, like she's been waiting to say this to me for a while now.

"Just a little." I wipe my sweaty palms on the front of my thighs. "But they have their eye on me . . . What exactly does that mean?"

"It means I have friends who know that I count you as one of my top dancers, so they're looking forward to your audition." Marisa puts her hand on my arm and squeezes. "You were one of my very first students after I opened the studio," she says, looking at me with eyes as kind as her words. "Back then, I knew you would go far and I've never stopped believing in you, Theo. Not for a minute. If anyone can do this, it's you."

My toes are throbbing as I walk back to the dressing room a half hour later and when I sit down in front of my locker, lower myself to the floor so I can stretch, I see it. I sit with my legs straight out in front of me and push my fingers to the end of my feet, to the crimson blemish on the box of my pointe shoe.

Bleeding feet are no real cause for concern around here. It's impossible to avoid when you're on them all the time, when the skin across your toes is a canvas of ever-present blisters. It's nothing new for someone who dances this much. But I haven't bled *through* my shoes since I first went on pointe. I stroke the satin and look at my thumb, now stained a faint red. The smell of metal courses through my nose.

I'll never forget the day I was rummaging through my dance bag and Chris saw my pointe shoes again. But by then, they were almost dead; the satin was dirty and starting to rip, and the platforms were nearly too soft to support me. Dried brown spots decorated the toe, and when I waved the shoe jokingly in front of his face, he pushed it away from me, told me not to be gross.

I unlace my right shoe and slip it off carefully, followed by the padding. My toes sting as I run my fingers across the top of the open blisters, wipe off the blood caked into the crevices around the nails.

I used to have nightmares about *The Red Shoes.* The fairy tale, not the movie. I imagined myself dancing to exhaustion but unable to stop. But I was never like Karen, the girl who wore the enchanted shoes. I didn't beg for mercy from an executioner; I was so captivated by my red pointe shoes that I couldn't stop, wouldn't stop under any circumstances. I always woke up before I saw what eventually happened to my feet.

Looking down at my bloody toes now, I wonder: if those magical shoes existed, would I slip them on? I used to think I would, if the alternative meant never dancing again. A year ago—even six months ago—I would have laughed at anyone who said I might not pursue a career in dance. Now I know anything can happen, that life can change so quickly, the plans you thought were set in stone can crumble into nothing. That I could be stuck here for another year, then apply to colleges like everyone else.

*There are plenty of wonderful dance programs at regular universities, even public schools.* That's what Marisa tells the people who aren't good enough to go pro.

Sometimes I think it would be easier if Donovan *had* chosen to run away with Chris, and never come back. I'd be able to practice in my spare time without the guilt, kiss Hosea without the nagging memories of Chris. I don't know how I'd ever get over that kind of betrayal, but at least I wouldn't have to ruin my life in the process.

If Chris *kidnapped* him—well, then of course I'm happy he's back. Safe. But if I told people about our relationship, I know what they'd think every time they looked at me. They'd never be able to read an article about Chris or see his picture without thinking of *me*.

Marisa raps on the dressing room door ten minutes later and I'm still staring at my toes. She asks if everything's okay because she needs to lock up soon, but all I can do is look at the rust-colored smears where my thumbs brushed away the blood.

# CHAPTER TWENTY-TWO

I WAKE TO THE AROMA OF PIES TWO DAYS BEFORE Christmas.

Sweet potato and pecan and key lime, too. My stomach rumbles and I think about how I used to race downstairs as soon as the smell of pies wafted up, needling my mother for a breakfast sample before she'd taken them out of the oven.

Now, I lie in bed for a few minutes. Awake but with my eyes closed, savoring the smell because that's as close as I'll get to the pies. I don't know why she makes so many. We always have leftovers because there are only three of us and I never take dessert if I can help it. Of course we don't have to worry about food going to waste with Phil so close by, but it seems a bit decadent.

Still, I can't help but breathe in and remember the taste. The buttery crusts and the tang of the limes and the richness of the pecans. I pinch my side hard and think about the costume fittings in my future. Then I get out of bed.

Downstairs, Dad is sitting at the kitchen table with his laptop blatantly open in front of him. I look around for Mom because no way is she putting up with this, but she's nowhere to be found. The three beautiful pies cooling on racks at the end of the counter are the only indication she was ever here.

"Morning." I lean in to kiss Dad's cheek. "Where's Mom?"

"Delivering Christmas baskets with her coworkers," he says, looking up long enough to flash me a smile.

I stick a piece of bread in the toaster and dig around in the fridge until I find an egg from the stash Mom boils each week. "On a Sunday? Aren't most people around here at church?"

Not us. We're very much the Easter Sunday/Christmas Eve type of Christians, and even then we visit the closest nondenominational church and leave as soon as the service is over. I used to think it was weird since most people I knew went somewhere on Sunday, whether it's a temple or mass or the AME church in the city where Donovan's family used to go. Then I met Sara-Kate. Her parents are atheists, and in the Midwest, that clearly made them the weirdest people in town.

"The baskets are going to the shut-in," Dad says, pushing up the sleeves of his flannel robe. "You're up awfully early for someone on winter break."

"You're being awfully bold about doing work at the table.

And the day before Christmas Eve? Mom has eyes around here, you know." I blink at him with an exaggerated gaze.

He laughs, holds up his hands in defense. "I'm not doing work, I swear. Just reading the news."

I peel the egg as I wait for my bread to toast and scoop out the round yolk over the garbage disposal when he's not looking. Then I sit down with my slice of toast and hard-boiled egg whites, which I chop into tiny pieces. The toast would taste better with butter but so would a lot of things.

"Don't forget we're meeting with Donovan's lawyer next week," Dad says, looking up from his laptop. "He wants to brief you on the questions you'll be getting, from him and during the cross-examination."

I push cubes of egg whites around my toast. "What's he like?"

"Mr. McMillan?" Dad looks off into the distance, squints his eyes as he thinks. "He's nice. Professional. Really passionate about what he does. Donovan's in good hands with him."

Mr. McMillan is going to ask me about Chris and unless I can talk to Donovan by then, I'll have to lie.

"He keeps saying how much he's looking forward to meeting you." My father takes a sip of his coffee, sets the mug carefully on the table as he looks at me. "He knows how close you were to Donovan."

My eyes land on the pies again and I sit up with a start. I have an idea.

"We should take one of those pies over to Donovan's house," I say. Nonchalantly, so it sounds like something nice I thought of and not a ploy to get him alone.

Dad glances at them over his shoulder. "We can ask your mother when she gets home. I'm sure she won't mind."

"We should do it while they're still warm. It's a nice gesture." I make one last halfhearted attempt at my toast, swallow hard around the dry crust, and stand up to take my dishes to the sink. "He's been back for two months now. And it's the holidays."

"I guess it wouldn't hurt." He's distracted by something on his computer. I love it when he brings the laptop to the table. He doesn't notice as I dump half my breakfast into the sink. "Do you want me to go with you?"

"I can do it." I turn my back so he won't see the smile splitting my face. "I'll go over after I brush my teeth."

Ten minutes later, I'm standing on my front porch, holding a foil-wrapped pie and sweating profusely. I can't believe how easy this was. Stars aligning. Fresh-baked pies. Preoccupied Dad, who won't overthink it like Mom would. We'd still be sitting at the table, making a pro-con list for leaving a pie on the neighbor's doorstep if she were here.

I walk down my steps and start heading over.

The day is winter-wet. The kind of damp that hangs in the air from morning to night, when old snow melts into slush under the sun and cools into ice after dark.

I walk down the driveway and the sidewalk, stopping to look at Donovan's house from the street before walking up the path. The welcome-back debris has been cleared off the porch, but it still stands out from the others. Every other house on the street is draped in strings of twinkly lights with tasteful holiday decorations dotting the yards. The Pratt house is nothing more than dark windows and a desolate lawn. The porch sits like the empty, ominous mouth of the house, waiting to swallow up anyone who comes too close.

I keep walking.

I'm cloaked in déjà vu as my boots take me up the path to the porch. Is it déjà vu if you're not reminded of one particular time, but thousands? Walking to Donovan's house was a regular part of my day when I was a kid—like going to school or brushing my teeth. Still, my heart thumps faster the closer I get.

I wonder if they're watching. If *he's* watching. If he's happy I'm coming to see him. If he wonders why I've waited so long. Or if he'll refuse to talk to me, if he's angry because he didn't really run away and I was the one who let Chris get so close to him.

I balance the pie on the edge of the neglected wooden swing to the left of the door, take a deep breath, and push the doorbell. I lick my lips and practice a smile, wait for the familiar tread of footsteps on the way to the door. Actually, it's weird, waiting. I barely ever had to ring the doorbell at this house before.

But I hear nothing. So I ring it again. I stare at the windows, try to look through the dark curtains to see if the Christmas tree is in its old spot. Every year in the same position with the same ornaments, winking its rainbow of lights through the glass. Now all I see is black.

Still nothing. I guess my great idea wasn't so great after all. Maybe my mother was right when she said we should give them time. She indulged me with those first couple of phone calls after he came back, but I haven't told her how many times I've tried to call since then. That I've been staking out his house when I'm home, hoping for even the smallest glimpse of life behind these curtains.

I place the pie on the dirty welcome mat and turn to go back home. I need a Plan C.

Then a click and a latch and:

"Theo?"

Mrs. Pratt's voice is music.

I turn around. She stands behind the screen door, but I can't discern any part of her except her silhouette. She is very thin, that I can tell. Her elbows stick out like bird legs in sharp points. Her head looks smooth, like it's wrapped in a scarf.

I retrieve the pie from the mat, stand in front of her with my arms outstretched like a peace offering. "My mom made pies," I say. "We wanted you to have one. Pecan."

"Oh, that's very sweet of you, honey." She steps closer to

the door but makes no move to open the screen. I think she's wearing a bathrobe. "Your mother's pecan is so good."

"I . . . I wanted to say hi, too." I bring my arms back to my chest, holding tight to the pie tin. "It's been a long time."

"It has. You're almost grown up now. A beautiful girl."

I'm glad she can see me well enough to make that statement, because she's just a shadow to me, stuck behind the screen. The house is dark. I keep expecting Donovan to poke his head around the corner, but no. It's silent.

But I think I heard a ghost of his mother when she spoke. A bit of that smile that always started in her eyes.

"Thank you." I clear my throat, breathe in fast so the cold air hits the back of my throat with a sharpness. "I was also wondering . . . Is Donovan home?"

"He is, honey, but I don't think he's up to having visitors right now." Her voice is kind, but generic, like she's repeated this sentiment hundreds of times. Maybe she has, but not to someone like me.

"Are you sure, Mrs. Pratt?" My own voice is pleading. Pathetic. Desperate. "I know it sounds silly, but I just want to see him with my own eyes. It feels—it feels like he's not really here if I don't. Could you ask him? Please? It's just me. I promise I won't stay long."

As vital as it is to talk to him, to ask him what I'm supposed to do when we go to trial in four weeks, my plea is sincere. Vague news updates and estimations from my parents aren't enough. I need to see the Donovan who came back. I'll feel so much better if I can just see that he's okay now.

Mrs. Pratt sighs, but her silhouette turns away for a moment as if she's looking behind her. Looking at someone. Considering. "Just a minute," she says, and closes the door instead of asking me inside.

The street is empty but I feel like I'm in a one-woman show. It's so conspicuous, standing on the Pratts' front porch. The paparazzi and news vans have been gone for a while now, but it's impossible to not look at the house when you leave or enter your own. I know because I do it every time, and I've seen my neighbors do it, too.

The pie has cooled, and my hands are cold. My fingers crinkle uncomfortably around the foil. I should have worn gloves. I should have thought of a more eloquent way to ask for Donovan.

The big door swings open again. My knees jiggle and I lock them, plant my feet firmly beneath me.

The outline of Mrs. Pratt's head is moving back and forth. His answer is no.

"Not now, Theo. I'm sorry. He's not ready yet."

She really does sound sorry, so it must be him. Donovan doesn't want to talk to me. Our history is useless.

"Don't take it personally," she says, running a hand over her scarf-clad head. "And please don't give up on him. He's getting better every day."

I want to ask if he'll pick up the phone if I call and he knows it's me. If he'll write me back if I bring over a letter or send an email, but I can't. I simply nod because there is no good way to respond to that, nothing I can say that will ever make this better for her.

"Here's your pie." I hold it out awkwardly, as if she can grab it through the screen.

She unlocks the door, opens it just wide enough for me to slip it into her hands. I catch a flash of red terry cloth, a glimpse of brown skin and taupe slippers before the door shuts again.

"You'll tell your mother thank you for me?"

"Of course."

"You're a good girl, Theo," she says softly, her face already halfway hidden by the big door. "Merry Christmas."

"Merry Christmas."

I turn before she can see the tears in my eyes.

Doesn't he know I want to help him? Doesn't he know I'm flipping my shit, wondering what he and Chris were doing all that time?

I descend the porch steps. Walk down the path. Up the sidewalk and back to my house. Kick off my boots when I step inside. Pass Dad on the way up to my bedroom.

He's holding his closed laptop under one arm and a fresh cup of coffee in the other hand. Steam billows from the top in playful curlicues that fade in the air.

"How'd it go?" he asks, pausing where I'm standing by the bottom of the stairs.

"He's still not talking." I slide my hand along the banister. I can't wait to go back to bed. It's the only way I'll stop thinking about this.

"I'm sorry, babygirl." He sighs as he looks at me. Throws a hesitant smile my way. "This won't last forever. He'll come around and I bet you'll be the first person he calls."

I used to think that was possible. But he's not the same, and neither am I. There was a time I wouldn't have been able to shake Donovan if I tried, and now that everything depends on talking to him, he can't be bothered with me for even a minute.

I run my index finger along the side of my rib, exhale silently as I find that familiar oval of tender, bruised skin hiding beneath my shirt.


Hosea calls in the afternoon.

I nearly drop the phone when I see that it's him. We've only texted until now; an actual phone call seems like a step forward. I smooth down my hair before I answer, as if he can see me through the phone.

"Doing anything for Christmas Eve Eve?" His voice is a little thick, as if he just woke from a nap.

I hear people talking in the background. His television. A few more seconds reveals it's a show with a horribly obnoxious laugh track.

"Nothing," I say quickly.

Too quickly. Maybe I should have invented plans so it doesn't look like I was waiting around for him to call.

"Me either." Hosea clears his throat. "Grams will be away until tomorrow night, so . . . you want to come over later?"

"Over to your house?"

I sound as if I've been invited to have tea with the queen of England, but I couldn't be more surprised if that's what I'd been asked. Going to his house is almost like a date. The closest we can get to one right now. There are only four more weeks left until he might not want me, after all.

"Yeah, I thought we could hang out without any . . . distractions."

He coughs away from the phone and I wonder if his face is hot like mine.

Still, I try to play it cool. Pause for a moment, try to keep the elation out of my voice as I say, "Sure. What time?"

I have to get a little creative to leave the house later. Nothing crazy, but I usually spend most nights around the holidays at home with my parents, and so do my friends, so they're curious about where I could be going the night before Christmas Eve.

"I need to drop off Sara-Kate's present," I say, and then go on before I lose my nerve to continue with the lie. "She leaves tomorrow to go to her relatives' and I want her to have it before Christmas."

It's not completely untrue. They *are* going to her grandparents' house—but her grandparents live a few miles away in the city and Sara-Kate and her family are just spending the day with them.

Dad and I have just finished cleaning up after supper while Mom has her cup of post-dinner coffee and pores over a stack of holiday cookbooks. As if she doesn't already have her favorite recipes picked out, ones she's made dozens of times now. Dad and I told her about the pecan pie together. She wasn't mad. She hardly said anything at all, except to sweep her hand over the top of my hair, kiss my forehead, and say, "He just needs time, sweetheart." I think she felt bad for me.

"You won't be in their way while they're packing?" she says now, flipping the page to some sort of elaborate baked dish that looks heavy on the melted cheese and bread crumbs. A dish that would make my mouth water so much, I'd have to pinch myself on *both* sides.

"They're all packed. She invited me and it's just for a little bit." I lean against the counter and try to appear not at all invested in the conversation at hand. "I'll be back by curfew."

"That was never up for debate," my mother says without looking up from her cookbook.

I glance at Dad, who's trying to hide his smile. "Go," he says, waving the dish towel at me. The long sleeves of his plaid shirt are rolled up to his elbows. "Wish Sara-Kate and her family a merry Christmas."

I spend a long time getting ready because what do you wear when you'll finally be alone with the person who occupies half of your thoughts? I go through my entire wardrobe, wish I could call Sara-Kate. She'd know exactly what I should wear tonight, could march into my closet and pull out four excellent options in less than five minutes.

But I can't ask for fashion advice or she'd know I was going to hook up with Hosea. And I can't listen to the judgment in her voice, so I work with what I have: nerves and indecision. When I walk out the door, I've finally decided on a cream-colored cardigan over a red silk tank top that glows against my skin, and a pair of jeans that gives off the appearance of an ass.

The drive to Hosea's is quick, just a little over five minutes on the empty Sunday-night streets. He lives on the left side of a mint-green duplex. I park a couple of houses up from his and sit in the car with the engine still running. I dig a fingernail into my wrist to make sure I'm here. On Hosea's street, only a few feet away from the front door of his house, where we'll finally be alone.

I check my reflection in the rearview mirror, smile with my mouth wide open to double check that I brushed away any food in my teeth. I didn't want to put on too much makeup in case my parents noticed before I slipped out of the house, but it's just enough, I think. I apply more lip gloss before stepping out of the car.

I look around as I'm walking up the path to his house, as if someone followed me here. As if Ellie will be standing just inside the door, ready to confirm her suspicions.

I ring the bell and stick my hands into my coat pockets as I wait for him to answer the door. It could be colder but I'm grateful when I hear footsteps coming toward me. I hold my breath as he fiddles with the lock, get a quick rush in those moments of anticipation when you can feel the other person, just inches away.

"Hey," he says warmly when we're standing in front of each other.

He's wearing a black T-shirt and jeans and he smells good. Fresh, like he just got out of the shower, but his hair is dry. And beautiful.

"Hi." I smile at him as I step inside the little foyer, which contains a table with a tray for mail and a small, horizontal rack above it to hang keys.

Hosea closes the door and reaches for my hand, pulls me all the way into his house. I barely have time to take in the living room before he's pushing my hair back from my face, brushing his lips against mine in a kiss hello. I close my eyes and lean into him as I kiss him back and we stand like that for a while. Slowly kissing in his grandmother's living room, like we have all the time in the world.

"I'm really happy you came," he says in that same warm voice that melts right through me. I look up at him, sketch the contours of his face with my eyes. I remember the night we talked at Klein's party, how I really looked at him the first time. Noticed the way his eyes softened and the tension seemed to relax from his strong jawline when he was talking to me.

"I am, too." I squeeze his hand.

And I am happy—I am—but I'm mostly nervous. Maybe

even more so than when I was getting ready earlier. Hosea will be my first since Chris. What if I don't remember what to do? I thought I would feel different going into this. Worse about planning to be with him, about helping him cheat on Ellie. But I'm not sure how I can feel bad about it when I know he's supposed to be with me.

I look around now. It's your typical living room: love seat, recliner, couch, and coffee table. It's almost too much furniture for the room and there's barely enough space to walk around but it works because there's no clutter. Not even a stray sweater or a discarded pair of shoes on the thin carpet. Just a couple of old photography books on the table next to the TV remote. An artificial Christmas tree sits in the far corner, small and white with silver ornaments and garland. I look under the tree, see a couple of wrapped gifts, and flush when I think of the mountain piled under the massive tree we brought home the first week in December.

A piano sits in the opposite corner. That makes me smile.

"Want the tour? It's small," Hosea says almost apologetically.

"I'd love a tour." I unbutton my coat and drape it over the arm of the couch before we move into the next room.

It *is* a small place, with just the front room, a kitchen, and two bedrooms and a bathroom off a short hallway. But it's clean and tidy and it smells nice. It smells like Christmas, like fresh pine and warm cinnamon, and I only notice the scented candles burning in the kitchen as we're leaving the room.

"And this is my little hole," he says, pushing open the door across the hall.

The room could belong to anyone with its beige walls, bare except for a calendar of landscapes hanging from an orange pushpin. A bed with a plain navy comforter is shoved up against the far wall, across from a three-drawer bureau and a small desk and chair. His room is clean, too, and I wonder if he cleaned for me or if it always looks like this.

"Where's all your stuff?" I ask, looking for any sign that this room belongs to him.

That's when I see it. A picture on top of the bureau. It's not in a frame. It's just a loose photograph, leaning against a dark wooden box. It's slanted at an angle so there's a bit of a glare, but I can still make out him and Ellie. They're at a party, outside in the summer. Or maybe a festival. His arm is around her and she's standing close to him, her body pressed to his side. Ellie's mouth is open in a wide smile. She looks pretty. Hosea is smiling, too, the glowing orange tip of a clove barely visible between his fingers. They look comfortable together. Happy.

"When I moved in, I wouldn't put up anything because I was convinced I wouldn't be here that long." His voice surprises me. When I look at him, he moves to the right, blocking my view of the picture. "Guess you can see how that worked out."

"It kind of looks like a guest room," I say, trying to shake the image of that picture.

I gaze at every wall and corner, want to burn this into my memory in case I'm never back here again. I make a special point to not look at the picture but Hosea is still there, still standing in front of it. My eyes slide to a different side of the room. I wonder where he keeps his pills, but it doesn't seem right to ask. It's not the first thing that comes to mind when I think of him now.

He flips the light off once I'm finished looking around. "Grams says it looks like a serial killer's room."

"That's nice," I say, laughing as we walk back into the hallway.

"Yeah." He cracks a smile. "She's . . . Like I said, I don't know if I'll ever forgive her for making me come live with her, but she's not so bad. She gives me my space."

"Where is she now?"

"Her sister's, down in Lincoln." He stops at the doorway to the kitchen. "You want something to drink? Or eat? I can't cook but she left some lasagna."

"I'm fine," I say. "Already ate."

And it's true, even if dinner was only three bites of pasta that I swallowed, four that I spit into my napkin, and the rest pushed around my plate until my parents had cleaned theirs.

"Or toast." He nods at the little silver toaster plugged in on the counter. "I make perfect toast."

"As impressive as that is, I'll pass this time." Again, I examine every crevice of the room because I still find it hard to believe I'm standing in Hosea Roth's yellow-and-blue kitchen, holding his hand. My eyes stop on him. "But I *would* like to hear you play."

"You've heard me play lots of times," he says in a strange voice with a strange look. One I've never seen on him. Flustered.

"Yeah, the stuff we've danced to for a million years." I shake my head as I move back to the living room. "I want to hear *your* music."

He stands in place so long, I wonder if he heard my response. Then he follows me, eyes the piano for a bit before he slides onto the bench, as if it's an impostor or he's sitting down for his first lesson. I perch on the edge of the couch as he turns and says, "Whatever I play sounds like shit on this thing. It's really cheap and out of tune, just so you know."

He could probably play "Chopsticks" for an hour straight and I'd be thrilled.

"Stop stalling," I tease. I'm a little nervous, too, though, and I don't know why. I guess because I don't know what to expect. All he's ever played in front of me is Tchaikovsky and Minkus and Gershwin—the music we know by heart, can play with our feet. Maybe I won't like his music as much.

He twists his wrists, stretches his fingers, and without warning he launches into a piece so startlingly gorgeous that I slide from the arm of the couch into the cushion. I watch his fingers move deftly over the keys, stare at the back muscles straining under his shirt as he pours every last bit of himself into his music. It is a cross between contemporary and classical, inter-woven with surprising patches of dark chords that resonate down to my core.

I wonder what he thinks about as his fingers dance across the keys. If, like he said back in the gazebo at Klein's house, he's thinking about how his song makes me feel, if I'll be that one person in three hundred who is unduly affected by his talent.

I look at his jaw from the side, set in its hard lines as his creativity flows through him. I pretend that he will never play this song for anyone but me. I could sit in this tiny living room and listen to him make music forever. But then he's finished and the room is silent and when he turns around I don't know what to say.

"What do you think?" he finally says. And I can't believe how anxious he sounds, how nervous he looks when his eyes meet mine.

"That was your song?" I stand up, smooth my hand down over the front of my top.

"Yeah. I mean, I composed it. Yeah," he says again. Then, as he stands, too: "Did you like it?"

"Not liked. Love." I take a couple of steps toward him, which in this little room means two more will bring us close enough to touch.

"You could be famous," I say softly. "If other people heard you play—"

"I'm not that good. I'm not anywhere close to being that good." He actually blushes, his cheeks flushed by my words.

I decide that particular shade of pink is outstanding.

He looks away and then down at the floor. "I still have so much to learn and I need to save up for a better piano and—"

"You'll find a way. You're special," I say. "I can't believe nobody knows this about you."

"It's enough that you know." He sticks his hands into his pockets and he's still not quite looking at me. "It wouldn't be fair if you didn't. I get to watch you dance all the time and you're pretty much perfect out there."

"I'm not as good as Josh. He's the best. Ruthie's really good, too. And I still have so much to work on before my auditions—"

"You look perfect to me." His eyes lock onto mine again with such intensity it almost frightens me. "*Everything* about you is graceful."

This time I turn my head because I don't know how to look at him after he's said something like that. He closes the space between us and still I don't look at him, don't move even an inch. My breath quickens the closer he gets and then he's in front of me. Blocking the light, reaching out to me, tracing his fingertips along my cheekbone. My eyes roam over the loose strands of hair that frame his face. He swallows and I watch his Adam's apple bob, wonder if he'd like it if I kissed him there.

Somewhere along the way we slipped from want to need and it's in every part of our kiss. In the way he bites down lightly on my bottom lip, gently coaxing my mouth open. It's in the way my hands press into his back, always pulling him toward me, always wanting him closer. I savor it all—the quick catches of breath, the warmth of his lips, the sugar-sweet taste of cloves on his tongue.

The need is why I take his hand without question, why I follow him down the hallway, why I find myself undressing him moments later. We take turns. His black T-shirt. My cardigan and tank. I feel a tiny bit of relief as my fingers brush against the top of his jeans and find buttons in place of a zipper. He lets me unclasp my bra and he stares as I do it and I hope he's not disappointed, that he doesn't care I have little use for one. But I relax as he swallows, as he meets my eyes and tells me I'm beautiful.

We lie down on his bed and he pulls me close, slides my body across the cool, soft comforter. His hair hangs in front of him, tickles my collarbone and teases my skin like the silky strokes of a paintbrush. And I can't believe how much room we have without the confines of a car. How much softer his bed is than a backseat, how his piano hands sloping along my spine are such a nice change from a door handle digging into my back.

He is gentle with me, so much gentler than I thought anyone could ever be. His lips travel across my neck, my shoulder, my navel, and when he stops to ask me if I'm okay, I take his face in my hands and I kiss him. Hard, so he won't see the tears in my eyes. No one has ever asked me that.

It's uncomfortable at times, but it's never unbearable. I keep waiting for his rhythm to change, for him to treat me like the rag doll I sometimes felt like with Chris. But Hosea is sweet—the whole time. He interrupts his kisses to ask if this feels good or that feels better, to make sure I don't want to stop at any point. He is extraordinary and right now, tonight, he is mine.

Afterward, I go to the bathroom and I sit on the toilet and I cry. Shoulder-racking sobs that I bury in my hands and hide under the rush of the faucet. I can't let him hear me but I can't lie there with him, hold it in while he is so kind. Stroking my hair and kissing my neck and saying how happy I make him. I press a pink hand towel to my mouth and I choke down sobs, because tonight can't last forever and he's not mine.

Not really.

# CHAPTER TWENTY-THREE

THE LAST TWO WEEKS BEFORE THE TRIAL SNEAK UP ON me so fast that I gasp when I look at the calendar and see I have twelve days left.

Because of winter break, it's the first time I've been in the studio with Hosea since we slept together, and I'm not sure I've ever been so conscious of someone in the room. Every shift on the piano bench, every turn of the sheet music, every twitch of his wrist makes me think of being with him.

Ruthie can tell something is up. She keeps eyeing me during class, which doesn't help, because my timing is already off. I can't focus when I keep wondering if Hosea sees me now and thinks of what my feet really look like under these shoes. I tried to keep them out of view that night, but he looked at them as we were getting dressed.

My feet should be displayed on a warning poster in a podiatrist's office. They're hideous. I can't remember the last time the skin on them wasn't thick and dry, hardened by calluses and blisters. My toenails are obscenely short because if I let them grow out even a bit, I will pay for it. Not to mention the scars from where the skin has cut open and bled and healed itself. If I end up in a professional company, I will give up the chance of ever having semi-normal feet.

I asked him not to look at them, but he wrapped his hand around my ankle, pulled my foot onto his lap. He slid his palm over the top of my foot, brushed his thumb along the slope of my arch. I let out a breath without making a sound. His long, beautiful fingers were touching my deformed feet when all I'd ever wanted was to hide them. He curved his fingers around my toes, pressed lightly on a callus as he said they show I'm committed to my craft. Then he leaned in and kissed me and as I kissed him back, I wished so much for time to stop. Just a few extra minutes where everything was good and special and ours.

After class, I time how long I'm in the dressing room perfectly because Hosea is just walking through the lobby as I enter from the hallway. The only person standing around is the girl at the front desk, and she's older, not interested in what we're doing. So I hurry to catch up to him, put my hand on his arm.

He looks surprised to see me, even though we just spent an hour and a half in the same room. Though he's been as close to me as only one other person. Ever. Closer, even, if you count our emotional connection. Something I never had with

Chris, not if I'm honest with myself. How can you have a true connection with someone if everything they ever told you was a lie?

"Hi," he says. And he smiles, but I don't miss the hesitation behind it because—right. We're at the studio. In public. I glance back at the girl behind the front desk. She's not even looking at us, but we still have to be careful. Even a city as big as Chicago is a small world; people know each other and things could get back to Ellie easier than we think.

So I take my hand off his arm and I keep space between us as we walk out to the street. Around the corner, where the only people who can see us are ducking in and out of the adjacent drugstore. It snowed a couple of days over winter break and most of it has melted in the city, but not all of it. Little snowbanks still sit against some of the buildings, blackened from cigarette butts and garbage and dirt from the city streets.

"Hi," he says again, and he kisses me swiftly on the lips now that we're kind of in the clear. "How are you?"

"Tired. But good." I shrug. "How are you?"

If good means sweating through my sheets and waking up with night terrors, wondering how I'll know what to say in my testimony. If it means staring at Donovan's house way too long and too often, wondering if he'll talk to me if I go back and try again. If it means only eating enough to stave off suspicion and pinching my side until pain rips through me each time I even think about food, then yes. I'm good.

"I'm good, too," he says, nodding. "Fine."

This all seems so oddly formal. He's seen me naked. Run his hands all over me, kissed me until I was weak against him. But now he looks at me expectantly, like I should have something specific to say if I want to approach him.

"Are you, um . . . Are you going to winter formal?"

It's the first thing that pops to mind. I hadn't been thinking about it. Not really. But it's next Friday, and people are making plans and I want to know his.

"I don't want to. I mean, I wouldn't, but Ellie—she really wants to go since it's our last year." He sighs. "So I told her I would."

"Oh." God. Of course he's going with her. "Right."

"Look, I hate these things," he says. My eyes fixate on the piece of hair hanging in his face, next to his ear. The same ear that I've kissed. "I wish I didn't have to go . . . I wish I could be with you instead."

"You could," I say. With so much hopefulness it makes me sick.

He pushes his boot against a pile of hard, grimy snow. "You know I can't cancel on her now. She . . ." He doesn't finish his sentence and when I don't say anything, he says, "I should get going."

Sort of distractedly.

Sort of in a way that squeezes my heart.

And it must be all over my face, because there's a rueful

note to his tone as he says, "I have to meet Ellie. I'd give you a ride to your car, but—"

"I don't need a ride." I dig my gloves from my pockets so I'll have something to do besides think about how I just sounded too proud.

"Theo."

I'm not fooling either one of us, so I stop fiddling with my gloves and look at him.

"This doesn't change anything, okay?" His gray eyes are tender as they meet my gaze. "I want to see you as much as possible, but she can't know about us."

Right. I told him I could handle this. I promised I could share. So when he says, "We're still cool?" I nod and let him hug me and I squeeze my eyes closed very, very tight as my nose presses into his chest.

And it's a good thing I manage to keep it together as I walk back around the building after we've said our goodbyes, because I forgot my dance bag. I'll have to go back in the studio and I can't let anyone there see me cry. I've always prided myself on not crying so they won't see me as weak. Especially Marisa. And it's hard to keep it in sometimes, but I'm not about to break my fourteen-year streak now.

I run into Ruthie at the door. My dance bag is saddled over her right arm, on top of her own, and her face lights up when she sees me. "Oh, good. I was just about to call you. I wasn't sure if you'd already left . . ."

She looks around vaguely, but she's obviously looking for Hosea. I don't take the bait. Instead, I take my bag from her and I say, "Thanks, Ruthie," and when she offers me a ride I say yes right away.

Ruthie lives in River Forest, the next town over from Ashland Hills, so I'm not that far out of her way. Besides, the walk to the station would be brutal—I've only been outside for a few minutes and my toes are already going numb.

Ruthie and I start walking across the lot and down the street toward her car. I expect the first question out of her mouth to be about Hosea, but she surprises me when she says, "Do you ever think about giving up on this? All of it?"

I stare at her in stunned silence for a second. "Ballet?"

"Well, I don't mean soccer." Ruthie retrieves a pair of red wool gloves from her coat. "Yes, ballet. The summer intensives, the hours in the studio . . . What would you do if you didn't dance?"

I give her a funny look. "Nothing, I guess. I don't know how to do anything else."

"Me either." Ruthie clicks the remote on her car and we get in after it beeps at us. Then she turns on the heater and buckles her seat belt. "Is that weird? That we don't know how to do anything else?"

I shrug, reach behind me to pull my own seat belt across my chest. "I don't think so."

"It just seems like everyone else has been involved in, like, a million things since we were kids," she says, waving her hands in front of the vents as she waits for the car to warm up. "Sports and music and clubs."

"Yeah, but they always end up dropping them to focus on something," I say. "We just knew what we wanted to do a long time ago."

"But what if we were meant to do something else? We'll never know." She pauses, runs a hand through her golden curls as she looks at me. "Don't you ever wonder if you should have been . . . I don't know, a gymnast or a volleyball player or something?"

"Is this about summer intensives?" I look at the key chain dangling from Ruthie's rearview mirror. A single, miniature satin pointe shoe, as perfectly sculpted as the ones we wear in class.

Ruthie checks her mirrors, turns on her lights, and pulls out of the metered space on the street. "No. I don't know. I want it. I really do. But what if I fail? Or what if I make it and I'm the worst one in my program? Everyone will think it's a pity spot and no one will ever take me seriously."

"Ruthie." I roll my eyes. "You'd never be a pity spot. I don't even think they give out pity spots. Tons of people audition every year. They don't have the room."

"I'm not sure how much that means, coming from the teacher's pet."

I say nothing and she's silent for a while. Pulling her curls out in a straight line and letting them spring back to her head.

Flipping through songs on the radio for so long I want to slap her hand away from the dial. I've started to think she's forgotten I'm in the car at all when she says, "At least ballet will get me out of this place. I don't care if I have to dance for a company in the fucking Appalachian Mountains. I'm leaving."

"What happened now?"

"Nothing new," she sighs. "I'm just tired of always being on everyone's bad side. I need a fresh start."

"Just one more year of high school," I say. "Unless you make it into preprofessional and then you can leave even sooner."

"But what if I don't?" Ruthie's eyes are on the road ahead, but I can see the fear behind them and the thought of Ruthie being scared scares me. I didn't think she was afraid of anyone or anything in the world. "What if I don't get in anywhere? Not even a summer program? Then what? I stick around here and go to DePaul and meet even more people I hate? I can't do that, Cartwright. I can't."

"I'm scared, too." I flick my index finger against the pointe shoe hanging from the mirror, watch it bob back and forth as we travel along the dark expressway. "Really scared."

I catch a glimpse of her narrowed blue eyes as she glances at me. "Of what?"

"Everything you just said. And . . . making the wrong decisions. Fucking everything up."

I pinch myself. Above the elbow this time. Hard. My mouth is moving faster than my brain.

"Making the wrong decisions. Hello, vague city. Aren't we all afraid of that?"

I ignore her smirk and ask, "What's the worst thing you've ever done?"

I slide my hand up my throat to make sure I'm the one talking. Tiny vibrations pulse beneath my fingertips, so I guess it *is* me. Ruthie is saying something back, so it had to be me.

"If this is a blackmail scheme, Cartwright, you're being pretty transparent right now." She moves to turn down the heat and I wish she could also turn back this conversation so I never asked that question.

"I wouldn't do that." I look at a champagne-colored mini-van in the lane next to me on the expressway. The interior is lit up by a rectangle hanging between the front and back seats. A DVD player, but I can't tell what it's playing or who's watching. "I just want to know. What's the worst thing you've ever done?"

Ruthie tilts her head to the side, sucks in her bottom lip, and pushes it back out. "If you tell anyone this, I will *murder* you. That's not a figure of speech. I will track you down wherever you're dancing and pretend to care how you're doing, but I'll really be there to poison you."

"Poisoning?" That seems tame for Ruthie.

"Let's just pretend the anger management sessions will be working by then." She clears her throat. "But I'm serious, Cartwright—"

I twist my body in the seat so I can face her. "I'm not going to tell anyone, okay?"

She speaks very, very slowly, so I can't miss a word even if I tried. "In sixth grade, I got in a fight with Skye Richardson. It was bad. She pulled out a chunk of my hair, and I bit her arm so hard, it broke the skin."

I shudder.

"My parents grounded me, but it was right before school let out, so part of my punishment was that I couldn't go to summer camp that year." She throws me a glance. "Look, I know a lot of people think camp is lame, but I was twelve and I really liked it. I felt like the people who came back every year . . . they were the people who really got me, you know? And I wouldn't be able to see them for another twelve months because of my parents. It's not like they would have let me fly across the country to visit."

I can't imagine Ruthie at summer camp, let alone enjoying it and making friends. She barely keeps it together at the studio.

"It was my mom, mostly. I know my dad would have given in, but she was really pissed." Ruthie sighs. "They were calling me Cannibal Girl at school and it got back to her and . . . there's one thing you need to know about my mom: she has bipolar disorder."

Oh, shit. I have a bad feeling I know where this is going and Ruthie must sense it, too, because she pauses before she says the next part.

"She was really open about me knowing, though. They told me when I was little. I wanted to be helpful, so she made up this routine where she'd start the coffee in the morning and I'd get her pills from the bathroom. Set them next to her mug. It's just what we did and she always trusted me and . . . I started messing with her pills. I switched them out." Ruthie pauses again, never takes her eyes off the road. "I was so mad at her. I'd actually watch her take the medicine, knowing it was the wrong pill, and I didn't feel a thing. It's like I was in a fog."

She stops for a minute and I want to ask her what happened next, but I don't dare speak before she does. She's going to finish. Ruthie is nothing if not thorough.

"She ended up in the psych ward for, like, two weeks." Her eyes blink deliberately a couple of times, as if she's firmly placing herself in the present. "They thought she wasn't taking her meds, and my dad was a wreck, trying to figure out what had happened. It was a mess and it was all because of me," she finishes, letting out a long, low breath.

"You didn't know—" I begin.

"I knew what I was doing. I haven't seen one of her meltdowns because she's been taking her medicine regularly since I was adopted. But I've heard about them and they don't sound pretty. I didn't think about the fact that she could die. Apparently her lows are really low."

I run my hand along the smooth leather of the car seat. "Did you ever tell her?"

"No. I mean, I've thought about it. A lot." Ruthie looks

in the rearview mirror as she changes lanes, starts making her way toward the exit for Ashland Hills. "I'm almost eighteen, so I know it's not like they'd give me back to the agency or anything, but . . . sometimes I worry that they think I'm a bad seed. They've had me since I was a baby and I turned out like this anyway. It must be in my blood. If I told them about the pills . . ." She shakes her head. "I couldn't. That's too far, even for me."

I don't know what to say. I didn't realize Ruthie was quite capable of what she just described. She's a fighter; everyone knows that. But I didn't know she was calculating. Vindictive when she can't solve a problem with her fists.

For the next few minutes it's just me guiding her to the Ashland Hills train station and her nodding as she goes straight ahead after the four-way stop or makes a right onto Magnolia. I point her toward my car. It's fairly nondescript, a hand-me-down from my mother when I turned sixteen, but she studies it like a fancy sports car as we drive up.

"So you really *do* drive. I was starting to doubt it."

"My parents would like me to believe my car turns into a pumpkin if I drive into the Chicago city limits."

She gives me a distant smile, then says, "Now you know my deepest, darkest secret. I almost killed my mother. Who's basically the nicest person alive. Probably would have made an excellent TV movie, huh?"

"Something like that." I return her smile even though we both know there's nothing funny about it.

Her blue eyes go very serious. "Do you think I'm terrible now?"

"No. Everybody makes mistakes."

It would have been really bad for Ruthie if she'd gotten caught, or if something even worse had happened to her mother. But she *didn't* get caught and she *didn't* tell anyone.

"What's your worst thing, then?" Ruthie prods. "It must be pretty bad if you're asking about mine."

Her tone is just gentle enough to jar something. Like earlier, my mouth seems to be opening on its own with no direction from me. The words crawl up from my stomach where they've been hiding, boxing at my insides until I am sore and raw.

They creep through my rib cage and skate by my heart and when they burst free from my lips I feel like I'm breathing air for the first time in months.

"I dated someone who might have done something really bad."

A warm rush flows through my body, followed by chills. I said it. I've put it out there and now there's no going back.

But I said it so fast that Ruthie is confused. "*He* might have done something really bad or you might have?"

"Him. I don't know for sure. I still don't know if he did it, but I think he might have." I press my hands against my thighs. "And things might have been different if I'd told some-one about him. Nobody knew we were together . . ."

"Maybe it's not too late," Ruthie says, her tone encouraging but not forceful. Perhaps that's what I heard in her before, a little hint that I can trust her. I don't know what it is but it keeps me going.

"He got caught," I say, gulping in more air. Breathing in until I feel as if my lungs might pop. "He'll be in trouble anyway, but if I tell someone about us . . . *all* about us . . . it might help people."

One person in particular.

"And if you don't, you have to live with it." Her voice is clear but when I look over, her eyes are cloudy and I know without asking that she's reliving the ambulance ride to the hospital and the way people kept telling her it would be okay because she was just a little girl and little girls shouldn't worry themselves with things like this.

". . . Donovan."

"What?" She turns her eyes on me and she's back in this moment. "What did you say?"

Shit.

But I try again. I am still sick and scared when I think about facing Chris in the courtroom, regardless of what I say. But at least I will have said this part to someone already, even if I never say it again.

"My ex-boyfriend. He's the guy accused of kidnapping my friend . . . Donovan."

I whisper but it's quiet in the car and Ruthie doesn't have to strain to hear me. She remembers when he disappeared, has seen the news like everyone else. Her face pales in the light from the parking lot lamp and there it is. *That's* what it looks like when you tell someone the worst thing you've ever done. It's mostly Ruthie staring at the same spot on the windshield for so long, I lose track of time.

"I read an article that said he's thirty." She pauses, then adds, "Years old."

"He told me he was eighteen." I swallow. "He didn't look old. He was my first, he . . . I loved him. So much, Ruthie."

She lets out a breath so long and loud, it would be comical if we weren't discussing the worst thing I've ever done.

"God, Cartwright. He . . . So when you were together, he was . . ." I can see her doing the math, adding it up, calculating just how stupid I was four years ago. "Have you told anyone else?"

I shake my head and when I look at Ruthie I'm sorry that I do.

Her eyes are brimming with pity. I don't know what I was thinking by telling her. I *wasn't* thinking. I had no control over my body, over my own vocal cords. I had to let it out somehow but Ruthie doesn't understand. Why would she?

"Cartwright, I—"

"I know." My hand is already on the door handle, ready to escape before she has to tell me what she really thinks of my confession. "It's gross. I'm leaving. Thanks for the ride."

"Stop," Ruthie says in a scary voice. Her fighting voice. Then it softens as she says, "I'm sorry. I am so, so sorry."

So she's not angry. Just sorry for Donovan. Maybe sorry she ever became friends with me.

"Cartwright?" Ruthie is giving me a sad look that seems almost as out of context as the words that follow. "I mean I'm sorry about what happened to *you*."

"That he lied? Yeah." I rub my eyes. I'm tired. Of talking, of thinking about Chris, of regretting everything I didn't do four years ago. "I'm sorry he wasn't the person he said he was, either."

"That's not what I—" She presses her lips together for a while before she asks, "You had sex with him?"

I nod, but even as I answer, "He was my boyfriend," I get a sick feeling in the pit of my stomach.

She stares at my face so hard, I want to look away but I can't. That's not part of the deal. You don't get to look away when you're talking to someone about the worst thing you've ever done. You're either all in or you're out.

"It doesn't matter if you liked him or not. He still . . ." Ruthie hesitates but she doesn't look away because she knows the deal, too. She swallows. She blinks twice as she says my first name for the first time in ages, as she talks to me in a voice so pained, it chokes her.

She says: "Theo, don't you know he raped you?"

Rape.

Rape.

*Rape.*

No. That's a word for what happens to women who get jumped on street corners or girls whose dates won't take no for an answer. I was in *love* with Chris. He didn't force me to be with him or drop something in my drink so I didn't have a choice.

Sure, he was a little too rough sometimes, but rape? It's what people think he did to Donovan, but he didn't do that to me. We had sex and he left without saying goodbye but he *didn't* rape me.

I have to get out of here. My shaking hand jiggles the door handle and I step outside so I can get away from Ruthie, from that same pathetic expression she's been giving me since I brought up Chris's name. I can't handle her looking at me like I'm the one people should be feeling sorry for.

Ruthie gets out of the car, too. Her curls catch the watery beam of the parking lot light as she stands by the hood. They glow whitish blue like the sky at dawn and she looks like an angel now more than ever.

"Cartwright—"

"He was my boyfriend. He didn't . . . You can't go around telling people he—" My tongue twists around my own words and I can't say the one that makes my chest constrict. "You can't, Ruthie."

She lets out a deep breath, a translucent cloud that curls over the hood of her car and disappears into the night air.

"You can't tell, Ruthie. You can't. You can't tell. You can't say *anything*." I repeat this over and over until she's standing in front of me, until Ruthie Pathman's arms are wrapped tight around me in the empty parking lot of a train station.

"Promise you won't say anything." My face is smashed into the shoulder of her wool coat, my voice muffled, but there is no doubt what I said. "Promise me, Ruthie. You *have* to promise. You have to—"

"I won't say anything." She pulls back to look at me, to look dead in my eyes as she says this, and I believe her.

Perhaps I'm being foolish. I have to believe there's someone I can trust.

# CHAPTER TWENTY-FOUR

I WAS SUPPOSED TO RIDE TO SCHOOL WITH DONOVAN the last day I saw him, but he ditched me.

We rode the bus during winter because it was cold and our parents didn't like us traversing the icy roads with our flimsy bike tires. But once spring hit, we were free to bike to and from middle school, and we always took advantage of it.

The bus smelled like dirty gym socks on a good day and there was always some sixth-grader crying in one of the front seats. Plus, riding our bikes gave us more independence. We didn't have to be outside immediately after the last bell rang, and we could stop off at the convenience store if we wanted to waste some time before we went home.

And once we met Chris, that's what we always wanted.

I'll never forget the Monday we showed up after school and Chris wasn't there. Mondays were his afternoons behind the register, but the gum-smacking cashier told us he'd quit.

Quit?

"Yeah. Just stopped showing up," she said, flipping through

the back half of a tabloid. Tiny star tattoos swam around her wrist and her hair was a watered-down red that frizzed to a stop at her shoulders. "Told Larry not to hire him."

"Why not?" I crossed my arms as I stared at her.

"Because I knew he'd pull some crap like this." She paused on a picture of an actor sporting a house-arrest ankle monitor. "He was lazy and I think he was *stealing,* too. Thought he could get away with it 'cause he was cute. Wasn't *that* cute."

The cashier shook her head. I looked at the name tag hooked above the pocket of her yellow polo. Her name was Penny.

"Larry called him a couple hours ago," she said around a mouthful of strawberry bubblegum. I could smell the artificial flavoring across the counter, see the pink wad as she twisted and pulled it around her teeth. "Says his phone was off."

Donovan and I exchanged a look. He must have been in trouble, like a car accident. Or maybe he was sick and that's why he couldn't answer his phone.

"Did he . . ." I paused, not wanting to give away too much. Just in case he showed up and got his job back and Penny started asking questions. But I had to know, had to do as much as I could while I was there. "Do you have an address? We . . . we need to talk to him."

"Couldn't give it to you even if I had it. Confidentiality and all that." Penny straightened behind the counter and gave me a careful look. "Got yourself a little crush? Trust me, pretty boys like him are a dime a dozen."

"I don't . . ." But I didn't know how to finish. I couldn't tell her that I wasn't some little girl who came in after school to hang on the counter and stare at him while he was working. I was his *girlfriend*. The crush stage had passed months ago.

Penny swapped her tabloid for one on the counter behind her. "He's gone, girl," she said, giving me one last look. "And I don't think he's coming back."

Donovan disappeared exactly two weeks and a day later.

After he was so short with me, so secretive ("We don't have to do everything together"), I marched back down the stairs and out the door and got on my bike, trying to fight back the tears. First Chris had disappeared, and now Donovan was being weird. Too private.

Everyone was pulling away from me—but nobody was telling me what I'd done wrong.

Later, when I was in the principal's office, there was nothing I wanted to do more than pull away myself. I was seated across the desk from Principal Burns and next to Donovan's mother. The office was freezing and I was starving. I hadn't eaten lunch. I'd sat in the cafeteria with Phil and stared at my cheeseburger and fries until they were cold, sitting on my tray in a soggy, abandoned pile. Not eating felt good. It made me feel strong. In control.

"Theo, can you tell us one last time what he said to you?"

Principal Burns had a kind face. I knew I wasn't supposed

to think so, but the lines around his mouth and eyes were comforting, like a grandpa. And he made sure to tell me right away that I wasn't in trouble, but when I saw Donovan's mother, saw the worry behind her eyes, I knew something was very, very wrong.

I took a deep breath before I began telling them what I'd already said at least five times. "He said he had to take care of something. But that he would show up later and we'd ride home together."

There were only two more periods left, though, and I think all of us were pretty certain Donovan wasn't going to show up to finish the school day. I'd expected him before lunch and clearly that hadn't happened. He wasn't answering his phone; it went straight to voicemail. And no one else had heard from him—not Phil or Donovan's parents or any of his friends from the baseball team.

"What would he have to take care of?"

Mrs. Pratt wasn't looking at me as she said this, but her eyes were wild as they moved around the rest of the room. She was barely sitting in her seat—perched on the very edge—and she kept twisting her hands in her lap.

"That doesn't sound like him, keeping secrets." Her eyes landed on me then, and I wanted to look away but I couldn't. "Why would he keep secrets from you, Theo? You're his best friend."

Principal Burns moved a glass paperweight from one side

of his desk to the other, cleared his throat. "Theo, is there any-where you can think that he might have gone? Somewhere out-side of town? Someone's house? Maybe there was a place he went to get away from everyone?"

"Well." I gazed down at my lap, at the hole that was starting to tear in the knee of my jeans. "We used to go to the convenience store sometimes. After school . . . the one on Cloverdale."

Mrs. Pratt's head whipped toward Principal Burns, but he must have been well versed in dealing with hysterical parents. He was already calling out to his secretary to get the store on the phone. A couple of minutes later, he was talking to the owner. Larry.

Yes, Larry had seen Donovan; he'd been in the store about thirty minutes after I saw him, and he was alone. But no, he didn't know where he was off to after he left the store on his bike. He'd bought snacks while he was there—beef jerky and potato chips and soda and licorice. And a comic book, but Larry couldn't remember which one.

Why was he at the convenience store when Chris no longer worked there? Sure, we'd stopped in a few times, when we were bored or dying of thirst or hunger. That was the way we'd met Chris, after all. But why stop for snacks, like he was going somewhere and would need food later?

Mrs. Pratt was inconsolable. My mother showed up to take both of us home a little while later. Honestly, I would have preferred to stay at school, even for those last couple of hours, because it meant I didn't have to confront the dread that was slowly spreading from the Pratt house to ours to the rest of the town.

When Donovan still hadn't shown up by eleven that evening, my parents sent me to bed. As if I could sleep, not knowing where he was. If he was coming home, why hadn't he told me where he was going?

They kissed both my cheeks, held me an extra-long time in their arms before I went upstairs that night. I turned off my light and got into bed, but on top of the covers with all my clothes on. I uncurled my phone from my palm and pushed the button for Donovan's number. I held my breath, waiting for him to pick up, to tell me he'd lost track of time and he was coming home soon.

I got nothing. Not even one ring, just straight to his voicemail, where the tone he used around grown-ups told me he couldn't come to the phone right now, to please leave a message and he'd call me back.

I didn't leave a message because I'd already left so many. One more wouldn't make a difference.

I called Chris, though. Just one last time, to see if his silence had been a mistake, if he missed me, too, and wanted to see me.

But all I got was the same message I'd been getting for the last two weeks:

*I'm sorry, but the number you've reached is no longer in service. If you believe you've reached this recording in error, please hang up and dial the number again.*

I didn't fall asleep until two in the morning. I slept with my phone on the pillow next to me, but it never rang. Not during the night, or the next day, either.

My phone never rang again with calls from Chris or Donovan and I never stopped wondering what I'd done to deserve it.

# CHAPTER TWENTY-FIVE

WINTER FORMAL.

Decidedly less cheesy than homecoming and more relaxed than prom, yet it's done little to earn my respect over the years.

But Ashland Hills High School takes its dances very seriously, and the specially appointed student council committee starts planning immediately after homecoming, more than two months in advance. This year, it's the Friday before the trial. I have three days until it starts, and I think that's as good a reason as any to skip it, but Sara-Kate and Phil aren't having it. Like last year, we go together. Dateless, but not alone.

This year I thought they might go together, as actual dates. I don't think anything has happened beyond the rampant teasing I've witnessed at lunch, at Casablanca's, and virtually anytime the three of us are together. But it's there. It's in the way Phil always jumps to hold the door open for her or give her the best seat at the movies, in the gaze that never stops appreciating her hourglass figure. And it's in Sara-Kate's extra-sweet smiles and the constant patience she reserves for his excessive complaints about the injustices of the world.

So I let my mother take me shopping for a dress and I get ready with Sara-Kate, let her doll me up with the miracles hidden in her makeup case. I feel beautiful when she's all done, when I'm slowly turning in front of her full-length mirror, admiring my long, plum-colored dress with the low back.

"Is Hosea going tonight?" she asks, sitting on the edge of her bed as she looks at me looking at myself.

"Yeah." I catch her eye in the mirror as I slide my hands over the smooth fabric. "I mean, I think so. He said Ellie wanted to go, so . . ."

"So you're still talking to him. Of course." She gives a quick nod, and I know I shouldn't be offended by that nod, by the way she says "of course," but I am. And that's exactly why I haven't told Sara-Kate that I slept with him. She doesn't understand, and I don't know how to make her see that he's worth it.

"Are you mad at me for . . . liking him?"

We're still looking at each other in the mirror. She clasps her hands in her lap, glances briefly toward the window. The night is black and cold behind her white lace curtains. We're all going to freeze tonight because nobody likes to wear their coats over pretty dresses and fancy suits. I hold my breath as I wait for her to respond.

"I'm not mad at you, Theo," she says to my reflection. "I just think you can do better. You deserve someone who doesn't have to hide his relationship with you."

I don't know what to say to that, so I look away from her. Step away from the mirror.

Two seconds later, her arms are around me, in a hug from behind. She slips her chin into the nook between my neck and shoulder. "But I still love you, and I want you to be happy."

We stand like that for a while, and I feel so good wrapped up in Sara-Kate love, and I wonder if she'll feel the same way about me if she finds out about Chris.

I think Phil is going to stroke out when he sees Sara-Kate in her evening finery. Honestly, his eyeballs nearly pop from their sockets behind the black-framed glasses he's donning for the occasion. For good reason. Sara-Kate's hair is the whitest shade of platinum blond, a stark contrast to the navy chiffon dress that hugs her hips. Her lips are painted ruby red and she looks like a modern-day version of Marilyn Monroe.

"You look . . . *Wow*" is all he can say as she approaches.

"Is that the official Philip Muñoz Seal of Approval?" Sara-Kate teases, her mouth turning up in a wide smile. She touches the rhinestone barrette clipped to the front of her hair.

"Yeah." He gives a lopsided smile of his own, a smile so goofy, it looks foreign on Phil. "Something like that."

He tells me I look good, too, and I can't stop wishing it were Hosea saying it instead.

Everyone usually goes to a nice restaurant to eat dinner before the dance. Like Rizzo's, the fancy Italian place with an actual maître d' at the front. They make reservations and take their parents' credit cards and try to sneak glasses of wine with their fake IDs.

We go to Pizza Bazaar, which is hardly fancy enough to be considered a restaurant. It basically consists of a long counter with bar stools at one end, a few booths, and some wobbly-legged tables scattered around the black-and-white tile floor. The lighting is bad and the pizza is just okay. But it's empty and affordable and it makes Phil and Sara-Kate feel as if they're not taking this dance thing as seriously as they are.

Phil goes up to put in our order. Slices of pepperoni and sausage for them and a small house salad—sans dressing—for me. I look down at the laminated menu caked with dried marinara sauce and sticky droplets of soda. The pizza here is mediocre but it's hard to fuck up a slice of cheese, which is what I really wanted to order.

But the less I eat, the stronger I feel. A few flashes of weakness, constant rumbling in my stomach—it's worth it. If I can sustain my willpower with food, I can do anything. Like face Chris in court next week. Decide what I'm going to say. Survive.

Phil takes his time at the soda machine, making sure he gets the precise ratio of ice to soda in each cup.

"Has anyone ever cared so much about a drink?" I ask as I watch him measure out root beer for Sara-Kate.

"I think it's sweet," she says, and when I look over and make a face, she shrugs. "It's not like any of the other guys at school pay attention to detail. Or anything, really."

I give her a curious look as Phil hunts for the right-size lids among the stack overflowing to the side of the soda fountain. "Still nothing with you two?"

Her cheeks redden, right on cue. "Nothing declared. But I . . . I think something might happen tonight. Maybe?" She starts to chew on the end of a cherry-red fingernail, then remembers her fresh manicure and stops. "It seems like something could happen. But who's supposed to make the first move?"

"I don't know." I take a couple of napkins from the silver holder to my side, set them in a neat stack at the end of the table. "It just sort of happens when it feels right."

She glances at me with anxious eyes as Phil makes his way back to the booth, slowly weaving his way through tables and chairs as he holds carefully to the three sodas. "Is that how it was with you and . . . you know?"

I can't figure out if she's being coy because she doesn't want Phil to overhear or if it's because she hates the idea of us so much that she can't say his name.

"Yes," I say, looking at her carefully. "It was exactly like that."

"Like what?" Phil sets the sodas down with a flourish and nary a spill. He takes a bow and we clap for his effort.

"Like you should look into getting a job here, you did such a damn good job with those drinks," I say, and I wink at Sara-Kate when he's not looking.

Phil shakes his hair out of his eyes and removes his glasses, wipes the lenses on a paper napkin. He's wearing a gray vintage suit with a skinny tie and onyx cuff links. Sharp as always, and as I look at them across the table, I think how good he and Sara-Kate look together with the old-Hollywood glamour thing they have going on.

"You all set for the big trial next week?" he asks.

I reach for my Diet Coke and take a long sip before I answer. "Not particularly."

"It should be pretty easy, though, right?" Phil jams a straw into his cup. "You just get up there, talk about the morning you saw him and what he said, and then wait for them to prosecute the shit out of that dickbag." I don't say anything, so he looks at me a little closer and says, "Right?"

"Guys, I . . ." I look around to make sure no one else is listening, but we almost have the entire place to ourselves, except for the older man waiting for a take-out order at the counter, his newspaper spread before him. "Do you think Donovan was abused?"

Phil frowns. "You think he wasn't?"

"I don't know." I wrap my hands around the cool, smooth paper cup. "Everyone thinks so . . ."

"But?"

"Not *but,*" I say, shaking my head so he won't get the wrong idea. "It's just . . . there's no proof and he's still not talking and what if things didn't go down like we think they did?"

"Okay, but let's think about this." Phil is using the voice

teachers employ when it's clear how wrong you are but they want you to come to the conclusion on your own. "How many kidnapping cases do you know where kids go back to their families, totally unharmed? And I'm not talking about custody battle kidnappings—just regular old cases like this one. Can you remember any? I can't think of *one.*"

"I'm not saying it didn't happen." I press my palms flat against the table. "I just . . . How will we ever know what happened for sure if Donovan isn't talking?"

"That's what the trial is for," Phil says, shrugging. "And Donovan's lawyers are trying to make sure they have as much evidence against this guy as possible . . . *because* Donovan isn't talking."

"Also." Sara-Kate has been sipping on her root beer this whole time but she looks at both of us now, says, "Also . . . don't you think it means something? I looked up *selective mutism* and he fits the profile. People with PTSD get it all the time."

"Yeah," Phil says with finality. He fingers the slanted edge of his black tie. "I don't think there's any other explanation."

I look down at my soda and nod. This wasn't helpful. Ruthie says Chris raped me every time we were alone in his car, but if that's true, why didn't *I* stop talking? Why didn't someone see the same signs in me?

Rape isn't supposed to be this vague notion. It's a harsh reality and everyone knows what it is, can define it in two seconds flat. Chris didn't rape me.

The stocky guy at the counter calls the number for our order, looks around the place like it could be anyone, even though the take-out guy left and we're the only people in here now.

Phil stands up to grab the tray but stops to look at me first. "I know it sucks thinking about what happened to him," he says. "It makes me want to strangle that guy myself. But you're just nervous. Even if Donovan doesn't talk . . . things will work out. They have to. No one in their right mind would let that piece of shit go free after what he did. I mean, Jesus. He kept someone's kid for *four years.*"

My phone buzzes in my purse and I've never been more grateful for the interruption. I look down at a new text. A text from Hosea.

*Meet me later in the lab?*

I thought I was quiet but Sara-Kate catches my little intake of breath, glances over, and asks what I'm looking at.

"Nothing," I say as I key a message back to him *(What time?)* with shaking fingers. "Just my mom. She wants me to check in with them later."

Sara-Kate looks away quickly and I know she doesn't believe me, but the truth won't make her happy. And we can't discuss this right now. Because the truth is that my life could change forever in a few days, and I have to live in the moment, and I'm not going to feel bad about it.

Phil returns to the table with our dinner, slides the Styrofoam bowl of salad in front of me. I nod thank you, pretend to be extremely engrossed in the pale mixture of iceberg lettuce and shaved carrots that came from a bag, but really all I'm thinking about is Hosea, wondering when his response will come through.

And when it does: *I'll text you later. Keep your phone on.*

I pause for a moment, look at Sara-Kate to see if she's still interested in what I'm doing. But she's examining the pizza with Phil, trying to assess who got the larger slice of sausage and whose piece has more discs of greasy pepperoni.

As soon as I determine they're not paying attention to me, I write back: *What if you get caught?*

Not three seconds later: *You're worth it.*

I slip the phone back into my purse and try to ignore the gooey slices of pizza in front of them. The smell of salted meat and melted cheese is so damn good, it's offensive. But I touch my fingers to my side, pinch and pinch until the pain makes me forget my hunger.

I spear a forkful of dry salad, let it hover over my bowl for a moment as I consider what Phil said earlier. *I don't think there's any other explanation.* I don't know what to believe, but I do know I have to make the most of this evening.

The dance is held in the cafeteria, which has been transformed into An Enchanted Evening, according to student council. The room still reeks of boiled meat, but the dance committee hung giant silver stars and sparkly snowflakes from the ceiling so we'll forget about it, at least temporarily.

Everything's a little hazy, though. We smoked a bowl on the drive from Pizza Bazaar to school and I'm feeling it. I almost passed; I don't want to be too out of it when I see Hosea or risk the chance of missing him because I forget to check my phone. But I won't forget—how could I possibly forget when seeing him will be the highlight of the whole evening?

Besides, I'm just the right amount of stoned to get through this thing. Bryn Davenport accosts me at the entrance to the cafeteria—and so it begins.

"Theo, your dress is *amazing*," she says, reaching out to touch the strap.

Her shining eyes match the smile on her mouth and she looks nice, too. She's in a simple black dress that only looks simple because of how expensive it is, and a tasteful white rose corsage decorates her left wrist.

"Yours is really nice, too, Bryn." I return her smile, then gesture toward the corsage, ask about her date.

"Oh." Her face flushes but she composes herself just as quickly as the blush rose to her cheeks. "David Tulip. I mean, it's not like a *date* date. I'm pretty sure he's taking shots with Joey in the bathroom right now. But he asked and no one else had, so . . ."

She shrugs as if to say, *What's a girl to do?* Then her eyes sweep over my bare wrist and she looks behind me, says, "You're here with Sara-Kate and Phil?"

"Also not a *date* date," I respond with a wry smile.

"Yeah, but what's *their* deal? Are they together now or what?"

I look over my shoulder to find Sara-Kate pinning something to Phil's suit jacket. "After tonight? The answer will probably be yes."

"Good," Bryn says with a quick nod that sends her shiny black hair swaying by her chin. "They belong together, don't you think?"

I look back at them again. Sara-Kate gave him a boutonniere—a plastic one in the likeness of a mounted deer head. It's so miniature and even from here, I can tell it's incredibly detailed. Phil is beaming and can't stop looking down at his lapel to admire it.

"Yeah," I say, turning back to her. "They do."

I don't have much time to figure out the feeling that flared up in that moment—jealousy that they can be together without any complications? Worry that they'll forget about me once they become an official couple?—because David and Joey walk up to us then. Stinking of tequila. I can't believe they didn't bother with chasers or breath mints, but as Joey's shoulder slams into the wall I think maybe the smell won't be what gives them away after all.

David comes up behind Bryn, slides an arm around her waist. He nods at me, then moves his head close to hers. "What do you say we go out there and tear up that dance floor?"

She moves her nose out of the line of his tequila breath, but she smiles. "Only if you promise to hold off on the rest of that until we get to Klein's?"

"Of course," David says, already leading her toward the dance floor. "I was saving it for you."

"Hey, Joey." I tug on his elbow to stop him before he follows. "Do you have any more?"

"The te-kill-ya? Oh, yeah." He pats the inside of his suit jacket.

"Let me borrow it?" I say, batting my eyes as I look up at him. Joey is a total pushover for a damsel in distress, even if the "distress" is needing to get as fucked up as possible.

He lumbers over me, swaying like a drunken giant, and I think maybe *I'm* doing *him* a favor. Taking it off his hands and all, because one more shot and he'd be facedown on the linoleum.

"Sure thing, Theo." He turns his back to the cafeteria entrance, blocking us from everyone's view as he deposits a silver flask into my beaded, black clutch. It fits perfectly, settled into the satin lining between my phone and a tube of lip gloss. "Finish it. Man, I am *blitzed*."

He totters off to the cafeteria, and I walk over to Sara-Kate and Phil, who are being so cute, it makes me self-conscious about being here with them. If it weren't for my plan to see Hosea later, I would wish I hadn't come at all.

"Bathroom," I say, then pantomime taking a drink.

"Seriously?" Phil's fingers run over the edges of his boutonniere. "I'm pretty baked right now."

"I think I'll pass, too," Sara-Kate says, her eyes apologetic.

But I don't think she's all that stoned. She only took a couple of hits; she just wants to stay close to Phil. Suddenly, it's like I'm not here with them at all.

"Okay, well." I shrug. "I promised Joey I'd take good care of the tequila, so I can't let him down. I'll be back soon."

The bathroom at the end of the hall isn't empty, but I walk past the girls retouching makeup at the sinks and sneaking cigarettes by the window and lock myself into the handicapped stall. I lean against the stall divider with my clutch in one hand, Joey's flask in the other. The pale blue walls were repainted at the start of the school year and they're already covered in graffiti. Declarations of love (LB ♥ JW 4EVER) and random phone numbers and a couple of unattributed quotes from the poets among us.

But the accusations. There are so many. Scrawled onto the wall with permanent black marker and layers of black and blue ink. Who's a whore and who slept with him or her and whose number you should call for a real good time. I recognize some of the initials. Some names are crossed out and replaced with new ones—a slut-shaming war taking place on the wall.

God. If people found out I dated Chris, they'd *never* run out of things to say, no matter how many times the custodian painted over them.

If I had a marker in my clutch, I'd scratch over all of this. Cover it up until no one could see how hateful people are. The very people who walk through these halls every day. But I don't have anything besides a tube of lip gloss and my keys, so I'll have to drink.

The tequila burns my throat like hot fire, but I tip my head back and take a drink for every girl who was called a name on that wall. Then I double up for good measure.

I float back to the cafeteria. Silver and lace and chiffon and flowers. Shiny pop music and cologne-infused sweat. And the unmistakable smell of liquor. A whole smorgasbord on the breath of my classmates, so I'll blend in if nothing else.

Mr. Jacobsen is one of the chaperones. He wears a tan sweater over a collared shirt and tie. His hair is slicked back with some kind of gel or water and he keeps patting at it as he talks to Mrs. McCarty.

I move along the perimeter of the cafeteria, avoiding them. I'd get tangled up if I tried to cut through the dance floor. Too many people.

I'm glad Sara-Kate and Phil are nowhere to be found when Hosea enters the room, because I'm pretty sure the look on my face is completely readable. But it's not my fault. He's wearing a dress shirt and nice pants and a tie. And his hair is down and he looks gorgeous.

My eyes follow him. He waits at the entrance for Ellie to catch up to him in her skintight dress, but she's digging through her clutch two feet away from him, too preoccupied to see that he's holding out his hand for her. Finally, she looks up and they trail slowly across the room to the opposite wall, with Klein and Trisha close behind.

Even though I know he cares about me, I wish it didn't hurt to see them together. But I get to be alone with him later, if only for a few minutes. And that's what gets me through the next hour as I wait for his text. That, and the tequila buzzing through my veins.

Sara-Kate and Phil come back from the dance floor. They look sweaty and happy. Phil goes off to get paper cups of punch while Sara-Kate pats at her face with the tips of her fingers.

"You should come dance with us," she says. "I don't like you standing over here by yourself."

"I'm fine," I say. Then I sway and thankfully it's into Sara-Kate's shoulder and not the other direction.

But maybe not, because she looks at me too closely. *Peers* at me. Says, "Doll, are you wasted?"

"Tipsy," I say with a shrug that's meant to be nonchalant but comes off as defensive. I think. I am so warm right now. So spacey and dizzy and loose.

"Theo—" she begins with this really worried look in her eyes, but I cut her off.

"I'm *fine*. I promise." I run my right hand up and down my left arm. "Please don't—just have fun with Phil. I don't need you to babysit me while you're on your date."

Then I walk away because I don't want to be a bitch to her, but the alcohol loosens my tongue and I don't know how to stop. I amble through the horde of students, familiar faces at every turn. Familiar faces that want to dance with me, so I let them. Leo, wearing shiny black cowboy boots under his suit pants, tries to line dance with me during a fast song. Then Joey and I meet up again, and I think he confuses me for his date, but I waltz around with him anyway until Erika Healy comes by to claim him, gives me an apologetic smile as she lugs him away.

I wonder if Hosea sees, if he's watching me like I've been watching him all night. Trying to keep track of his whereabouts and holding my breath anytime his hand so much as grazes his pocket.

He dances with Ellie a couple of times. Only slow songs and only because she pulls him onto the dance floor. I watch his hands, how they curve around her hips. I watch the way she looks behind him, scoping out the people around them instead of talking to him or resting her head on his shoulder. Klein and Trisha are out there, too, and they move toward Hosea and Ellie so they're dancing side by side. So Trisha and Ellie can talk while they sway along to the music with their boyfriends.

Four songs later, I finally move off the dance floor. Sara-Kate and Phil have disappeared again, so I'm zoning out a few feet away from the refreshment table, staunchly ignoring the new plate of cookies McCarty just set down, when Klein saunters up. Sans Trisha. His eyes are rimmed with red and he teeters from one side to the other as he walks, but he makes it over to me and sets his feet deliberately in place as he stops.

"Purple is definitely your color, Legs," he slurs, digging his fingers into my shoulder like a vise grip. However much I had to drink, Klein has surely exceeded it. Not to mention whatever else he's on.

"Thanks," I say as I shrug him off. And then, because I'm feeling good, I say, "You look nice."

It's partially true. The suit is nice. Dark gray, cut well, and paired with a jewel-toned shirt that would bring out the green of his eyes if the whites weren't so red. His collar is streaked with dark marks and it takes a minute to realize it's Trisha's makeup.

"Hey." He looks over his shoulder, about as stealth as a parade float parked in the middle of the cafeteria. Then he scream-whispers, "You wanna get out of here?"

"No," I say firmly, crossing my arms.

"Come on, Legs. Got some new shit from Hosea," he says, patting his pocket. "The *good* shit. Don't tell me you're not down."

"I'm not," I say. "Actually, I was just getting ready to—"

My phone vibrates in my clutch and I stop. I don't even try to send Klein away before I check my phone. It's Hosea. I know it. And when I look down, there it is:

*Five minutes? You go now. I'll get rid of Klein.*

So he has seen me, and he's watching me right now. I give the room a cursory glance, but it's dark and I've been looking away from him too long to see where he ended up. I make sure Klein can't read the screen as my unsteady fingers type back a simple *See you then,* and I drop my phone back into my purse.

"I have to go," I say, already turning my back to him.

"Atta girl," he says with a wicked grin so large he'd make the Joker proud.

"Not with *you*. I'm going to the bathroom."

The hallways are ominous at nighttime. The window panels between the strips of lockers cast shadows across the floor and walls, angular and sort of eerie. I walk slowly, take my time as I travel down the corridor and when I get to the end, I turn around to see if anyone is watching. Nope. I slipped through the back door in the cafeteria, the one the cooks use to exit the kitchen.

I hang a left and move down the hall, sticking close to the lockers until I reach the door to the science lab. It pushes right open and I nearly fall into the dark room. I'm waiting for my eyes to adjust to the low light coming from the back when I see him. Standing by the light, a little lamp on a lab table in the back that's not visible from the hallway. The beam is so muted, the lamp so small that it's barely visible from the front of the room.

"You made it," he says with a smile I can't see.

"I did." I start edging my way around the tables, trying not to snag the delicate fabric of my dress on their sharp corners. It's harder than it looks when you've drunk half a flask of tequila.

Ever so faintly, I hear the chords of a slow song starting up in the cafeteria. I like that we can hear the music back here—in our place; that it's like we're at the dance together, if only for a little while. It feels magical.

Hosea is walking toward me. "You look . . . ," he starts in a low voice, but he doesn't finish. He shakes his head as if he can't find the words and I give him a shy smile because he's looking at me.

So intently that my skin warms, as if I can feel his gaze lighting on different parts of me, sliding from the curve of my neck to the slight dip in my waist. Now I know what Sara-Kate felt like earlier and I was silly for being jealous. This is more than worth the wait.

He pulls me to him and his fingers find the open back of my dress, send shivers through me as he rubs the small of my back in slow, gentle circles.

We kiss. Slowly. With my arms wrapped around his neck and his hands sitting low on my hips. I tangle my fingers in his hair as our mouths find each other in the dark. We step to the faint strains of the music, swaying so slowly, our bodies are hardly moving at all.

I look at his chest as we pull away, start to rest my head there as we dance. I jerk back at the last minute. Hosea stops for a second, looks at me, confused.

"My makeup," I say, touching my carefully done face. "It'll get on your shirt."

"Oh." He lets out a breath and then nods. "Right."

I want him to tell me he doesn't care, to put my head there

anyway because that's how you dance when you're with someone you really like. Someone special. I want him to tell me he
doesn't care if he gets caught, that maybe it's time Ellie figured
out what's going on between us.

But then his hands move away from me, move to his collar,
where he begins unbuttoning his shirt. He shrugs out of it,
lays it on the table to his right. His eyes never look away from
me, not even as his fingers move down to his belt. I slip a dress
strap over my shoulder. Then the other. The satin drops to the
floor and pools around my feet.

"Theo," he says, reaching out to touch a lock of hair by my
ear. His eyes crinkle with warmth.

And as we stand there, nearly naked and staring at each
other, I want to say so many things to him.

*Please don't stop liking me, no matter what happens.*

*Please break up with Ellie.*

*Please always look at me this way.*

"You're so perfect." He kisses my neck and I breathe.

Hosea breaks away to peel off his undershirt, to wipe down
the black top of an empty table behind me. Then he turns and
lifts me by the hips and sets me on the edge, nearly in one motion. His hands trail down my neck, my breasts, the flat plane
of my stomach. His lips follow.

The table digs hard lines into the backs of my thighs, but it's
the best kind of pain. He straightens up again to kiss my lips
and I wrap my arms around his neck. Pull him into me, until
he's nearly crushing me. Wrap my legs around his waist. I need

him to be as close as possible. I need to never forget this night. I need—

"Theo," he says, even softer this time. His fingers hook around the waistband of my underwear, tug them over my hips.

I melt at the sound of my name because it means something when he says it.

"Theo, I—"

But I never get to hear what he was going to say.

Hosea's words are cut short by the commotion at the front of the room. Interrupted by the door bursting open and agitated voices that should be familiar to me but are unrecognizable in the moment of confusion. Unrecognizable until the light is flipped on and I match the voices to their faces.

Klein.

And Ellie, standing next to him with her mouth hanging open because Hosea and I are still intertwined. I'm practically naked, and Hosea is wearing only boxers. We freeze, melded together like a clandestine version of that sculpture *The Kiss*.

The scene doesn't last long. Our reaction may be delayed, but once it kicks in we jump apart like we don't know each other. Klein's face is painted with a self-satisfied smirk and Ellie's mouth is still wide open. Catching flies, Phil's mother would say.

"Told you," Klein says.

My face burns with the heat of a thousand fires as I pull up my underwear, then cross my arms over my bare chest. I slide down from the table and desperately search the area for my dress. Thinking maybe it wouldn't be so bad if I died right here on this floor.

Hosea shrugs back into his button-down, not bothering with the dusty undershirt. He steps into his pants, leaving the belt undone. I watch him from the floor. He's looking at the front of the room.

"How the fuck did you—" he begins, but Klein cuts him off.

"I showed you this place myself, dude," he says, his voice *so* fucking smug, I want to kill him almost as much as I want to disappear from this earth right now. "You think I didn't know where to look for you? After you were both being so shady and disappeared at the same time?" Klein pauses. "You think Lark didn't figure it out that day she saw you in the bathroom, Legs? She said you were flaunting that clove like you wanted people to think you were his fucking girlfriend."

My stomach turns and when I look at Hosea his face is nearly as pale as his shirt. I'm afraid to stand up and face Ellie. Terrified. She's been quiet just long enough to formulate what to say to make me want to crawl into a hole, to figure out how she's going to get back at me. Maybe even how she's going to hit me.

The corner of my dress sticks out from the lab table across the aisle. I know they'll see me, but I have to get to it, so I keep one hand over my chest as I make a mad dash. Something rips on my dress as I yank it toward me, but I don't care. I hide behind another table as I get dressed in record time. I'm out of their sight, yet I've never felt more conspicuous. Sick and exposed, like someone threw me onstage in front of a full house before I'd learned the choreography.

But I can't let Hosea go through this alone, so I run a dusty hand through my hair and stand up as Klein begins talking. Again.

"Look, I'm sorry you had to see this, but I felt like it was my responsibility to show you," Klein says to Ellie as he rubs her back in an exaggerated fashion. "We're friends and you should know what's going on right under your—"

"Get the *fuck* away from me," Ellie says in one of the scariest voices I've ever heard. Low. No, guttural. Crawling up from the back of her throat like every single word is a challenge.

I look down at the floor, at the bottom of my dress, where the fabric ripped. Away from the taunting eyes of Klein, from the worry sketched across Hosea's face. When I look up again it's only because I hear Ellie crying.

Tears stream down both sides of her face as she looks at us, back and forth like if she stares hard enough this will all undo itself before her eyes. And it's a weird thought, but she looks pretty as she cries. Vulnerable and sort of . . . soft.

She turns her swollen eyes on Hosea and keeps them there. "Why would you do this? Do you not care about me at all?"

"Ellie—" Hosea starts, his face still white under the buzzing fluorescents.

"I don't know how you could do this after we've been together so long." Her voice breaks as a fresh batch of tears brims over her eyelids, sends ebony ribbons spilling down her cheeks. "You text me every night just to say you love me. I can't believe you would let me look like a fucking fool instead of breaking up with me."

Nightly texts? He still *loves* her? No. She's lying.

My head spins. I close my eyes and that makes it worse, so I grab onto the edge of the table. I wish I'd stayed on the floor.

"No one else knows," Hosea says in a hollow voice.

Ellie snorts as her eyes dart over to Klein. "Not for long."

"Hey, I haven't said shit to anyone," Klein says, holding up his hands. "Like I said, I was just looking out for—"

"Shut. Up. Klein." Ellie pushes her palms into the surface of a lab table as she says this, as if she's trying to gather strength before she speaks again. She stares at me for a while. Long enough for everything to turn cold. Then she wipes at the mascara pooling under her eyes, takes a deep breath, and walks out the door.

No *fuck you,* no threats of my life being over at this school. Not even a foreboding look thrown over her shoulder. And somehow, silence is scarier than anything I expected from her.

Hosea wipes a hand over his face. Looks at me and then away with damp eyes.

I go to him. "It's okay." I rub his arm. Up and down. Frantically. He can't love her. "She had to find out about us eventually, right?"

What we have isn't going away anytime soon. He knows

that. The look in his eyes before they busted in—he doesn't look at her like that, does he? That look was *special*. It was for me. This *place* is special. It's ours. He can't love her.

Silence. Even Klein decided to shut the hell up for a minute.

Hosea isn't moving. He isn't looking at me. He isn't talking, which makes my mouth work overtime.

"We're going to be okay, Hosea." I slide my hand around his biceps and squeeze. I want Klein to leave so Hosea can wrap me in his arms again. So we can pick up where we left off. We'll both feel better once we're together again, alone. "She's pissed now, but it'll blow over and maybe one day she'll—"

"Look, Theo, I like you. A lot. You're sweet and beautiful and—you're perfect. Special. You are." He swallows hard. His shoulders are rounded, his hands braced against the lab table.

He doesn't go on, but I know. From the tilt of his head and the squint of his eyes, I know what comes next.

"She doesn't understand you. Not like I do." My voice works hard to claw its way up, but it still comes out so very small.

"Maybe that's my fault," he says, with a long, heavy sigh. I look down at his hands. They tremble as they squeeze the edge of the table.

Klein coughs. We ignore him.

"Do you love her?" It chokes out of me in a ragged burst of air. Because it feels like someone is crushing my throat, like those could be my last words.

He's hunched over the table, but his face says it all, reflects an emotion too painful to acknowledge but too serious to ignore: regret. "I . . . We've been together so long and—"

"Do you *love* her?" I stamp my foot against the floor. Like a child.

"She's my *girlfriend,* Theo." He's still staring down at the table, but I don't miss the irritation behind his words. Like I'm a nagging fly he's been trying to swat away for months. Like he never felt anything for me at all.

He stands up straight, instantly shoves his hands into the pockets of his dress pants. Then he hesitates before delivering one last crippling blow. "Yes . . . I love her. I have to try to work things out. I can't—we can't be together. This is done."

He blinks at me a couple of times before he starts walking toward the door. Chasing Ellie. Leaving me again. Forever, this time.

"Hosea, *please*—" I follow him. I grip his elbow before he can walk away from me. I failed with Chris, but I can make this work with Hosea. "I need you. Please stay and we can figure this out. We *can,* I know it."

He shakes his head as he looks back at me one last time. "Theo."

That's it. My name used to sound like a promise from his mouth and now all it means is no. He doesn't want me. He won't love me. We are done.

He bumps into Klein as he passes. Hard. Shoulder to

shoulder. A challenge. But even Klein isn't stupid enough to screw with him now.

My body is leaden. So weighted down with disappointment and longing that I don't think I'll be able to walk back to the cafeteria, to find Sara-Kate and Phil and tell them to take me home.

My knees buckle and I crumple to the floor of the dirty science lab in my pretty purple dress. I could be sick right here, think I might actually vomit. But nothing would come up.

I'm empty.

I press my cheek to the cool linoleum as I wait for Klein to leave, for my breathing to return to normal, for my stomach to stop churning with shame. I have nothing left now. Ellie is right—everyone will know about this by Monday, if not by the end of the dance. I was Hosea's secret because he didn't want me as much as I wanted him. I was a diversion and he walked away from me as easily as Chris did.

I lie in a heap between the abandoned lab tables until Klein's footsteps shuffle off down the hallway. I lie there alone and I think of all that I've lost and I wait for the tears to come but they never do.

# CHAPTER TWENTY-SIX

THE MORNING I TESTIFY IS BITTERLY COLD.

An unforgiving Wednesday, with a wind that chills your bones as soon as you step outside, no matter how many layers of scarves and hats and gloves are wrapped around your body.

I watch the sun rise. Tucked behind the clouds, but it's there. Lightening the sky's inky canvas as the stars burn out like teeny-tiny lightbulbs, one by one. I'm standing in front of the window because I was tired of lying down. I didn't sleep, not for more than a half hour or so at a time. The last couple of nights were like this, but last night was different because today I'll be called to the stand.

Dad gets up to start the coffee. Once his footsteps have faded down the stairs, I pad across the hall to their bedroom. It smells like stale air and sweat. Sleep. My mother's eyes open when I say her name. Slow and fluttery and a little confused.

Then she sits up and motions me toward the bed and I crawl

in on Dad's empty side. Mom pulls up the duvet to cover my shoulders. "How are you feeling?"

I curl into a ball, try to become as small as I feel inside. "Tired," I say in a little voice. "Scared."

Her hand smooths down the back of my hair as I close my eyes. "I know. But it'll all be over soon and then things can go back to normal."

*Normal.* Maybe. Maybe not. I'm no closer to a decision about what to say than I was four days ago. I even called Donovan's house one last time, on Saturday night, and they ignored the call one last time.

"You're going to do just fine," Mom says, her voice soft and smooth as satin. "Do you remember your first recital?"

I remember it. Vaguely, but I do. I was three years old and I completely choked. Somehow, even though we'd practiced on the stage in the high school's auditorium, it looked bigger that night. Enormous. And the seats were full of adults I didn't know. And the lights were too hot and too bright. I'd clung to the heavy stage curtain like it was my salvation.

"I wanted to pull you offstage, bring you down to sit in my lap, but your father wouldn't let me," she says. "He told me to let you stay up there, that if you didn't want to go back to class after that night, we'd know ballet wasn't for you. But if you still talked about it, you probably just had a little case of stage fright that would work itself out."

"He said that?"

"He did. And he was right. Because the next year you were up there without a care in the world, front and center." She bends her head to kiss my temple. "You were brave back then and you'll be brave today. I know it. I love you, sweet girl."

I take in a breath, exhale beneath the covers as I wonder if she'll feel the same way when I'm done with my testimony. "Love you, too."

We lie there in a cocoon of warmth and silence until the aroma of coffee wafts up the stairs, until Dad calls out that we need to start getting ready. We don't want to be late.

Mom makes thermoses of coffee for her and Dad, one with green tea for me. Even my father looks like he has trouble eating this morning. He chews each bite of toast for a ridiculously long time. I manage two bites of a cereal bar and am genuinely surprised when it doesn't come right back up.

We drive into the city with the soothing voices of NPR as our soundtrack. The cold, gray expressway matches the cold, gray skyline, as if all of Chicago is observing Donovan's trial.

I look down at my phone, at the text from Phil telling me to kick some judicial ass, at the email Sara-Kate sent last night that says she loves me and knows I'll do awesome. There's even a text from Ruthie, sent late last night, telling me to call her if I needed to talk.

Nothing from Hosea, of course. I haven't talked to him or seen him since the dance. I haven't talked to *anyone* since winter formal. Opening statements were Monday, and my parents let me stay home because we knew I'd be called either the second or third day and it's not like I could concentrate much on schoolwork anyway.

When I told Phil about Hosea, I think he was more annoyed than anything else—that he didn't know we were hooking up, that it seemed like I didn't trust him enough to keep my secret. Sara-Kate could have easily gone the "I told you so" route, but that's not her style. She said she was sorry things ended so badly, and I knew she meant it.

If I close my eyes and think very hard, I can still feel his arms around me in the science lab. I can feel his warm lips pressing against mine, remember the way his heart beat steady and strong against my chest.

The reporters and photographers are stationed outside the courthouse because nobody can stand to miss a moment of this. We get a few looks as we walk up the steps; a few of the reporters shuffle over after they see photographers snapping pictures of us, figure we must be at least marginally important.

My parents shield me from them, and Donovan's lawyer meets us on the front steps of the courthouse. Graham McMillan. He's supposedly one of the best prosecuting attorneys in the Midwest. Some reports say he's the best in the nation. Before I saw him on the news, talking about the case in a press conference, I expected him to be tall and imposing, gruff-voiced and fierce. But he's short and has a baby face with chubby cheeks, and when I met him a few weeks before the trial, his eyes disappeared into half-moons when he smiled, when he shook my hand and said it was nice to meet me.

We didn't talk much yesterday; there was a chance I could be called but I wasn't, so I spent the day sitting in the hallway outside the courtroom, doing homework and listening to music and almost wishing I was inside so I could get it over with.

But this morning he's clearly waiting for me, stops pacing as soon as he sees us. He greets my parents, then says he needs to steal me away before the trial starts. They hug and kiss me, say they'll see me inside.

McMillan and I walk through the halls of the courthouse. Sterile and stately and old.

We ride the elevator up to another floor. It's quiet. I think we might be the only people up here this early. McMillan walks to a machine that dispenses hot drinks and buys me a tea. I'm not thirsty but I hold on to the steaming paper cup and watch him pay for his coffee.

We blow on the tops of our drinks as we walk. I follow him until we reach one of the hard wooden benches at the end of the corridor, perch on its cool, worn edge.

McMillan takes a sip of coffee and grimaces. He looks at me. "Are you ready for this?"

I look down into my tea but I don't drink from it. "Not really."

"Just remember to take your time. Remember what we went over before—all you have to do is talk about that morning."

He leans forward with his elbows on his knees. "I'm going to ask you some questions about the last time you saw Donovan, and then about how well you knew the defendant."

The defendant.

I haven't seen him in person yet, but you can't turn on the TV or open the newspaper without seeing his face. He's cleaned up for the trial. Shaved the bushy beard he had when they found him with Donovan so he looks more like he did when I used to know him. Younger. Friendly. He was wearing a suit the last two days, with a tie and all. I'd never even seen him in a button-down shirt.

The first day we drove out to the park, he asked if I'd ever had a boyfriend. I looked at him shyly as I said no, as I wondered if he'd think I was a baby for being so inexperienced and turn the car around. But he just looked over and smiled. Rested his hand on my knee as he said he was glad, because I was special and he wanted to be my first.

I didn't know what to say to him, so I'd said nothing. Sex had always been so far away and suddenly it was in the car with us. Or the concept, anyway.

"Would that be okay, Pretty Theo?" he said, trailing his fingers lightly up and down my knee. "If your first time was with me?"

I knew I had to say something then, so I whispered yes. I wasn't sure exactly what I wanted, but I was equally excited and frightened as I thought of the illustrations in the book Donovan and I had looked at so long ago.

*You'd have to keep it a secret, though. Some people would say we shouldn't be together, but they don't know how mature you are for your age. They don't know you like I do. Can you keep a secret, Theo?*

His fingers moved up my leg, traveled to the inside of my thigh. His touch sent a tingling sensation through my entire body, even through the fabric of my jeans.

*Yes.*

My stomach twists when I think about seeing him. In probably less than an hour. I wonder if I'll feel different when we're finally in the same place again. I wonder if I'll be able to talk at all just knowing those amber eyes are across the room.

"Pretend you're talking to me instead of the jury," McMillan says, looking at me with his kind but serious eyes. "That it's just you and me, like right now."

I nod, take a couple of sips of tea. It's bland, almost bitter, but I keep drinking. Drinking means I'm not talking, not tempted to tell him there's a little part I may have left out when we met a few weeks ago.

McMillan is still looking at me. I swallow, and then I open my mouth, think the words might dribble out like tea running down my chin, but nothing. Just silence and nothing. So I close my mouth and nod again for good measure. *Yes, I know what to do once I get in there. No, you don't have to worry about me, Mr. McMillan.*

"I'd better go check in with the Pratts, but is there anything you want to go over before we head back down?"

He stands, holding on to his phone with one hand and the bad coffee with the other. He looks down at me with those half-moon eyes and this is my chance.

I look at his hand wrapped around the coffee cup. He's wearing a wedding band: plain, smooth gold. I wonder if he has children. If so, how many? Does he have a girl? What would he think if his daughter got up on the witness stand and told everyone that her ex-boyfriend was the guy on trial?

My mouth sticks. The words are there, the sentences formed, but I can't say them.

So I shake my head at McMillan. "Okay, then," he says. "Let's go back down. Judge Richey will have my ass if we're late." He glances down at his phone before he looks at me sheepishly. "Sorry."

My mouth works again, but only to give him a small smile. Only to say in a weak voice, "Nothing I haven't heard before."

I learn of Donovan's arrival long before I see him. I'm sitting on a bench in the hallway, waiting for the trial to start so they can call me in. The energy in the building changes, even around the corner and all the way down the hall from the front doors. The rustling turns to murmurs, which turn to a clear declaration of his presence in the courthouse. Donovan is here, and I will finally see him in person.

My parents sit on either side of me. Mom holds my hand and Dad sits closer than usual. Like he's protecting me. Normally it would annoy me that they were being so clingy, but right now, it's all I want. I look over at them every few minutes, try to memorize their faces because I don't know what they'll look like after I get up from the stand.

The prosecution team heads down the corridor, a cloud of business suits and stony faces surrounding Donovan. They slow down as they pass us and then they stop. Mrs. Pratt edges her way out of the middle. She wears a cheap red blouse and tan slacks that hang loosely at her hips. Makeup doesn't cover the bags under her eyes, but she looks better than the shadow I talked to behind the screen door. Her hair has been done and she's smiling. She steps aside to let Donovan through and I stop breathing.

I stand, slowly. Dad puts his hand on the small of my back, pushes me toward this ghost. I close my eyes to match him up with the photograph I've committed to memory. I open them and he's still there. My arms and legs are cast iron. I'm afraid that if I move, he'll disappear again. I saw pictures of him, video from the first couple days of the trial, but it's nothing compared with him standing here in front of me. He's truly here, truly alive.

He's so tall, much taller than me. The dreadlocks are gone. His hair is shaved close to the scalp with clean edges, just like he used to wear it. His suit is new and his shoes are so shiny, I could probably see my reflection in them. He's the version of my friend I couldn't imagine, not even after the last few months of knowing he was back. I search his exposed skin for scars, visible marks to indicate any abuse he may have endured, but that's stupid. His pain would be on the inside now. The types of wounds you can't measure just by looking.

I wrench my cast-iron arms from my sides because he isn't real if I don't touch him. I know I probably shouldn't, but I have to. My fingers brush over his sleeve, his collar, but I stop myself before they can get to the cleft in his chin—because he flinched. Like he doesn't know me.

A part of me wilts. I never thought Donovan could be uncomfortable around me. Even now, after four years apart, I never thought that. I look at him, stare at him, will him to look into my eyes. I don't know if we still have the same connection after so many years have passed, if his eyes will tell me anything at all. But I have to try.

"Hey," I say in the softest tone possible. "Hey, Donovan. It's me. Theo."

It works. He's looking at me and then I wish he wasn't. His eyes are the deepest, brownest pools of sadness. I swim in them. Wade through the depths of hurt and anger and confusion. Each wave is deeper than the next. Murkier, harder to see through. But when he looks away, I know one thing for certain: Donovan didn't run away.

I reach both arms out to him and then I stop. Because he doesn't move at all. Doesn't look at me. Doesn't say anything— of *course* he doesn't say anything. I should probably just walk away, compose myself before I'm called inside. But instead I step closer and wrap my arms around him like someone who has never been taught to hug, like someone who doesn't know you're supposed to let go. I hug him until I think my ribs will crack and his spine will crumble and my arms will snap like twigs. I hug him so hard and I whisper, right in his ear: "I'm sorry."

He just stands there. Paralyzed in my arms. And I know I have to let him go. But I can't. Dad steps forward to pry us apart, his hands gentle as he pulls back on my arms. I stare at Donovan, try to look into his eyes one last time, but he's gone in a second. Swallowed up by the prosecution team like a human tornado.

I watch them walk down the long corridor as Dad gently squeezes my arm, as Mom murmurs, "You'll see him again soon, honey. Do you want some water? Maybe you should go to the bathroom before—"

I don't catch the rest because I'm breaking away, running, trying to reach Donovan and his lawyers before they get to the door of the courtroom. My flats pound the concrete floor, the slap of the soles echoing against the walls. People milling about the hallway stare at me like I'm crazy, but I don't care. I have to talk to McMillan before it's too late.

"Mr. McMillan!"

Nothing. There are too many people ahead of me in their huddle, too many footsteps and voices bouncing along the hallway. And there's no way I'll be able to get through. Most of them are much taller than me. I'd have to fight my way through a wall of navy and gray and black suits and I'm smart enough to know that's not happening.

*"Mr. McMillan, I need to talk to you!"*

Everyone stops. My voice echoes through the silent hallway like I'm speaking through a megaphone. McMillan is at the front of the pack and something tells me he's not the guy you summon by screaming in a courthouse. But what other choice did I have? Let them walk through those doors without knowing what could be the most important piece of their case against Chris? Let Chris take a lighter sentence because I loved him once upon a time?

Love doesn't change the fact that he was too old. Too old to be talking to me. To both of us. He was too old to spend his free time with a couple of thirteen-year-olds.

A murmur spreads through the group in front of me, and then the suits at the back are stepping aside and McMillan emerges. He looks peeved, to say the least. No half-moons this time.

"What is it, Theo? We really have to get in there now," he says, his eyes flickering toward the courtroom door. "Judge Richey—"

"There's more."

It comes out so calmly, like it's an afterthought. Like this hasn't plagued me for months, like I haven't already broken down exactly how my life will play out after this. I think it's McMillan's face that keeps me calm. Even when he's not smiling—when he looks so annoyed—I feel safe with him. It will be hard to get it out now, but it would be even harder if I went into this at the last second, totally alone.

"What do you mean?" His eyebrows sink down toward his nose, but his eyes are still open and honest.

I'm doing the right thing. I am.

"I have more to t-tell you," I say, looking down at my flats. "I have to talk to you before you g-go in there. It's important."

"Theo, this—"

"It's about Chris Fenner. There's more."

I'm shaking.

Because if Chris was capable of raping Donovan, then what he did to me could be rape, too.

McMillan looks at me for a long moment, then says something to the man behind him in a low tone. The suit looks surprised. He must be shocked that McMillan is taking me so seriously. But he just nods and moves toward the front of the huddle.

McMillan puts a hand on my shoulder, looks at me with curious and cautious eyes. "We don't have long. You're sure this is essential to the case? To your testimony?"

"I'm positive," I say as we start walking toward the elevators again.

I've never been more sure of anything in my life.

## CHAPTER TWENTY-SEVEN

THE COURTROOM IS FREEZING.

My parents sit in the second row, directly behind Donovan's family. Their heads swivel as the heavy door thumps closed behind me. They have to wonder why I ran after McMillan, why we sat talking so long, and why he called in a couple of his colleagues after I'd told him everything there was to tell.

The thing is, as much as I know McMillan hates that I waited so late to tell him, it's worth it. Because as soon as I told him Chris Fenner was my boyfriend, he got a gleam in his eyes. And I'm pretty sure that meant he had enough information to do some serious damage to the other side's case.

"But what if they *expect* me to say something?" I asked when we were sitting in an empty room upstairs. It seemed like someone's office—small and boring with a desk, a chair, and some filing cabinets. No windows. A lock on the door. My heart still wasn't beating normally at that point, even after I'd gotten everything out. It would probably be the theme for the day.

"Well, there's a chance he did tell his lawyers about your 'relationship,'" McMillan said, scribbling something down on a yellow notepad. "But Theo, what did you tell me when you first described him?"

I looked at him, confused, but he didn't wait for me to make the connection.

"You said you were in love with him and he knew it." He paused, his pen hovering over the paper. "And since you didn't go to anyone until now, he probably thinks you won't tell."

"Unless they think we've been hiding it this whole time on pur—"

"Don't overthink it. Look." McMillan leaned forward with the most solemn expression. His eyes were the biggest I've ever seen them, which isn't very big at all. "This guy, he . . . he took a lot from you, a long time ago. And you didn't tell anyone, not until the day you had to testify. He probably thinks he still has you wrapped around his finger. If he's counting on Donovan not saying anything, he's probably counting on the same from you."

McMillan was right. Donovan and I used to believe everything Chris told us, do anything he said. If only to make sure we weren't doing anything wrong, anything to make him stop liking us.

So now, as I walk from the back of the courtroom to the front, as my shoes make tiny clicking noises on the floor, I try to remember this. McMillan is right. My testimony is going to shock everyone—my parents, my friends, everyone in this town—but it will shock Chris most of all. And him thinking I'm not strong enough to go through with it, not strong enough to stand up for my friend and myself . . . well, I guess it's typical Chris. But I'm not typical Theo.

I see the back of his head from the corner of my eye. His dark hair is cut short so it stops at a clean line above his collar. I wonder who paid for that haircut. His lawyer? Or maybe someone did it in prison? He's been there this whole time, after all. I guess he doesn't have any friends or family with a spare million dollars lying around for bail.

He cracks his knuckles at precisely the moment I walk by. I flinch. I hate myself for it, especially since he can see me. But the only thing to do is keep walking, so that's what I do. I refuse to turn my head. And somehow, I make it up to the witness stand in one piece.

I hold up my hand as I'm sworn in.

*. . . the truth, the whole truth, and nothing but the truth . . .*

I sit down and breathe deeply to center myself, like I do before every dance performance. Take stock of what I'm about to do, think about how far I've come to get here. Then I glance at Judge Richey—a very tall woman with fluffy dark blond hair—and the jury, which is made up of a hodgepodge of people. Skinny and average and fat. College-age and senior citizens. Mostly white, but token minorities take up a few of the seats, one to check off each box: black, Latino, and Asian.

I force myself not to look at Chris. I can't look at him until I start talking about him. I can't lose my nerve. Not after what I've already put at stake, what I've put McMillan through this morning. Not after what I saw in Donovan's eyes.

McMillan starts by asking standard questions: my age, where I live, where I go to school. I wish I didn't know they got increasingly worse, that the most personal ones, the hardest questions to answer, are yet to come.

*Take it one question at a time,* McMillan told me only a few minutes ago, though it seems like days. *Don't worry so much about anticipating the next question that you lose your train of thought and get flustered. One at a time is all you can answer.*

I take another breath.

"Ms. Cartwright, do you recognize this young man?" McMillan steps aside so I have a clear view of the table behind him, sweeps his arm out just in case I missed Donovan sitting there. I look at him. He's facing me, but he doesn't make eye contact. He's looking at a point beyond me. Anywhere but my face.

"Yes, sir," I say, pushing through my dry throat. There's a cup of water to my right but I'm too nervous to pick it up. Afraid I'll knock it over on the table, or worse—spill it down my shirt.

"How do you know him?"

"He's my neighbor. Donovan Pratt."

How long have I known Donovan? How well did I know him? How much time did we spend together each week, if I had to guess? This goes on for a long time but when McMillan gets to the day in question, it's so simple. Like he could be asking about the day I started junior year. He asks what I was doing the morning Donovan disappeared, but he doesn't mention Chris's name or the abduction.

I relay what happened when I stopped by Donovan's house. Finding him upstairs and dressed for the day, listening to him tell me to go on without him because he had things to do. I relay our conversation to the best of my knowledge and I don't look at Donovan because that makes it too real, like I'm walking down his stairs and out the front door without saying goodbye all over again.

I let out a breath when it's over, but I'm not sure why. This is far from over. Our mock testimonies were thorough but not this detailed. He talked about the day Donovan went missing for so long that I thought he'd never get to the actual point. But then he does and for a moment, everything stops.

For a moment, I'm still just plain old Theo Cartwright. Seventeen. A girl who lives and breathes ballet, who loved Trent Ryan Miller. Former best friend of Donovan Pratt. Daughter of the man and woman with the very kind faces sitting in the second row of the gallery—the people whose names will forever be connected with my shameful story after I speak.

"Ms. Cartwright, are you acquainted with the defendant?" McMillan asks, and when I look at him, his face has changed. It's harder but his voice is the same. Even. Affable. If you couldn't see his eyes you'd hardly know he was gearing up for anything special.

"Yes, sir," I say, and my mouth instantly fills with sand.

I can't fight it anymore. I reach for the cup, pick it up with an unsteady hand. But not so unsteady I can't lift it. I wet my lips and the tip of my tongue before I set it back down. I don't trust myself to do more than that.

"And how do you know Mr. Fenner?"

*Take it one question at a time.*

"He worked at the convenience store that was on Cloverdale." I bite my lip. Now? No, not yet.

"Big Red's Gas n'More on Cloverdale?" McMillan asks, threading his fingers in front of his chest.

"Yes, sir." Not yet, not yet. I train my eyes on McMillan's face, don't dare glance at anyone in the jury. Certainly not in the gallery.

"And how did you meet Mr. Fenner?"

"Donovan and I would go there sometimes after school. To Big Red's."

"And Mr. Fenner talked to you while he was working?"

"Yes, sir." I clear my throat. "Sometimes."

McMillan starts pacing again. He takes long strides for such a short guy. It makes him look taller than he is. "What did you talk about?"

"A lot of things." I practically whisper. I need to speak up but I can barely hear myself, can hardly make out my own words over the sickly pounding of my heart in my throat. "School, our friends, my dance lessons. What it was like working at the store. What high school would be like."

"Were you aware of the defendant's age at the time you met?"

"Yes, sir."

"And how old did you think he was?"

"He—he told me he was eighteen."

There it is. A shift in the air. Rustles in the gallery. A few people breathe in sharply. I can't peg who it is, but I'm not looking out there. I'll never be able to go on if I watch the disappointment and disgust make its way across their faces like the world's fastest epidemic.

Jurors lean forward to make sure they can hear every word out of my mouth from this point on. There's movement at the defense table, but I only see it from my peripheral vision because not yet.

"Ms. Cartwright, how would you describe the nature of your acquaintance with Mr. Fenner?"

I get the feeling that when McMillan recounts this part of the story to his wife, to his colleagues and his friends, he'll say this is the point where the defense knew he had them by the balls.

"We were friends," I say. "We'd hang out while he was working and on his breaks and sometimes on his days off. And then . . ."

McMillan nods at me to go on, but I can't. My throat has closed up. I can't swallow. My tongue is this big, dry lump parked in my mouth like a useless ball of dough and how will I speak if it can't move? I don't know what to do. I look at McMillan again. His eyes shift to the cup of water.

Right. I reach for it with grateful hands, force myself to take an actual drink. A long one, and then another. I set down the cup and look at McMillan again. He gives another short, simple nod. Continue.

Now. *Now* I look across the room to the defense side. I look right at Christopher Fenner. Lock my eyes on his face to let him know I'm not scared anymore. I'm not scared of getting him in trouble and I'm not scared of how many ways he can break my heart.

What we had was never special. He used me to get to my friend.

"We were friends first, and then he said . . . he said if we had sex, we'd be boyfriend and girlfriend." I swallow hard around the lump in my throat. Water won't help this.

McMillan's voice softens. Just a bit, but enough to make a difference. "Ms. Cartwright, did you have sexual intercourse with Mr. Fenner?"

Every corner of the room is silent. So silent I hear Judge Richey's quiet, even breaths to the right of me. Even the stenographer is still, his fingers poised over the keys as he waits for me to speak.

"Yes, sir. I wanted him to be my boyfriend. I loved him." I pause. "I'd never had a boyfriend before. I was only thirteen."

## CHAPTER TWENTY-EIGHT

THE DAY I MET CHRIS SEEMED MEANT TO BE.

It was the winter of our seventh-grade year and school had been shitty that day. No, shitty didn't begin to describe it. I'd gotten a C-minus on my math quiz—which I'd skipped lunch to study for, so I was starving. I was late to my class after lunch because I'd gotten so wrapped up in studying, I didn't hear the bell in the library and was loudly informed by Ms. Batson that this was my "final warning."

Earlier, I'd been in a bathroom stall where I overheard Trisha Dove debating whether or not to invite me to her birthday sleepover. She and Livvy Franklin were standing in front of the sinks, basically listing my pros and cons as they refreshed their lip gloss. As nonchalant as if they were discussing the weather; they didn't even check under the stall doors. The consensus was that I was nice and had never done anything to piss them off, but I didn't have a lot of girls for friends and I was a little too obsessed with "that dance thing."

God. I had known both of them since kindergarten. It's not like I was a new girl they had to feel out. Just because I spent most of my free time at the dance studio or with Donovan and Phil didn't mean I was a weirdo.

By the time I met Donovan at the bus lines after school, I was fuming inside my parka. I wanted to get home because I had the night off from dance and it meant I could spend the evening curled up on the couch in front of the TV. My parents would make a fire and we'd watch mindless sitcoms and the intense hospital dramas they loved and I'd forget about every shitty part of my shitty day.

But Donovan wanted to stop by Big Red's on the way home to check out the new X-Men. I wasn't in the mood. I was still new to pointe work and the lesson the night before had been brutal. I was half limping because of my sore feet and I didn't feel like standing around watching him look at comics while one of the grumpy cashiers watched both of us.

Donovan was insistent. He promised to buy me anything I wanted if I'd come with him. I knew that wasn't saying much—after all, the most expensive items at Big Red's Gas n'More were things we'd never buy anyway, like jumper cables and bottles of liquor. And it's not like his allowance was so extravagant. But it was still a nice offer. And I *was* hungry from skipping lunch, wouldn't mind spoiling my appetite for dinner with a candy bar or chips and a soda. So I went.

The glass door of Big Red's had barely suctioned shut

behind us before Donovan nudged me. His eyes were trained on the front counter, but I'd already noticed. In place of the middle-aged woman with the bad skin, or her husband—Larry, the owner, who was just as inexplicably cranky—was a new guy. He was older, but not by a lot. Maybe college-age at the most.

His head was bent over a cell phone, his thumbs moving rapidly over the keys, but he looked up as the bell on the door jangled above us, as we stomped the lingering bits of snow and ice from our boots. He looked up and he smiled. Said, "Hey, guys" so warmly, like he'd known us forever. Like we were friends.

Donovan and I were speechless, almost frozen in place. No one had ever greeted us like that here, if they greeted us at all. Larry and his employees had no problem reminding us that we were just dumb kids who were lucky enough to have money to burn or else they'd kick us out in an instant. They were always more concerned with their magazines or the person on the other end of the phone. We were an inconvenience, another reason they had to pay attention.

But something about this guy seemed different. He was cute, for one thing, with a grin that made me look away and then back at him, a grin that made me feel grown-up and nervous at the same time. He ran a hand through his thick, dark hair as he looked at us, as he asked, "Anything I can help you with?"

My God. He was treating us like adults. Or at least actual teenagers, which I appreciated, since I knew I still looked like more of a child than a girl on the verge of womanhood. Or whatever that video said in health class last year.

"Uh, no, thanks," I said, stepping out of his line of vision. Sort of hiding between the racks of candy and gum because he was the cutest guy I'd ever seen in person.

It was stupid to be so nervous. He was probably just a high schooler who was being nice to us as some kind of joke.

Donovan didn't say anything. He walked around the corner to the comic books almost cautiously, as if we were being set up. I made my way down the candy aisle, then slowly down the next one, inspecting noodles and ice cream and tuna in a can. I was pretending to look for the item Donovan had promised to buy but I couldn't concentrate; every part of me was consumed with the new guy behind the counter.

Guys had never really paid attention to me. I got looks sometimes and no one seemed like they wanted to puke when I was partnered up with them in class, but no one ever asked me out, either. I was always the friend. Known for ballet and being sidekick to Donovan and Phil. I'd never been kissed, not even in a game of spin the bottle or a sneak attack during elementary school recess.

I moved to the back and stood in front of the refrigerated wall of drinks for a while, perusing my options as the coolers hummed steadily on the other side of the doors. Nothing. I moved on to the freezer with the pints of ice cream and frozen treats lined up in neat stacks. I don't know why ice cream sounded good when it was forty degrees outside, but it did. So I was standing there, so intent on choosing between an ice cream sandwich and a wrapped ice cream cone that I didn't hear him come up behind me.

"Finding everything okay?"

I jumped. Then I looked up at the open glass door in front of me, my fingers clutching the handle. "I'm sorry." I slammed it shut so quickly, the whole case shook.

It was Larry and his wife's pet peeve. If you had the door open longer than two seconds, they would scream out from the front counter that you'd better close it unless you wanted to pay the store's electric bill that month.

But this guy just flashed his grin and said to let him know if I needed any help. Then he moved down the aisle, whistling a clear, cheerful tune that stuck in my head for the rest of the week.

At the register, he made a big show of ringing me up before Donovan, made a sweeping gesture with his arm as he said, "Ladies first." Which was kind of silly since Donovan was paying for my ice cream, but I let him do it anyway. And that's when, up close and able to stare at him while he was preoccupied, I noticed just how gorgeous his eyes were. A magnificent shade of amber, so clear and beautiful that it looked like his pupils had been trapped there by mistake. I could get lost in them. I already was.

"You guys go to the high school?" he asked as he swiped the bar code of my ice cream sandwich package across the scanner to his left.

"*Us?*" Donovan practically snorted in his face, because he looked just as young as I did. His voice was only starting to change and he was still skinny and small back then. "No way. We're only in seventh grade."

I shot him a look. I didn't want this guy thinking we were babies, because then he'd start treating us like babies.

"Really?" He handed the sandwich to me then, and I moved aside as Donovan threw his comic book, a bag of chips, and a soda up on the counter. He kept his eyes on the register. "Haven't seen you guys around, but you don't seem like seventh-graders," he said. "You could definitely pass for freshmen."

"You go to the high school?" I asked, surprised and pleased that he wasn't as old as I'd thought.

"I graduated early," he said with a quick smile. "At my old school. I had a lot of credits, so now I'm just taking some time off and working until I figure out what I want to do."

"I can't wait to graduate," Donovan said, digging money out of the front pocket of his backpack. "Then I can do what I want all the time without answering to anyone. Ever."

"Yeah, but then you'll have a job, and you have to answer to your boss at a job." He told Donovan the total and looked at him as he handed over the money, as their fingers brushed against each other in the exchange. "What would you do all day if you could do whatever you wanted?"

"I don't know." Donovan was flustered at being put on the spot and that's when I realized he thought the new guy was as cool as I did. He normally didn't care what anyone thought of him, didn't pay much attention to what other people said. "Look for rare comics. I'd go on trips all over the country to find the really good ones because you can't always trust people selling them online. And I'd go to a baseball game in every city that has a team. Even the bad teams."

"Huh." The new guy looked thoughtful and paused before he reached into the register to make change. "You like fishing?"

Donovan wrinkled his nose and scratched under the collar of his puffy winter coat. "Not really. I mean, I don't think so."

"You ever been?"

Donovan's head shook after a moment. "It doesn't seem right, killing all those fish like that. They never did anything to us."

The guy leaned forward on his elbows, bringing his face even closer to ours. Even though I didn't know him, I was jealous. Why hadn't he asked *me* what I liked to do in my spare time? Then I thought of Trisha and Livvy in the bathroom earlier, thought maybe it was better if he didn't know about how much I loved ballet.

"You don't have to kill them," he said. "You can throw them back and they're as good as before you took them out of the water."

Donovan looked skeptical.

"Maybe we can go sometime," the guy said, his voice easy

as he stood up straight and handed Donovan a couple of dollars and some coins. "It's too cold now but once it warms up a little, my buddies and I make a day of it. Take a cooler full of food. One full of beer"—he gave a sideways grin when he said this, as if he knew he shouldn't be mentioning beer, but thought we were mature enough to handle it—"and we just goof off. Sometimes we catch something to bring home and cook, sometimes we don't. You wouldn't have to catch anything. You could just chill with us."

Donovan turned over the idea in his head as he deposited the money in his backpack, slid the comic book carefully into a thin zippered pouch on the other side. "You'd let me hang out with you guys?"

"Of course," the guy said. "You seem like a cool dude to me. Cool people are always welcome."

I stood off to the side, feeling very unwelcome and very uncool until he looked at me and said, "No girls allowed on our fishing trips. Sorry." And then he winked one of his brilliant topaz eyes. "I'll have to find a way to make it up to you."

Those words ran through my head the rest of the week and I kept telling myself it didn't mean anything but when he kissed me two weeks later, I felt validated. As if I'd known all along that he was meant to be mine.

We had both fallen for him. He made both of us feel special in our own way and that just didn't happen with someone like him. Older, cooler, and more experienced. And it never happened to me, not with guys that good-looking.

We were both so enamored that we didn't realize he hadn't told us his name. We didn't realize until the transaction was complete and the conversation had wrapped and we were making our way toward the glass door.

"Hey, I'm Trent, by the way," he called out from the counter. "Trent Miller."

"I'm Theo," I said quickly, wanting to get it out before Donovan could speak.

"Theo? That's an interesting name for such a pretty girl." He winked at me again and I normally hated winking but on him, it was cute. Sexy.

My face flushed as I explained, "It's short for Theodora." I'd said it a thousand times but it felt different when I said it to him. It made me feel older, somehow, like maybe I wasn't such a little girl with an old-lady name after all.

"Nice to meet you, Theo." He turned to my friend. "And . . . ?"

"Donovan. Donovan Pratt," he said, copying Trent by adding his last name.

"Theo and Donovan," he said, nodding very slowly, as if he were packing it away in an important place. "I'll try to remember. That is, if you guys come back and see me?"

"We'll try," I said, attempting to play coy at the same time Donovan said, "Definitely. We'll be back, Trent."

He said it with so much enthusiasm that it embarrassed me. I knew from hearing girls talk in the locker room before gym that I was supposed to play hard to get. So I didn't even say goodbye that first day we walked out. I tried to pretend it didn't matter if Trent Miller liked me, but I looked back at him through the glass once we were on the other side, and I knew that was the furthest thing from the truth.

# CHAPTER TWENTY-NINE

I DON'T KNOW EXACTLY HOW LONG MY TESTIMONY lasts, but it feels like a long time. Hours.

I have no idea what my voice sounds like as I croak out my story. Or what my fingers look like as they press a fresh tissue to my face every few minutes, reach down to cradle the cup of water more often than that. I couldn't tell you which of the jurors gasps when I tell them, in detail, what Chris did to me in the backseat of his car and what he had me do to him. I'm not sure if it's the Asian woman with the silver bob or the white man with the purple birthmark that covers half of his face.

I don't see my parents' faces, don't wonder if they are horrified or mortified or both, because I can't look at them and watch all the respect they had for me drain away before my eyes.

I try to be a grown-up. I attempt to say it all with no emotion, without showing how terrified I am of these questions. The detail is astounding—in McMillan's wording and how much I'm supposed to reveal in my response. I have to close my eyes sometimes, shut out everyone in the room and talk like I'm relaying the plot of a movie. I don't shake so much if I think about someone else in the role of Theo Cartwright. My voice wavers a few times, but McMillan just tells me to take my time, waits patiently as I stop to take in a few deep breaths or sip from my water.

Chris's lawyer isn't so nice. He spits questions at me rapidly, so quickly that my body grows too warm and my thoughts become muddled. But I keep up with him. I have to, because the sooner I answer his questions, the sooner I can get out of this hard seat and away from all these probing eyes. His own are an icy, crystal blue and they peer at me the whole time he's cross-examining, daring me to doubt him. I knew from the second I saw him that he'd be anything but easy on me. He keeps asking if Chris ever flat-out told me he was going away with Donovan, or if I ever saw anything inappropriate between them with my own eyes. He asks if Chris threatened me, if I ever felt like my life was in danger when I was around him.

McMillan objects a few times—maybe one time too often, because the judge admonishes him and almost seems ready for Chris's lawyer to get back to it. But I appreciate that he's looking out for me, that he knows how hard it is to sit in front of a courtroom and have my past laid bare.

I glance at Chris a few times and it's hard to believe how the tables have turned. It feels amazing to have the power over him, and I become stronger as he sinks a little lower into his seat with each admission. He's done. Ruined. And maybe my life is, too, but at least I'm not going down alone.

I wonder when he decided—that it was going to be me, and then Donovan, for as long as he could have him. Did he know how it would play out as soon as we stepped through the front door of Big Red's? Or did he wait a few days to feel us out?

I think the part that bothers me the most is not knowing if he'd targeted us specifically or if he would have done the same thing to any two kids who walked through the door.

I don't want him to have that choice ever again and that's how I pull through the questions from Chris's attorney. Even the hateful ones that imply I was stupid and probably deserved what I got.

Maybe he thinks that. A lot of people might think that when they find out. But I told the truth. I did what I could for Donovan and people can call me all the names they want, but selfish won't be one of them.

# CHAPTER THIRTY

I SLEEP FOR WHAT FEELS LIKE A WEEK, BUT WHEN I finally get out of bed it's only four in the morning.

I'm groggy. Disoriented. I crawled into bed as soon as we got home from the courthouse, and the trial comes flooding back in a rush.

The defense attorney's accusing tone as he fired the most embarrassing, personal questions at me. Questions no one should ever have to hear, let alone answer in front of a crowd. The hushed sounds of shock from the gallery. Chris's eyes. Always Chris's eyes.

McMillan and the suits escorted us to our car, protected us from the throng of reporters shouting questions and shoving microphones in our faces. We made it home in record time only to find the same type of scene outside of our house. Once we were inside safely, I walked directly to the stairs. I hadn't said a word to either of my parents since I stepped off the stand.

They talked to me, though. Even when I didn't talk back,

they kept going. They must have said they loved me no fewer than twenty times on the drive back, then assured me it wasn't my fault, that I should never think it's my fault. They told me that what I did was brave, that they were proud of how grown up I was on the stand.

Dad chimed in, but Mom did most of the talking. I wondered why, until I saw his eyes when he opened the car door for me. They were red and watery and he'd been hiding his tears from me the whole ride home.

I turn on my light and look down at myself. I'm still in all the clothes I wore to the trial: black pants and a gray blouse that reminds me of Hosea's eyes. My black cardigan lies on the floor next to my flats. My phone sits on top of my dresser across the room, turned off as soon as I got home. I couldn't take any chances. I still can't. Everyone must know the news by now.

I think of the reporters who greeted us on our trip back from the courthouse and I jump back over to the wall, slam my hand down against the light switch. I wait for my eyes to readjust to the dark, then creep slowly to the window. I crouch down so my eyes are level with the ledge and I slowly part the curtains, look out at the dark street below.

Still there. Not as many as before, and they're not standing outside, but a couple of vans are parked across the street. One is planted boldly in front of our house. I can't make out any shapes inside the tinted windows, but I can only imagine the men inside. Leaned back in the seats with their mouths open as their snores fill the cabin, or heads slumped over chests as they try to catch a few winks. They can't miss anything. For many, this is probably their biggest story yet and it was delivered straight to them, practically on a silver platter.

I pad downstairs to the kitchen in the dark and open the refrigerator, casting a halo of light around my face. Boiled eggs. Leftover macaroni and cheese—homemade, not from the box. A couple of aluminum-foil-wrapped slabs catch my attention. I peel off the top layer of foil, look down to discover leftover slices of frozen pizza.

I close the fridge and open the pantry. My eyes skim over bags of potato chips and boxes of fancy crackers and the package of British cookies my father loves. ("They're biscuits," he says in a bad accent every time he pulls out the package, just to annoy me and Mom.) Things I haven't touched in months, can barely remember the taste of. My stomach growls but I can't eat. I haven't eaten anything since the granola bar yesterday morning and most of that sits in the silver trash can across the room.

Maybe I'll never eat again. Maybe I'll just waste away in front of everyone because that seems like the easiest choice now. My ballet career—or the promise of one—is over. My friends must be furious at me for keeping such a huge secret from them. And Hosea . . . Well, he didn't choose me anyway, but now he must be glad he didn't end up with a girl who'd been sleeping with a pedophile.

I slip back upstairs, where I walk into the bathroom and

turn on the shower. It's likely to wake my parents but the hot water shooting down on me is just the right kind of pain and I stay in until the skin on my fingers prunes.

When I come out of the bathroom wrapped in a towel, a triangular beam of light peeks out from the door of Mom and Dad's room. It's cracked, just slightly. I pause in the space between our rooms, wonder if they'll call out to me. A couple of seconds later, Dad's muffled voice says, "You okay, babygirl?"

"Do you need anything, honey?" Mom asks.

I hear a pair of feet drop to the floor.

"I'm fine," I say. "I'm going back to bed now."

A long pause, then, "Okay, sweetheart. We'll be right here if you need us."

"We love you," Dad calls out before I shut my door.

I change into a fresh pair of pajamas, dressing in the dark, and get back into bed, feeling worse than I did forty-five minutes ago.

Two minutes later I get back out and walk into their room without knocking. They won't care. They've wanted me to talk to them for hours now. Mom is sitting up in bed, her back propped against their nest of pillows. Dad is pacing the room in flannel pants and a T-shirt. They were murmuring before I walked in, but they stop. Smile at me, gesture me in from the doorway. I stand in place.

"Sweetie?"

Mom's voice is soft. Tentative. Comfort. Love. All of the reasons I can't respond.

Dad walks toward me, says: "Can't shut off your brain, babygirl?" His voice is decidedly upbeat—even if it's forced—but I suspect from the bags under his eyes that he hasn't slept much tonight, if at all.

I shake my head. I know the routine. Yet I don't walk over to their bed and slip under the sheets between them, lying there as my mother strokes my hair and tells me everything will be all right. I yearn for their soothing voices, would like nothing more than to fall asleep to their placating words.

I lean against the doorframe for support, close my eyes for a moment to trigger the memories of that summer. Things could be different this time. It could be a totally different experience, knowing what I do now and I have to at least try because I'm not sure being here is an option.

I pinch my thumb and forefinger around the skin on my waist. Skin suctioned like glue to muscle and bone.

"I think I need to go back to Juniper Hill."

# CHAPTER THIRTY-ONE

THE HOUSE LOOKS COZIER WHEN WE PULL UP THIS time, but maybe it's because of the snow blanketing the peaks of the Victorian architecture like a real-life gingerbread house.

It's strange to walk up the steps in snow boots, to stamp the soles on the rough fibers of the welcome mat as we wait for someone to come to the door. Last time the air was thick and hot, the landscape buzzing with insects and fat bees that swooped in front of our faces. This time I can see my breath.

The check-in process is the same. Dr. Bender is there to greet us in her grass-green tunic with a purple shawl wrapped around her shoulders. Then she whisks Mom and Dad away while a counselor I don't know shows me to my room and checks my bag to make sure I haven't smuggled in something from their forbidden list.

My parents look sad to leave me a half hour later, but they have to be relieved. Even more so than the last time. I feel guilty thinking about what they'll go back to, because I know the reporters and paparazzi won't give up that easily.

I'll finish out the school year through a tutor who comes to the house three days a week.

Just like last time, I get letters from Phil. Every week without fail a flat, business-sized envelope is waiting for me in the mail slot with Phil's boxy handwriting on the outside. I can tell he's trying not to talk too much about all the fun he and Sara-Kate are having without me, but the happiness practically leaps off the pages of his handwritten letters, and I smile when I finish reading them. He deserves to be happy.

Sara-Kate's emails mention Phil, too, but most of the time she writes me poems. Long ones, short ones. Sad and silly and serious. They're beautiful. All of them, and she writes them just for me. I don't always understand what they mean, but I appreciate them. They're about us and they're not about us. I know they're the best way for her to deal with me keeping so much from her. She's been nothing but kind, yet I know how much I've altered the trust in our friendship and I hope she can forgive me.

One day, about six weeks after I've been at Juniper Hill, Diana pokes her head into a group session. They aren't supposed to be interrupted for any reason, so I'm pretty worried when she looks around the circle until she finds me.

She assures me that everything is fine as we walk down the hall and up the maple staircase toward Dr. Bender's office.

It's remarkably similar to being escorted to the principal. I try not to worry as I watch her curly black ponytail swing in front of me. I have to say, I was kind of excited to see Diana that first day. She looked happy to see me, too. She's my primary counselor again. It only makes sense; she knows the first part of my story better than anyone, even if it wasn't the whole truth.

Dr. Bender's office is empty. I expect Diana to follow me in, but she hovers in the doorway as she points to the phone on the desk, tells me to push the button next to the blinking red light. Says she'll be right outside as she gently closes the door.

I wonder if anyone has ever been allowed to sit alone in Dr. Bender's office. I make sure not to knock over anything on the desk as I reach for the phone, put the receiver up to my ear and push the red light winking at me.

I say hello softly, almost too softly.

The voice on the other end is deep as it says hello back to me. Unrecognizable, and a little cautious, as if I was the one who called. I curl the phone under my chin as I look out the window of Dr. Bender's office. It overlooks the backyard: the art shed, the garden, the river birch trees that dry clothes on a line in the summer.

It's snowing again. The country air whirls fat flakes against the window, pressing complicated patterns into the glass. I watch as I wait for the other person to speak, as I wonder if we'll just sit here and breathe at each other for the next few minutes.

The voice is stronger this time as it says hello again. As the person says he is Donovan.

My whole body goes cold.

"Donovan?"

He doesn't say anything, but he clears his throat, and I wonder how long it will take me to process that he has a deep voice now.

I squeeze my fingers tight around the receiver. Shut my eyes as I open my mouth. "I . . . Donovan, I'm sorry. I'm so, so sorry."

I can tell someone is in the background. Not speaking, but there for support. His mother, I'm sure.

Then I hear a long, loud breath. A sigh. It sounds like relief. It makes my eyes fill.

"I, um." He pauses. Clears his throat again. I imagine his mother touching his shoulder, encouraging him to go on. "I wanted to say thank you, for . . . Thank you, Theo."

The whole room is a blur as I stop trying to fight the tears.

But I feel light inside, like a three-ton weight has dislodged itself from my body.

I can finally breathe.


Christopher Ryan Fenner was found guilty.

After my testimony, Donovan cracked. Just a little. He gave a written statement, but our stories combined were enough to put Chris away for multiple life sentences with no chance of parole. He was charged with corruption of minors, dozens of counts of rape against a child, and transporting a minor across state lines to engage in sexual activity. He'll never see the outside of a prison again.

My name shows up in the news less frequently but it's still there more often than I'd like. Along with this year's school picture, stacked up against one taken of Donovan in court and Chris's mug shot. I know some people think I ran away until things die down, but there's no escaping this. Even with the limited Internet access and the absence of a daily paper, I can't forget that the whole world knows who I am now.

Chris broke up with me and disappeared, but all the while he was hiding out in a shabby hotel at the edge of town, waiting to make his move on Donovan. The city had thawed out by then and he'd called Donovan, invited him to come along on a fishing trip with him and his friends. He asked him not to tell me; he said he hadn't been sure how to break up with me and that I'd be upset if I knew they were hanging out.

There was no fishing trip. There was just Chris and his car and Donovan with the comic book and pile of snacks he'd picked up along the way.

A few days after Donovan's call, I swing by the mail room on my way to the house library. There's a package in my mailbox. A small, padded white envelope with no return address. It's been slit open because they check all the packages here before we get them. I shake it. Something plastic clacks inside but I wait to open it.

The library is a room on the second floor filled with books we can borrow and computers we can use for a limited amount of time each day. Pete is hanging out behind the desk near the door, pecking away at the keyboard in front of him and stopping every few seconds to stroke at his patchy blond beard. He looks up but doesn't even make me sign in before I head to the computer farthest away from him.

I set the package next to the keyboard, but decide to check my email first.

There's one bolded message at the top. It's from Marisa.

It's long, and it sounds so much like how she talks that I can picture her sitting down to type it out after a long day of teaching. She says everyone misses me, and not to worry, that summer programs will still be around next year and I'll still have her full support.

But the part I read over and over is the paragraph where she says it took courage to do what I did, and she admires me for being so strong. That a professional company would be lucky to have me one day.

I get permission from Pete to print off Marisa's email so that even on the lowest days, I can remember she still believes in me.

Then I pick up the padded white envelope. Turn it over so whatever is inside will drop out. It's a CD with FOR THEO printed on the front in black marker.

I pull a slip of paper from the clear plastic CD case, no bigger than an index card. In the same neat handwriting as that on the disc, it says:

THIS WAS ALWAYS FOR YOU.
—H.

My shaking hands slide the disc into the slot on the side. When I hit play, I'm rewarded with what I wished for so many weeks ago. As the familiar chords float their way into my ears, brazen and bashful, ethereal and timeless, I see Hosea on the piano bench, sharing something so heartfelt and personal, communicating how he felt about me the best way he knew how.

A few months ago—even a few weeks ago—I would have thought it was a sign. Even after winter formal, I still sometimes thought we were meant to be. I thought about him all the time when I first came here. But now . . . well. Things look a little different when you spend your days with a houseful of troubled girls and a cadre of helpful hippies.

He cared about me, but not enough.

Hosea said I was special, but words don't mean anything without actions to back them up.

And maybe I am special, but it's not because he said so.

I log out of my email and stand up, gathering the CD and packaging, and Marisa's printed email. I nod at Pete on the way out, but I stop in the doorway. The email in one hand, Hosea's CD in the other. I pause for a moment, then release my grip on the disc and listen as it drops into the trash with a resounding thump.

I keep walking and I don't look back.

# ACKNOWLEDGMENTS

I'M LUCKY TO KNOW SO MANY EXCELLENT PEOPLE who helped make this book a book:

Tina Wexler, you are an absolute gem. I'll never forget the day you pulled my query from the slush pile, and I'm so proud to call you my agent. Thank you for the unwavering enthusiasm, wisdom, humor, and professionalism. I appreciate all that you do.

To my editor extraordinaire, Ari Lewin: Working on this book has been one of the most challenging and rewarding experiences of my life. From the beginning, you understood the story I was trying to tell, and I'm so grateful for your fierce commitment to get it right. Thanks for always being an exceptional person and editor; you've helped make this lifelong dream truly special.

Thank you to Katherine Perkins for a keen editorial eye, and the rest of the Penguin team for creating a beautiful, tangible thing from a document that once lived on my computer.

Lisa Barley, I value your friendship, patience, and honesty.

Eternal thanks for reading the earliest drafts of this story, indulging me in endless conversations about the plot and characters, and never letting me give up. Much love to Lena Anderson for your loyalty, excitement, and nonstop support. I'm indebted to Stephanie D. Brown, Carrie Burns, and Erika Enk Rueter for reading early versions and providing helpful feedback and encouragement. Leila Howland and Vanessa Napolitano, your quick reads and brilliant notes during revisions were essential to the development of this story. Thanks also to Lesley Arimah and Kelly Kamenetzky for listening and rooting for me, always.

Amy Spalding, thank you for a stupendous amount of support and making me laugh when I need it most. Corey Haydu, Kristen Kittscher, and April G. Tucholke, I am so grateful for your emails and friendship; I'll never understand how you always know the right thing to say, but I do appreciate it. Alison Cherry, thank you for being so kind and faithfully cheering me on to the finish line.

Los Angeles and Chicago friends, thanks for putting up with my incessant babbling and disappearing acts while I was working on this book—and for being my family away from home. I'm incredibly grateful to Debbie Farr and Sonshine Performing Arts Academy for teaching me how to tap, and fostering a love and respect for all disciplines of dance.

To my big brother, Al: I constantly wanted to do what you were doing when we were kids, so I'm really glad voracious reading has always been your thing.

And to my parents, Jerri and Albert, I can't thank you enough for raising me in a house filled with good books, buying me all those notebooks and pens, and never forcing me outside when I'd rather be in a quiet room, writing. Some of my favorite memories are Saturday mornings spent at the library and bookstore—and also that time you gave me, at my request, nothing but a giant box of books for Christmas. I was seven years old when I told you I wanted to be an author, and you always said I could do it someday if I tried really hard. Thank you for believing in me.

# RESOURCES

IF YOU OR SOMEONE YOU KNOW IS DEALING WITH ANY OF THE topics in this book, *please* know that you're not going through this alone. Try talking to a trusted friend or family member about it, and if that isn't an option, there are many professionals with the resources to help, including the following organizations:

RAINN | Rape, Abuse & Incest National Network

www.rainn.org

1-800-656-HOPE (1-800-656-4673)

National Center for PTSD (Posttraumatic Stress Disorder)

www.ptsd.va.gov

1-802-296-6300

NEDA | National Eating Disorders Association

www.nationaleatingdisorders.org

1-800-931-2237

National Center for Missing & Exploited Children

www.missingkids.com

1-800-THE-LOST (1-800-843-5678)